One shell hit a gren

Without warning, the wag exploded with a sudden violence that took the Armorer by surprise.

And then it was over, almost anticlimactic. The convoy rolled on.

The Armorer looked at Eula, who regarded him impassively, as though the events of the firefight hadn't occurred, as though she were examining him in minute detail, trying to get inside his head, unconcerned by what had just happened.

J.B.'s sense of unease welled up with renewed vigor. There was something odd about the whole situation, something that could spell danger not just for him, but for all the companions.

Something for which only *he* could find the answer—if he could figure out what the question was....

Other titles in the Deathlands saga:

JAMES AXLER

DEATH LANDS®

Desolation Crossing

A GOLD EAGLE BOOK FROM

W☉RLDWIDE®

TORONTO • NEW YORK • LONDON
AMSTERDAM • PARIS • SYDNEY • HAMBURG
STOCKHOLM • ATHENS • TOKYO • MILAN
MADRID • WARSAW • BUDAPEST • AUCKLAND

Recycling programs
for this product may
not exist in your area.

First edition July 2009

ISBN-13: 978-0-373-62597-0

DESOLATION CROSSING

Copyright © 2009 by Worldwide Library.

Printed in U.S.A.

The only art her guilt to cover,
To hide her shame from every eye,
To give repentance to her lover,
And wring his bosom, is—to die.
                              —Oliver Goldsmith,
                              1728–1774

THE DEATHLANDS SAGA

This world is their legacy, a world born in the violent nuclear spasm of 2001 that was the bitter outcome of a struggle for global dominance.

There is no real escape from this shockscape where life always hangs in the balance, vulnerable to newly demonic nature, barbarism, lawlessness.

But they are the warrior survivalists, and they endure—in the way of the lion, the hawk and the tiger, true to nature's heart despite its ruination.

Ryan Cawdor: The privileged son of an East Coast baron. Acquainted with betrayal from a tender age, he is a master of the hard realities.

Krysty Wroth: Harmony ville's own Titian-haired beauty, a woman with the strength of tempered steel. Her premonitions and Gaia powers have been fostered by her Mother Sonja.

J. B. Dix, the Armorer: Weapons master and Ryan's close ally, he, too, honed his skills traversing the Deathlands with the legendary Trader.

Doctor Theophilus Tanner: Torn from his family and a gentler life in 1896, Doc has been thrown into a future he couldn't have imagined.

Dr. Mildred Wyeth: Her father was killed by the Ku Klux Klan, but her fate is not much lighter. Restored from predark cryogenic suspension, she brings twentieth-century healing skills to a nightmare.

Jak Lauren: A true child of the wastelands, reared on adversity, loss and danger, the albino teenager is a fierce fighter and loyal friend.

Dean Cawdor: Ryan's young son by Sharona accepts the only world he knows, and yet he is the seedling bearing the promise of tomorrow.

In a world where all was lost, they are humanity's last hope....

Chapter One

"A hard rain's going to fall," Doc muttered gnomically from the rear of the wag.

Mildred looked at him, also hard. The reference was lost on the others; but she, of an earlier age than them, wondered if some memory had once more filtered through Doc's labyrinthine and fogged mind.

Jak looked up at the clear sky above them and sniffed. "No rain. Not for too long…"

The sky was azure, the sun burning red-yellow as it passed its peak and they entered the afternoon. The heat seemed to bounce off the ground around them and radiate back up, meeting itself so that it created a haze of shimmering air that held them tight. The land surrounding the wag on all sides was barren for as far as they could see, a chiaroscuro of browns that disappeared into the false horizon of the heat haze. It was dotted here and there by patches of stark cacti, rising up freakishly as though a part of the land was reaching to the sky in search of escape. To their rear, diminishing steadily with the rhythmic turning of the wag's engine, lay the hellhole from which they had just departed.

"Rain, sun, who gives a shit as long as this damn engine doesn't stall," Ryan said through gritted teeth, grinding the gears as he ground his teeth.

J.B. and Krysty exchanged glances. Ryan had been in a foul mood since they had acquired the wag. Stranded in a pesthole that went by the name of Stripmall, they had been short of jack, short of supplies and short of work. Like others they had encountered in these wastes, the ragged-assed ville had been devoted to one primary industry: a gaudy house of large proportions, designed to service the trading convoys that had to make the arduous trek across the dustbowl lands.

There were many old malls that had been adapted in this way, and each followed the same basic pattern: the old storefronts had been converted into display cabinets for the girls and services within. Each held a different type of woman, displayed a different kind of pleasure. All tastes were catered to. And with the friends devoid of any kind of currency, there had been a tacit pressure exerted on the men to push Mildred and Krysty into work. After all, mutie women with prehensile hair were always at a premium, and there were few black women in this area of the Death-lands. Both of them represented a novelty, which made them potentially high earners.

And when Ryan and J.B., in particular, had paid no heed to the imprecations; when Millie and Krysty had made their own opinions known forcefully—the proprie-tor of one gaudy house now nursed two broken arms—it had become obvious that the choice to say no would soon be removed. So they had made it their business to get the hell out of the ville as soon as possible. A catalog of bad luck had landed them in Stripmall, and it hadn't got much better when they had been forced to trade what little they had left for a broken-down wag. It was cumbersome, too big for their needs and made a noise as if a dozen stickies were being chewed up in the pistons.

But it would serve its purpose. They hoped.

The wag was a big yellow school bus, the padding long since disintegrated or ripped away from the uncomfortable metal seats. The suspension was shot to hell. That wouldn't have mattered on the kinds of roads that it had originally been built to traverse, but the road out of Stripmall was little more than the beaten remains of a highway, more pothole and debris than smooth surface. Even the tarmac that remained was in a sticky, semiviscous state because of the heat. So the bald tires dragged, bumped and slewed across the surface.

The steering was also shot, each crevice, bump and deviation in the surface wrenching the wheel in Ryan's hands, tearing at the muscles in his forearms. It was less than comfortable on his buttocks, too, as the combination of poor road surface and even worse suspension catapulted him toward the ceiling of the wag with monotonous regularity. Back in the seats, spread down the length of the bus, the other friends found themselves bounced around like ball bearings, rattling with the same force against the sides of the bus.

To make it worse, Ryan was starting to get the feeling that they had been gypped over the amount of fuel in the wag. It was impossible to get an accurate reading as the fuel gauge was broken, and even though they had watched the toothless, scrawny guy they had bartered with fill the tank from battered gas cans, there was no way of knowing what the consumption of the beast may be—Ryan was beginning to fear it was a damn sight less than they had figured.

Stripmall vanished into the haze of the horizon, and now they were surrounded by nothing but dust, blue and cacti that looked uncannily as if they were moving across the ground. It was as though the companions were isolated from the rest of the world, with nothing but the whine and strain of the engine and the bone-jarring impact of the road to occupy their minds.

Which was perhaps why Doc's mind was starting to wander again. Drivel to most, but to Mildred something that struck an associative chord.

"We are just desolation angels on the road," he intoned softly, staring out the back window, his voice hiccuping in time to the jolting of the vehicle.

"Say what?" Krysty asked.

Doc looked around, his eyes barely registering that she was there for a fraction of a second before recognition returned to them.

"Did I say something?" he asked, dreamily.

"Something but nothing," Jak muttered, "same usual."

Mildred ignored them, and asked, "Where did you get that from, Doc?"

The old man looked puzzled for a second, then remembrance crossed his face and he grinned slyly. "It may have been during my subterranean life, or perhaps when I was on satori in Paris," he answered.

Mildred's face split into a grin. "I have seen the best minds of my generation ripped apart…no, torn apart…is that it?"

Doc raised an eyebrow. "Something like. I fear your memory may be as faulty as mine, my dear Doctor. Which is something that does not, perhaps, bode well for the future. Immediate or long-term."

"It has been a long time, Doc. Both for us, and for the rest of what's left of the world. I know I remember that from high school. We had a progressive teacher who wanted us to read more than just the syllabus in Lit classes. Not just Frost, but the Beats, as well. That was how I came across them. But you?"

Doc frowned for a moment, as though struggling to pull out a memory that sought to elude him, remaining just that touch out of reach. Then his face lit up as he was able to grasp it.

"It was when I was taken from my home, and deposited in that purgatory that existed before the purging fire of skydark. Though it has birthed this wasteland, I suspect that it could not have been that much better in many ways. The stench of corruption always filled my senses back when… But where was I? Ah yes, the road dreams of Kerouac and Cassady. The endless journeying, with no destination in sight and no real goal other than to move on. Perhaps there was an object once. Perhaps, at one time, there was a point to the interminable road. But somewhere along the line that became lost, and to keep moving was the only goal. What is it, I wonder, that has bought that back to me… Come to that, was the whole thing allegory or metaphor, or was it just the ultimate realization of the dream to be free?"

"Dream you talk sense one day," Jak muttered almost to himself.

"Doc," Mildred said softly, "I asked you how you knew about the Beats and Dylan." She turned to Krysty and J.B., who had been trying to follow the discussion with varying degrees of enthusiasm. After all, there was nothing but the land and sky outside to occupy them.

"The Beats," Mildred explained, "were a late twentieth-century group of writers, and Dylan was a singer and poet who wasn't part of them, but was kinda like them. All long after Doc was a young man."

"I disagree," Doc replied with a sudden and surprising vehemence. "I was still a young man. I am still a young man. That which you see is not the real me, but what their meddling has made of me. And yet…" He calmed down, grew more reflective. "And yet they were not all bad. There were some who were interested only in the experiments, and found themselves at the behest of those who had power and money. One of them, a doctor called Seeger, was not a bad man, just a misguided one who was out of his moral depth. He consoled himself by reading the books he had treasured as an idealistic student, by listening to the recordings that had fired him on. I recall asking him why he had chosen his path. He grew by turns angry and morose, but in the latter state he was able to give me at least some kind of answer."

"What did he tell you?" Krysty asked, fascinated by this small glimpse of a time she had not seen.

"He said that fate has a way of snatching our dreams and hopes, distorting them in its breeze, tangling them the way that the string of a kite gets tangled by the winds. He said that roads that we travel are not as signposted as we think, and that even if we think that the past has escaped us, for better or for worse, it still has a way of sneaking up, tapping us on the shoulder, and reminding us that those things we thought long since buried have a bearing on where we are now, whether we should like this or not."

"So was he right?" Krysty asked again.

Doc's face creased into a rueful grin that held more melancholy than joy. "He is long since dust, and I am here. How can I ask him?"

"Come to that, would he have a better answer than any of us?" Mildred murmured.

Doc's face creased a little more. "My dear Dr. Wyeth, a doctor of philosophy you should have been."

Mildred was sure it was a half quote from something else that she should have known. She was trying to recall the source when her attention was taken by a more pressing matter. Jak had moved past J.B., Krysty and Mildred, and was now on the backseat next to Doc, staring out of the back window.

Doc turned and faced the rear, trying to follow Jak's gaze. In the unfathomable manner he had of snapping from reverie to an alert present, he could tell that the albino youth had caught wind of something on their tail.

"What is it, lad? I cannot see," he muttered.

"Not see," Jak replied softly. "Hear, feel. Different buzz under wag noise. Feeling road change. Not much, but enough. Bastard heat," he added. Doc knew what he meant: the heat mist that obscured the true horizon, and bought a curtain down between them and Stripmall, limited their field of vision. If something was approaching, then it was not yet near enough to pierce that curtain, yet how much time would that cost them?

Even without the eerie miasma of the heated air, the motion and erratic progress of the wag would have made it difficult to discern what—if anything—had been in their wake. But such was the level of trust felt by Ryan Cawdor in the judgment of the albino hunter that he barked an order for the friends to be on triple red for whatever was about to approach them. And such, indeed, was the level of trust felt by the rest of the companions that they had already unsheathed weapons before the words had fallen from Ryan's lips.

J.B. moved forward to keep an eye on anything that could approach from the front of the vehicle: although it was unlikely, Ryan could do little to recce, his eye being riveted to the treacherous road surface directly ahead of them. J.B. could act as a roaming pair of eyes, just in case.

But in truth they knew that any danger would come from the rear. Mildred and Krysty were halfway down the bus, one on each side of the center aisle, arms curled painfully tight around steel seat supports to give them as much stability as was possible, sight intent on the wastes that stretched on each side, but the bias of their vision directed to the rear, where Jak and Doc were tight against the back window, as if the mere act of this could somehow force their hidden enemy to show themselves.

Enemy? Maybe not: but considering they had left Stripmall in some hurry, and that the women were highly prized by those who ran the gaudy houses, it was a fair assumption. A safe assumption. And better safe than chilled.

The progress of the old school bus became that bit more tortuous, the road that bit more treacherous: at least, that was how it seemed as translated through the steering grip of Ryan Cawdor. Maybe it was tension. Maybe the road really had worsened. It didn't matter: all that counted was that it was that little bit harder to cling on and keep rattling eyeballs in focus.

"Nearer," Jak murmured. He spoke low, but his voice carried to them with the authority of one who was never wrong. None of the others could distinguish the sounds he could hear, but they knew he was right.

They waited….

As though in slow motion and as though materializing from nothing, the pace of the pursuing vehicles caused them to shimmer and take shape as they broke the distance barrier and penetrated beyond the heat haze. There were three of them: two low-slung wags, like old cars that had been cut down and opened out to allow the shooters easy access and aim. Not that they would need it, judging from the size of the side-mounted machine blasters, each of which looked as though their weight could drag the vehicle to one side without the counterbalance of their opposite mounting.

The third vehicle was a motorbike bearing two men, the man on pillion carrying what looked to be a rocket launcher.

"Ryan, would it perhaps be possible to squeeze a little more pace from this vehicle?" Doc queried. "I fear they are starting to gain with some rapidity, and will soon be able to test their range."

Ryan couldn't look round—the road was in bad shape. But he knew one thing for certain. "It doesn't matter how quick they are, or what kind of firepower they've got. There's no way I can squeeze any more speed from this bastard. We're gonna have to fight."

Doc had suspected as much, but figured it was worth asking the question. Too much speed and the Lord alone knew how much precious fuel they would waste. Too much speed and the Lord was equally the only one who would have any notion of how the wag would stand up to the road surface.

Besides, it was too late to worry now. The bike had streaked ahead of the two wags that had previously flanked it, and the pillion rider had risen to his feet, swaying with the movement of the bike as he raised the rocket launcher and took aim.

"Bastard," Jak hissed, his tone saying far more than just the word itself could convey. As the roar of the discharged launcher reached them, a fraction of a second behind the muzzle-flash and the unsteady swaying of the pillion rider, the recoil kicking back at him, Ryan had already hauled the wheel to the right, taking them to the edge of the ruined blacktop and onto a dusty soil that was almost harder and surer than the road they had left.

The rocket hit the road about a hundred yards ahead of them, where they would have reached in moments, and where the impact of detonation would have shattered the glass of the windshield into Ryan's good eye, in all likelihood bringing chunks of rock, soil and softened blacktop with it.

Instead, the impact—now lessened by distance—hit them broadside. Krysty yelped involuntarily as she ducked, slivers of shattered window glass raining on her with some rock and soil. The side of the bus sounded as though it had been pelted with stones, but the damage was minimal.

Jak had already beaten out the glass of the back window with the butt of his Colt Python pistol, and had the barrel centered on the pillion rider, who was reloading while still standing. It was a neat trick, but stupe. With his attention on the rocket launcher, he wasn't looking at the bus. The rider was, and made to move the bike to one side. But he was hampered by the need to keep the balance of his passenger, and he wasn't quick enough. Jak snapped off one shot from the .357, the sound of the blaster almost deafening within the confines of the bus, despite the noise outside.

Jak had a hunter's aim. The pillion rider flew backward as the round hit him, the velocity of the impact multiplied by the forward motion of the bike. A red mist of blood spread around him.

The bike sheered as the rider attempted to cope with the sudden shift in weight and balance presented to him. He was good, but not good enough to deal with both this and the treacherous road surface. The front tire of the bike blew out on something unseen, and the bike slewed viciously out of control, the rider dragged underneath as the weight and momentum pulled it to one side. His torso had been bare, and he was in moments little more than a red slick on the road.

Simultaneously, fate had smiled on the friends. The pillion rider—now minus half of his viscera and quite chilled—had flopped back into the road, causing one of the wags to swerve to avoid hitting him. This attempt to keep hot on the trail would have proved successful, if not for the fact that the rocket launcher that the pillion rider had been carrying had parted company from his lifeless grip and skittered across the road and into the path the wag had taken to evade impact.

It merely swapped one for another; one of a deadlier effect. The front of the wag and the rocket launcher met with an impact that caused the detonation of the explosive that the pillion rider had been in the throes of loading. The resultant explosion rocked the air, causing the remaining wag to skid and veer across the surface of the road wildly before righting itself and continuing the pursuit.

IT GAVE RYAN a little more time to try to pilot the cumbersome wag across the hard-packed earth. It was bouncing and veering less than on the road, but it was still bone-shaking, and difficult for anyone to aim well.

The pursuing wag was almost on them, the machine blasters chattering and tracers of fire kicking up around them. The whine and clang of shots striking home were also a little too close for comfort. Short of stopping, there was little Ryan could do to give his companions a break when it came to return fire.

But maybe he could slow the opposition a little, and use the fact that the wag was large and cumbersome to its advantage. Without even thinking about it, he had been heading away from the ruined road, and had come within distance of one of the groups of eerie cacti that dotted the landscape.

He realized why he had been doing this, and without pause hauled the heavy steering column around so that the old school bus was headed straight for the center of the cacti. As they neared it, he could see that the plants were much larger, much taller than they had appeared from a distance. The actual span of the patch had to have been about 150 yards, and the plants themselves had thick bases at least six feet around. They needed them, if they were to support the branching arms of thick spikes that sprouted on all sides, reaching upward in mute supplication.

Despite the distances and sizes involved, there was no

way that he could get the bus through the maze they made without crashing into them.

Good. That was his plan.

"Away from the windows," he yelled.

Considering they were about to engage the enemy, it may have struck his people as a strange thing to say. One glance ahead told them why. They were in the aisle of the bus within moments.

Ryan slewed the bus into the middle of the cactus patch. The big yellow bus hit big yellow and green stalks that were as hard as wood. The front fender crunched, the headlights splintered, but the bus barged through, knocking some cacti over at a drunken angle, toppling others completely. Sap spurted and dribbled from branches taken off by the impact of the large wag.

The old school bus left a path in its wake, but one that was scattered with spikes like nine-inch nails, trails of sap and listing and fallen trunks.

The wag on their tail had been gaining all the time. The driver was hunched over the wheel, trying to keep a steady path so that the two blasters on either side—both manned—could lay down a barrage, which they had started to do as soon as the school bus had come in range. Their fire had taken out what was left of the back windows, and peppered the hide of the bus with dents and small holes. But they hadn't accounted for the fact that the old buses were built like tanks, for long and hard use. The main body of the vehicle could stand a lot more pounding than most nontrading wags the machine blasters were used to firing on.

Inside, stray shots ricocheted, and the din of the slugs on metal was dimmed only by the sounds of the cacti as the .wag collided with them. The old bus was taking a lot of punishment, and the companions were huddled in the aisle, unable to risk firing back.

The blaster-mounted wag hit the cacti patch close, now, on the tail of the school bus. Close enough to catch the splinters of cactus trunk, the spines like nine-inch nails and the sprays of sap.

The way in which the side panels and roof of the wag had been cut away to accommodate the mounting and firing of the machine blasters was ingenious, and skillfully executed. In normal circumstances it was to be admired. But these were not normal circumstances, and all it did in this situation was to leave the three inhabitants of the wag wide-open to the furies of the cacti.

The big heavy splinters of trunk wood took out the windshield of the wag, making the driver swerve erratically as he tried to avoid the stationary trunks, the flying wood, and still see where he was headed. His driving veered violently to the left as a splinter the size of his fist drove a hole in his shoulder, making him scream in red-hot agony.

But that was nothing next to the pain suffered by the exposed blaster firers. Leaning out of the vehicle on specially constructed bucket seats that took them directly behind the sights of the blasters, they were open to the sap and spines that flew freely in the wake of the old school bus.

The spines were razor-sharp, and flying at speed. They flayed and cut at the exposed flesh of the two men, driving into their arms and ribs with the drive of a knife being thrust home. One man got a spine right in the eye, puncturing the orb and allowing the viscous fluid to ooze down its length as it kept on going, through into his brain. A flicker of bright white light as the optic nerve shorted out, and he was gone, falling from his seat to roll lifeless on the hard earth, picking up stray wood and spines like a pin cushion.

The other man wasn't so lucky. He thought, at first, that he was. He had avoided the spines and spikes, more through luck than any attempt on his part to take evasive action. He had not, however, been so fortunate in avoiding the sap that was splashing the side of the wag. It touched his skin—just the forearm—and felt cool. He looked down, and could see that the coolness was caused simply by its burning through the surface nerves before they had a chance to register pain. The skin had melted from his arm, and already the corrosive liquid had stripped down to the bone. He made to scream, and another blob of sap caught in the air was sucked into his mouth as he drew breath. No scream issued forth as the coruscating liquid took the flesh from the roof of his mouth, continuing down his throat to strip his larynx. The effects also traveled up, eating into his nasal passages. His own blood began to drown him, although he was beyond noticing by this point, driven mad by the agony of being eaten alive by the acid sap.

As the second man also plunged to his doom, the driver was still attempting to pilot his vehicle through the carnage caused by the school bus. It was a losing battle as the pain from his shoulder injury rendered it useless, and his reflexes grew slower with every enforced turn of the wheel. As darkness engulfed his senses, he drove the wag into the base of one of the cacti. Already weakened by a collision with the school bus, it wavered then slowly tumbled forward, down onto the wag, igniting the fuel in the tank and engulfing cactus and wag in sheets of flame.

The enemy had been vanquished, but Ryan's main concern was getting the wag out of the cactus patch without any further damage. The labyrinthine path through the patch had seen him turn back on himself many times to try to squeeze the wag into gaps, and so he was no longer sure where the road lay, or indeed where the end of the patch itself could be found. He felt as if he was driving in dizzying circles, growing more and more confused, until he caught a glimpse of clear land beyond. He straightened the wheel and gunned the engine as much as he dared, foot down and headed for empty space. The interior of the wag echoed with the crash of cactus against metal, but there was no other apparent damage done as the wag crashed out and onto the flat, dry earth.

Ryan let the wag come to rest, the engine gently ticking over, and looked around. The cactus patch behind them was partially ablaze as the fire from the blaster wag spread. The road was to their left. The wag was pitted and scored by the impact of bullets, shafts of cacti trunk and spines, some of which had penetrated the roof of the wag, partially visible.

But the friends were intact. Gathered in the aisle, only now straightening and standing, they were in one piece. Wordlessly, they left the wag to survey the carnage. J.B. began to check the wag, noting the scoring away of paint and the stripping to bare metal where the acid sap had hit. Damn lucky it didn't hit any of us, he thought, tentatively approaching the scored sections of the wag body.

It was Doc who broke the silence.

"I wonder what it was that they actually wanted?" he wondered. "If it was to take our women, then it was a very strange way to do it…to blast us all to annihilation."

"Mebbe it wasn't that at all," Ryan mused. "Mebbe just sport. Mebbe the feeb we got this from thought it was still his. It doesn't matter. All that matters is that we get some distance between us and that pesthole."

He joined J.B. at the side of the wag. "Any damage?"

The Armorer shook his head. "Not anything more than surface. That bastard cactus juice is strong, though," he added, indicating the acid-eaten patches.

"Then we got lucky it never got inside," Ryan said. "Let's hope we don't have to ride that luck."

In a subdued mood, mindful of how close they had come to being overpowered by both man and nature in tandem, the friends boarded the bus. As Ryan clashed the gears and guided the vehicle back to the road, they sat detached from one another, each lost in his or her own thoughts. They hardly noticed that their driver elected to follow the line of the road, but not to actually venture onto the crumpled blacktop. The shoulder was rough, but actually less damaging than the potholed road surface itself.

They made slow, steady progress for more than ten miles, putting plenty of distance between themselves and Stripmall. The old highway seemed to stretch out before them like an endless ribbon, disappearing into the heat haze that was still heavy, even though the afternoon was wearing on. Some of it should have burned off by now, but out here the sun was so intense that any burn was minimal.

Which was why the sudden intersection of another

blacktop took them by surprise. It seemed to snake from nowhere and cut across the one they drove beside. Ryan pulled the bus up to a halt at the junction and turned to J.B.

"What do you reckon?" he asked simply.

The Armorer screwed up his face in concentration as he looked out of the shattered windows in both directions. He stood and, without a word, got off the bus, pulling the minisextant from a bag slung across his shoulder. He looked up at the sun, then took a reading before surveying the short distance available before the horizon blurred.

"That way's west," he drawled, indicating with his hand. "We were coming from the southeast to begin with, and the way I figure, there's more habitation to the west."

Ryan nodded. "West it is, then."

J.B. got back on board, and Ryan heaved the old wag toward the west. It was the first time since they had got back on the road that he had been compelled to put the wheel on full lock. As the wag groaned around, the steering became unsteady, and a whining, grinding sound began to come from beneath the vehicle. It veered sharply, and then tilted forward as a snapping, abrasive screech came from beneath, throwing all those within violently forward.

"Fireblast!" Ryan breathed as he managed to get the air back into his body that had been expelled by the sudden impact against the wheel. "What the fuck…"

"I would wager to suggest that perhaps we were not as lucky as we had assumed," Doc commented mildly, pulling himself up and ignoring the pain in his ribs.

"Yeah, Doc's right there," Mildred said with a sardonic tone. "Always knew our luck couldn't go on."

J.B. was already out of the wag and examining the damage. His head appeared in the doorway. "Nothing good to say." He shrugged. "Guess some of that sap shit must've got underneath, and turning the wag sharply hit the weak spot. It's sheered right underneath."

"No chance of being able to fix it?" Ryan asked, more from blind hope than anything else.

The Armorer allowed himself a ghost of a smile. "Not unless you got a torch and mebbe a replacement axle hidden somewhere in here."

It took them a few minutes to gather themselves and assemble outside, in the baking heat, where they could survey the damage for themselves.

"Shit, we gave our food and water for that," Krysty said as she looked at the irreparable damage, voicing the thoughts of all of them.

"We've just got to hit the road and hope we reach a ville before we run out," Ryan said. "No sense in heading back. May as well keep going west."

"You say that like we've got a choice," J.B. said, amused.

They gathered their packs, and were ready to begin when Ryan noticed that Jak had become distracted. The albino teen shook his head.

"Trouble. Wags coming from west, heading straight here. Heavy shit, should eyeball soon."

Ryan didn't doubt him. Even as he spoke, the sound of a convoy became audible from the distance. In normal circumstances, visual contact would have occurred first; but with this heat haze still rendering a false horizon, normal was a changed thing.

Ryan breathed heavily. "At least they're not from Strip-mall. They might be friendly, or at least inclined to ask first, fire second."

The old bus still had some use. It was a big vehicle, and could at least offer a degree of cover that was sorely lacking in the surrounding environment. The friends adopted positions around the bus that covered them from the oncoming convoy. As it broke through the haze, they could see that it was at least five wags strong, with a heavily armored vehicle at the front. They would have expected it to either fire on them from a distance—a "make-sure" defensive measure—or to approach them close up, knowing that the armored wag offered protection.

It did neither. Instead, the wag pulled up about a thousand yards away, the rest of the convoy coming to a halt at its rear. It sat there, immobile, for some time.

"What's his game?" Mildred asked.

"An interesting one," J.B. replied. "Is he trying to draw our fire?"

"Bastard strange way to do it," Ryan countered.

And then, just when they'd started to grow weary of the waiting, something happened. The offside door of the wag opened, and a squat, muscular man emerged. Dressed in a black vest and camou pants, with heavy boots and a khaki bandanna, he was holding a white cloth above his head. Slowly, he began to walk toward them. As he got closer, they could see that he was wearing the bandanna out of vanity for his bald head, although the rest of him was hairy, down to the bushy black beard flecked with gray that flowed onto his chest. His eyes were hidden behind mirrored aviator shades.

"He triple stupe or something?" Jak spit.

"Or triple smart," Ryan countered. "We're not going to fire on him when he's unarmed but has all that firepower at his back. That'd be like saying please chill me."

"Might be mutie stupes," Jak said. "Still taking big chance."

"Looks like the kind of guy that's based his life around taking chances," Mildred returned. "You don't get a trader with a wag like that unless you're prepared to walk the line."

As she said this, both J.B. and Ryan's thoughts turned to their old mentor, the man known simply as Trader. The one thing he'd taught them, above all else, was that life was a risk so you always had to weigh the odds with great care.

"They've got us covered," Ryan said decisively. "Must have."

"Probably long-range, mebbe they've even got one of those working infrareds or heat-seekers so they can see how many of us there are. We make one move, and we've bought the farm before he even needs to duck and cover," J.B. stated.

They laid their weapons at ease, as Ryan indicated. By this time, the heavyset man was in hailing distance.

"Looks like you've got trouble, there," he began.

Ryan and J.B. exchanged puzzled glances. No ultimatum? The lone man continued.

"I'm thinking that mebbe you could use some help."

Ryan paused before answering, "That's good of you to offer help, especially to strangers. But it's not the way things usually are. People in these parts usually come in blasting first, asking questions second. That's if there's anyone left to ask."

The heavyset man shrugged. "True. But there are some people I'm looking for in these parts, and I figure you may be them."

"How come?" Ryan looked along his people. Their faces echoed his own suspicion. They were rarely welcomed, or sought for anything other than retribution.

"I heard tell that a certain group of fighters were in these parts. I know their reputation. I know that they were last heard of in Stripmall, and that no one who isn't gaudy or paying mark is welcome there for long. And I know that there are six of you using that wag as cover."

"You're certain of a lot of things," Ryan yelled in return. "Means you must have good information and some serious tech."

"You're damn right I have," the man replied, his tone taking on a kind of pride. "I didn't get to be the best trader in these parts of the land without having a nose for useful shit. I like useful. I like good. And you people have a rep as being the best."

"How do you hear so much?" In truth, Ryan didn't care, but he'd ask anything to buy some time—time to figure out how they could cover themselves against the armored wag when they were either pinned down behind the old bus or completely in the open. Either way, it wasn't good.

"Tell ya something. I got this armorer, and she's obsessed by stories about you people. She's also got a nose for the ordnance like you wouldn't believe. She's got two big goals in her life, much as she'll let me know. One is to have the best armory of any trader. The other is to work with you guys. I trust her word on how good you are. But

listen, don't just take my word for it." Slowly, so as to show
that he had no concealed weapon, he lifted his right hand
until it touched the side of his face. "Eula, get your ass out
here, but slow." He carefully put his hand down, then continued. "Something she scoped out for me. Some old tech
equipment that enables us to communicate without having to carry a lot of shit. See, she's good. But don't take
my word for it. She's coming."

From beyond the heavyset trader, they could see someone exit the armored wag and start to walk slowly toward
them with a purposeful stride, and a gait that suggested she
was not to be trifled with. She was barely more than five
feet tall, and slight in build. She was dressed in black: vest,
skirt and leggings, with heavy boots that seemed too large
for her. Her hair was also raven-black, tied in a ponytail
that whipped behind her with every stride. She was carrying a 7.62 mm assault rifle that seemed too large for her.

When Eula was level with the trader, she stopped. She
didn't bother to look at him, but spoke unbidden.

"Been looking for you people for a long time, if you're
who I think you are. Got a lot to learn from you. We all
have. Especially J. B. Dix. Met him once. Remember him
well."

Behind the bus, Mildred looked at the Armorer. "You
know who she is, John?"

The Armorer looked puzzled. "She doesn't look all that
old. If it had been recent times, then all of you would know
her, too. But, if I do know her, then it must've been when
she was real small. Don't recognize the name, either."

"Well, she knows you," Mildred replied. "What's more,
that fact looks like it may save our asses for now. So you'd

better remember, in case she gets pissed at the fact that you can't."

"Well?" the trader yelled, "you gonna come out, or you still figure that we want to chill you?"

"Could have done that a long time back," Ryan countered. He indicated to his people. "We're coming out."

The friends emerged from the cover of the old school bus. As they did, they could see that Eula was scoping them. She turned to the trader and nodded. She was satisfied they were who they were supposed to be, which was some kind of comfort, Ryan figured. At least they were safe…for now.

Eula spent the longest time staring at J.B. Her expression was unfathomable, and it made the Armorer feel uncomfortable.

"You don't remember me, do you, John Barrymore Dix?" she asked. When he didn't answer, a smile played across her lips. "Don't worry. It was a long time ago. And no one noticed me back then. No one."

Chapter Two

The Past

Guthrie was a nowhere ville, a small pesthole of huts and small hovels constructed from the debris that could be scavenged. The people made some desultory attempts at farming, but the nature of the dustbowl soil meant that the few crops it could produce were stunted and lacking in nutrients. It was off the beaten tracks and ruined blacktops that still crosscrossed the midwest, and those who lived there had a legend that they only landed up there because they got lost on the way to somewhere else. The ville itself was named after the guy who was the first to erect a little hut that fell down many times before others stumbled on him and built a few little huts of their own.

J. B. Dix had ended up in the pesthole ville of Guthrie in much the same way as anyone else who arrived there: by accident, and less than willingly. The skinny youth was quiet, slight, wiry, and wore spectacles that he was almost always polishing. He never said a word if he could help it, although if a person got him talking about blasters, that was another matter. You couldn't shut him up, and he'd talk about stuff that no one else in Guthrie gave a shit about. So after a while they stopped asking. And he stopped talking.

What they really wanted to know was where he'd come from, why he'd landed in Guthrie and what the hell had happened to cause him to run. But any attempt to broach that subject was met with a greater silence than was usual. And it wasn't just a matter of his being a quiet kid. There was something else there, a kind of menace that said it would be a real bad idea to mess with him.

So no one did. Except for Jeb Willets, who was big and muscular and therefore so out of place in Guthrie that he was able to bully his way around the ville. He figured the little kid with the bad eyes would be an easy mark. And at first he'd seemed right. He'd taken him by surprise and landed a few blows that seemed to knock the hell out of the kid. But Dix was sly—a feint, a foot, a use of balance that the lumbering Willets wasn't used to, and the big man was on the ground, unconscious.

Then the thing that really made them leave J.B. alone: while Willets was unconscious, the skinny kid wired his shack to blow with some explosive he'd made. Then, when Willets was recovered, Dix took him at knifepoint and made him watch as the shack blew.

No one stepped in. The truth was, they all wished that they could have done that to the man. Willets was broken, and left the ville soon after.

And no one asked J.B. any questions. They left him alone. He liked it that way.

Of course, a man had to live. And one of the few things that he ever let out about himself was that he came from Colorado way, from a ville called Cripple Creek. He said nothing about family, but only mentioned it by way of saying that since he was young he'd been fascinated by blasters and explosives, and had educated himself in seeing what made them work, taking them apart and putting them back together again in better working condition than he'd found them. He knew the predark histories of the things, and he'd tell you about them while he was taking your beat-up old blaster and making it shiny like new.

The kid had a talent. It was the one time he didn't shut up, and no one wanted to know, but nonetheless you had to give it to him.

So most of the time you'd just leave the blaster with him, and let him bring it back to you when it was done. That was fine. You paid him jack if you had any, or else you gave him food or supplies of some kind. There were convoys that passed in or near from time to time, and there was usually some service or some goods that Guthrie could use for exchange.

It wasn't living, but it was existing. You didn't buy the farm, and that was enough for most people. It was enough for the young J. B. Dix, for now.

That changed when Trader chanced upon the shanty.

"WHY DO WE ALWAYS end up in shit heaps like this?" Hunnaker moaned, idly scratching at herself; she could already feel the bugs starting to bite. She looked out of War Wag One at the expanse of dust, ordure and ramshackle buildings that made up the ville. "We're supposed to be the best, so why do we bother?"

Trader bit the end off a cigar, spit it over her shoulder and out into the dirt, then clamped the smoke between a grin that threatened to split the graying stubble that covered the lower half of his face.

"Hunn, sometimes I can't believe how stupe you can be. For someone so smart, you don't do a lot of thinking. How do you reckon we got to where we are? I'll tell you," he went on, not giving her a chance to answer, "it's because we pay attention to detail. You never know what's out there until you've looked. That's how come I found the stash that set us up, and that's how come we keep getting bigger while all those other traders just bitch and whine and wonder how we did it."

"And you reckon we'll find something here?" she questioned, her tone leaving her doubt all too obvious.

Poet leaned over them both. "Ever known Trader to be wrong?"

She looked at both men, who were grinning at her.

"There's always a first time," she said flatly.

Trader and Poet were still laughing sometime later, when they took a look around the ville. By the time they'd finished, the smiles had gone and they were figuring that maybe Hunn had been right. There was nothing in this pesthole to interest them. They'd made some sparse business, just for the sake of it, and because Trader had a few commodities, he was overstocked with that he could afford to let go at a low rate. Never knew when they might come back this way, and they wanted a hospitable rather than hostile reception. Come to that, it would ensure they left on friendly terms, rather than in the wake of a firefight. Because these were mean folk, more so than in many other places. The misery of their existence saw to that.

So it looked as though this little detour would draw a blank, and it would be little more than just some wasted fuel.

Until the one thing that had been nagging at Trader the whole while suddenly clicked in his mind.

"You notice something about these folk?" he asked Poet in an undertone.

"Other than they're being meaner than a mutie rattle-snake with a jolt hangover?"

Trader's grin returned. "Yeah, other than that. Take a look at their blasters."

Poet allowed himself a surreptitious study as they walked, before answering. "Nice gear. Wouldn't like to have to face them down with those, even with all the ord-nance we carry."

"Too true, Poet. But think about it. This place is knee-deep in its own shit, with nothing to offer us in any way…to offer anyone who passes through. So how come they have such good ordnance?"

"Let me ask a few questions," Poet replied.

Which didn't prove too hard. There was only one bar in the ville, and although the brew it purveyed was of a poor quality—indeed, Poet felt he'd drunk better sump oil than this filth—it was all the locals had, and they were more than happy to let a lonely traveler spend some jack on getting drunk with them. He had plenty to spare, it seemed, and was more than happy to spend. Get him drunk enough and there was the chance of rolling him, boosting the local economy and getting one over an outlander, which was always a local favorite.

Except that Poet had drunk more, and far better, men under the table than lived in Guthrie. And for all its foul taste, the local brew was nowhere near as strong as some that he'd tasted over the years. So it wasn't long—and not so deep in his pocket as he'd feared—that Poet had turned the tables and had the locals on the subject of their hardware. A little flattery about how good their blasters were compared to some he'd seen on his travels, and they were soon telling him about their little secret advantage in the matter.

And it didn't take them much to start speculating on J. B. Dix, the taciturn and private teenager who'd arrived the previous fall had been a hot topic of conversation ever since. Tongues loosened, Poet had to put up with a whole lot of speculation that was of no use to him. But he did work out—among the drivel and drunken babble—that the young man had a rare talent that he figured Trader would feel wasted in this backwater.

So it was that the following afternoon, while Poet busied himself and those he had drunk with still nursed the mother, father, son and daughter of all hangovers, Trader made his way to the small shack that the mysterious J. B. Dix had made his home.

"Speak to you, son?" Trader had asked as he hovered in the doorway. The young man said nothing, hunched over an old Smith & Wesson .38 snubbie, meticulously cleaning and reassembling the blaster. The pieces he had finished with were immaculate; the pieces he had yet to reach looked as if they came from a different blaster. Trader was about to speak again, when J.B. finally answered.

"What do you want?" he asked in a tone that was neutral but brisk. He didn't bother looking up.

"I heard you've got a talent for this sort of thing," Trader said, realizing that niceties would be wasted, and that it would be best to cut to the chase. "I've got some ordnance that needs work. You care to take a look?" He didn't feel it necessary to add that the ordnance had been fine until he'd told Poet to work on it.

"It'll cost you," J.B. said simply.

"We'll see," Trader replied. "See what kind of a job you do."

"It'll be good," J.B. answered. He said no more. He was still absorbed in his work, and still didn't look up.

After a pause, Trader said, "I'll be back."

He left without another word from the taciturn teenager. As he walked back to War Wag One, through the filth and misery that was Guthrie, he mused on how come a man with such a talent should end up here. He hadn't originated from here, and he hadn't been here that long. So what had happened that had forced him to flee wherever it was that he came from and seek to bury himself in this back of beyond pesthole?

Trader was a student of the human condition. Not just because people fascinated him, but because it was a necessity in his occupation. You didn't learn to read people, and damn quick, then it was certain that you'd end up with a bullet or a knife in your gut, and all your jack in someone else's hands. So you learned to read people pretty quick. Generally. But this boy was something different. He gave so little away that it was hard to get any kind of a handle on him.

But Trader had a gut feeling. The kid did good work, and he obviously took pride in it. That attention to meticulous detail said something about his nature. And he seemed to be reserved by that nature. If something had made him run, it wasn't so bad that he was nervous about it. It really did seem as though he just felt it was no one else's business.

Okay, then, let's see how he does with the blasters, Trader thought. He found that Poet had finished his allotted task, and he sent him along to the kid with the screwed-up ordnance. Poet returned a few minutes later, shaking his head. Kid had said to come back tomorrow and hadn't even bothered looking up. Poet found him hard to fathom.

So how the hell the rest of them would take him—especially someone like Hunn—was an idea that kept Trader amused for the rest of the day.

Next morning, Trader felt that he should go and conclude this business himself. Mulling it over while drinking the night before, he'd almost made up his mind to ask the kid to join them without even waiting to see what his work was like. Hell, he could see that from everyone in this rotted ville. The only real question was how the kid would fit in. He'd either fit or fuck off pretty damn quick. So scratch that. The real question was whether the kid would want to fit with them.

Only one way to find out.

When Trader arrived at the ramshackle hut in which J.B. had made his home, he found that the kid was ready and waiting for him.

"Sit down," J.B. said, gesturing to a chair. Trader eyed it warily. It looked like it might collapse under his weight. He very carefully sat. The kid met his eyes, staring at him as though trying to work him out. It was rarely, if at all, that it was this way around, and Trader found it an unnerving experience. "So," J.B. said finally, "why are you jerking me around?"

"What makes you say that?"

The briefest of smiles—only the vaguest of amusement—flickered across his face as he gestured to the immaculately cleaned and restored blasters that lay on an oilcloth by the table.

"There was nothing wrong with your blasters. Least, there was nothing wrong till you or one of your people tried to mess them up."

"What makes you say that?" Trader repeated, keeping his voice even.

"Normal wear and tear, stupe assholes misusing ordnance…that's easy to spot. Just like it was easy to spot that someone had tried to make these blasters looked misused, and to fuck up the most difficult shit to fix. That just doesn't happen in regular use. Mebbe one in ten, if you're unlucky. But not every single one."

Trader grinned. "You got me. I wanted to see how good you were."

"Why?"

"Because I want you to join us. I don't know why you're stuck in this pesthole, and truth is, I don't care. But I do know this—you're wasted here. We could do with someone like you."

"Whoever messed those blasters for you knew what they were doing."

"True enough," Trader agreed, "but while they might have been able to put them right, they wouldn't have known that they'd been deliberately messed with to begin with. That, Mr. Dix, is a true talent. And I could do with true talent. I've got the best convoy in these lands, and I got it by keeping my eye open for opportunity. Way I figure it, we pick up armament to trade cheap that are fucked up, you fix them and we make a good profit. More than we do now. And with you one of us, we get to have the best armory of any convoy should anyone try to mess with us."

"And I get?"

"Good jack. I look after my people in other ways, too. You play straight with me, you won't find a better boss nor baron anywhere. I figure that if I treat my people good, they won't rip me off or run. Mind, you step out of line and I'll chill you myself."

J.B. said nothing for some time, just stared at the man in front of him. Trader felt like the young man was trying to stare deep into his soul, to work him out. It wasn't pleasant, but it was promising: someone this careful was liable to screw up easily.

Finally, Dix broke his silence. "As long as there's no more stupe tricks or tests like this one," he said, indicating the oilcloth of blasters, "then I'm in. It's about time I got out of this no horse shitheap."

Trader's face split in a broad grin. "Reckon you're about right," he said simply. "Welcome aboard War Wag One."

Chapter Three

The Present

In the moments since Eula had spoken, a silence had spread uncomfortably over the oddly clustered group. On one side stood Eula and the trader. On the other stood the six friends. J.B. was staring at the young woman. The others were dividing their attention between the Armorer and Eula, trying to fathom what ghost had just snaked from J.B.'s past, and how it would affect them.

J.B. was aware that whatever he said next would be of the utmost importance. The armored wag in the distance was linked to the trader—and probably the young woman who was the convoy armorer—by the discreet headsets they wore. Only now, up close, could he see the small stalk of clear plastic housing the mic as it sat in the trader's beard. Eula's was a little more obvious. No doubt they were powerful enough to be picking up every word that was said out here, so close were the two sides.

Problem was, he had never seen this young woman in his life, and had no idea who she was. The name meant nothing to him. The face, likewise. If he said as much, how pissed would these two people in front him be? And if they were, then how much would that affect the actions of the armored wag that lay some distance back? Take out these two and take scant cover, and what chance was there of surviving attack? With the mics, was there even the chance of taking that cover before being picked off?

They were outnumbered and unsure whether the supposed enemy actually was the enemy at this moment. The wrong word was all it would take to make the situation explode.

For a man whose way with words veered between minimal and clumsy most of the time, this was a no-win call. But he had to say something. The weight of expectation was upon him. That was a phrase he'd heard Doc mutter in the past, and he had never understood it until now.

"Listen," he began haltingly, "you say you know me, but I gotta tell you, I don't recognize your face, and you're not that old. I mean, I spent a lot of time with these people over the past few years, and you would have been a child, and…"

He could feel the others watch the trader and the woman, could feel the tension as they waited to read body language, the tightening of their posture as they prepared to act.

The trader looked at the woman beside him. She looked, in turn, with a level gaze at J.B.

"Well?" the trader asked.

She shrugged. "He's right. I remember him, but it was a long time ago, now. I was just a kid, and he wouldn't have noticed me back then. Always interested in ordnance. People came second. Bet they still do. Got a point, though. Blasters don't let you down like people do."

Was it Mildred's imagination, or did Eula look just a

little too hard at John when she said this last? Was there an undertone there that suggested she should be watched, that she should not be trusted?

Mildred looked along at the others, a sidelong glance intended to disguise her intent. It was hard to tell if they had also picked up on this. Back in the days of her youth, they called it a poker face. Her father would denounce the effects of gambling on a Sunday, but wasn't averse to a little poker on the Saturday night with a few friends. He always lost a little, but never gambled much. He said it was because he liked the social side of the game, and knew his face was too honest, too open. That was why to take it seriously would have meant ruin.

J.B.'s answer was important. No one knew that better than him. His words were measured, much more than he was used to. He knew that he had to pick each one as carefully as he, usually so dismissive of words, could.

"One thing you learn as you get older," he said slowly, "is that ordnance is important because it helps people. Get careful with that, and it can turn a firefight, defend a ville— a convoy—and someone sure as shit has to obsess at times, to make sure that can happen."

Eula, whose face had been thus far so set as to make the stony-faced friends seem open and readable, allowed a flicker of emotion to show. What it may be was hard to tell. Humor? Anger? Exasperation? Perhaps one, perhaps all. It was the briefest of muscle twitches.

"Yeah," she said slowly, "that's a good lesson to learn. Hope you didn't pick it up the hard way."

"Depends what you think is the hard way," J.B. countered.

Eula gave the briefest of nods—everything, it seemed,

was minimal to the point of almost nonexistence with her—before answering the questioning gaze of the trader.

"Yeah, I think we should ask them."

This last was cryptic enough to cause a ripple of bemusement to spread across the group. They were wire taut, expecting to have to act in less than a blink of an eye; and now, when they would have expected resolution and action, they were to be faced with a further dilemma.

The trader let a wry grin spread across his dark, bearded face. He raised his hand to his eyes and took off his aviator shades. A small gesture, but a conciliatory one as they would now be able to read his eyes. They were small, set in folds of wrinkled fat that showed a greater age than they would have guessed, and were of a piercing, ice blue. They almost twinkled with humor as he spoke.

"It's okay, guys. Listen, I've got to be straight with you, here. If we wanted to take you out, we could have done it without even breaking a sweat. We've got the firepower to do it, and it would have been easy to reduce that shitty little wag you were stuck with to a heap of melted junk metal. No problem. But our tech, and the intel we've picked up along the road, suggested that you were the people Eula here has heard of, and we need someone like you right now. So that's why we stopped and I offered myself up like this. Sure, you could try and chill me. I figure my wag would have taken you out before your fingers had even tightened on the those triggers. Mebbe that's a gamble, but you don't get anywhere by playing it safe the whole time."

Ryan let him speak. This trader was a little keen on the sound of his own voice, and a lot of what he was saying had already been said. But that was good. They'd already learned that the woman's name was Eula. Ryan was hoping that it would ring a few more bells with J.B.'s memory. Any help they could get would be appreciated. And the trader was letting slip that he was in trouble. Someone like him would only want people like them because he was short of muscle, which meant that he'd let slip a weakness.

"So what's your proposition?" Ryan said when the trader had left him the time and space to speak.

"Simple, really. I need replacements in my sec force. We had a little run-in with another convoy down the road apiece. It left me a little light on manpower."

"That's a mite careless for a man who's telling us about how good his tech is," Ryan posed.

The trader nodded. "Sure enough. Trouble is, the tech isn't always what you need. We don't have the night-vision shit working on the wag, and one of my rivals decided to pay us a little visit in the dark. His men crept up on us, and I guess I found that my boys weren't as sharp as they thought they were. Mebbe the tech has been too good to them—to us—and it made us a little soft."

Ryan was more than a little surprised that the trader had lasted long enough to be here. He seemed to give more and more away freely every time he opened his mouth, and he hadn't finished yet.

"I guess I should level with you. Eula knows of you because of J. B. Dix, but the stories about you spread across the lands. We should know, we spend most of our time on the road. You used to be with the Trader, right? Guy who was the biggest thing in convoys before he disappeared. Now, there are a lot of stories about him, too, and everyone has their own reason for why he went missing. I figure that mebbe he just made so much jack that he could afford to not lay his ass on the line every day, and that he's mebbe back where he got his shit in the first place, just enjoying every day."

He paused, scanning their faces to see if he was right. There was enough feral cunning with the loose tongue to perhaps be looking for a clue as to any great stash that he could uncover. He was far more transparent than he figured, and Ryan wasn't the only one who had to suppress a smile. Then again, he was the man with the tech and the wags, and they weren't. So if he was as stupe as he seemed, then he was lucky, too. And that was the most valuable commodity of all.

Their silence just encouraged him to run off at the mouth all the more. Sooner or later he'd tell them exactly what he wanted, but while he was letting this much slip, it wasn't worth telling him to cut to the chase.

"Yeah, well, if he is, then good luck to him. He earned it the hard way, and I'll tell you something—when I get the chance, I'm sure as shit gonna go the same way. Meantime, I've gotta earn that jack, and I'm down the number of men I need to cover my back. So I've got a proposition for you."

Finally, Ryan thought, but said nothing. The trader continued.

"We've got a run to do that some folks think is nothing short of asking to buy the farm. It's gonna take balls, but the way I hear it that's something you people ain't short of. Even the women. That's cool, if you ladies are anything like Eula, then I'm okay with that."

Mildred and Krysty exchanged glances. Each figured that this guy was ripe for having a new asshole ripped already, even though there was nothing wrong with the one he had, except that he used it for talking. Not even noticing this, he carried on regardless.

"I need replacement sec, and for a hard ride. I don't expect you to sign up for the long haul. Hell, I don't even want that myself. But I'll tell you what I can offer you. If we make the trip and you join us, there'll be good jack in it for you. More than that, it'll get you the hell out of here. 'Cause I'm thinking that right now you got no wag, and no way you can get out of this wasteland in one piece. I figure that does all my arguing for me."

Ryan considered that: they'd be trusting a man who was too full of himself for the one-eyed man's liking, and taking on the wild card that was whatever agenda Eula was bringing to the table. On the other hand, there was little to gain by staying where they were.

He looked at his companions. Mildred and Krysty had eyes that told him they would go with it; Doc raised one eyebrow in a manner that spoke volumes; and Jak shrugged, so slight that none but his friends would be able to see it. But it was J.B. whose opinion Ryan really wanted to know. He had known the Armorer longer than anyone, and the men had bonds forged in fire that went even deeper than their allegiances to the others in the group.

J.B.'s eyes flickered for a moment, as though indecision came from the need to search deeper within himself than he usually found necessary.

It was the slightest twitch of facial muscle, a nod that was barely a nod. But it was enough.

Ryan turned to the trader. He spoke slowly, as though he were still undecided. "Well, I guess you have a point, stranger. We're in a situation here that you could call no-win. Staying here is as good as buying the farm, just stringing out the agony, I guess. But we're taking a leap into the dark if—and it is if—we take up your offer. If we knew exactly what we were taking on…" He let it tail off, leaving the question unasked.

As he had hoped, the trader grimaced as he tried to hold his feelings in check and not let anything slip. But he was too garrulous, too open for that.

The man would be a sucker on poker night, Mildred thought, seeing where Ryan was leading him.

"All right, all right, I kinda wanted to get you signed up and with the plan before I told you too much, but if that's what it takes… Okay, it's this way. I've got a cargo of food supplies—some self-heats, dried stuff, fresh produce that we can keep that way with some old refrigeration units we plundered—and a whole lot of clothing. We're headed across this pesthole stretch of land, headed for the far side. It's a bastard of a haul, and there's shit-all in the way of stops along the way. At least, none that I would trust."

"If they're anything like Stripmall, then I can understand that," Ryan murmured.

"My friend, they make Stripmall look like a paradise," the trader said with a grim smile. "Point is, we don't have the fuel to keep the wags and the generators for the fresh stuff running if we make stops. We can only do it if we run hell-for-leather across this asswipe land. Hell, even stopping here is losing us valuable time. We can make mebbe one, two brief stops a day if we have to."

"So what's your problem?" Ryan asked. "Back in the day, when me and J.B. ran with Trader, we used to make long runs as a matter of course."

"You ever do the dustbowl?"

"We came this way a few times," Ryan mused. "Know Trader used to do it before I joined up."

"Yeah, but never in one long run," J.B. added. Ryan looked at him. He didn't know that J.B. knew anything about this territory. He'd certainly never mentioned it in all the years he'd known him. Nor had he said anything while they had been here.

The trader in front of them nodded. "There's a reason for that. These are the badlands, man. Rough riders and wag raiders. There's fuck all out here, so they have to do what they can, which means chilling and stealing anything that passes by and isn't defended by serious hardware. There's only one convoy that tried the straight run, and it didn't make it. So now it's our turn. We need new sec, and we want the best. From what I hear, that's you people. Reckon fate has smiled upon me—if not all of us—matching us up like this."

RYAN EYED HIM. The man was trying hard. Maybe a little too hard. So this other convoy hadn't made it? Ryan wondered if that was connected to the new refrigeration units they had acquired, and the loss of the sec men in a firefight with another convoy. Seemed too much of a coincidence. Still, if he made it seem as if they trusted the trader, then the man seemed too stupe to notice that they were holding out. The woman—Ryan looked at her, her face impassive and inscrutable all the while—was another matter.

"Figure you leave us no choice," Ryan said in his best ingenuous tone, "but even so, we'd be stupe if we said yes without knowing what kind of ordnance you had."

"Best you'll find," Eula interjected in flat tones. "Better

than J. B. Dix will have seen for many a year." There was
a note in her tone that suggested this should mean something to him; if so, it was too obtuse, and the Armorer was
left with nothing more than a vague sense of unease as her
eyes bored into him.

"You bet it is," the trader said quickly in a placating
manner. "Hell, it'd be impolite to ask you aboard without
showing you. Stand down," he added, holding his ear, obviously directing this into the headset, "we're coming
back. Everything is cool."

The trader turned, beckoning them to follow. Eula stood
back, still cradling the 7.62 mm blaster that looked too
large for her. Her impassive face still gave nothing away.
She was no threat at present—the manner in which
Krysty's sentient hair flowed free only reinforced this
impression—but she would still need to be watched.

The friends paused. The idea of having her, with that
blaster, at their backs was not something that anyone would
consider ideal. Subtly, Ryan indicated they should go with
it. Jak caught Ryan's eye, and as they fell in behind the
trader, the albino teen adopted the unusual position of taking up the rear of the party. Many places in his patched
camou jacket concealed his leaf-bladed throwing knives.
Reputation may have told how quick the albino youth could
be, but experience was the only way to really know the
swiftness with which he could move. As he passed Eula, he
knew he could move quicker than she could should the
need arise.

As they traveled the short distance between their
original position and the armored wag, they were able to
see more clearly the extent of the convoy. There were four

other wags. Two of them were large trailers, closed in on all sides. These were obviously the old refrigeration units. The cabs attached to them had been reinforced with mesh where any glass was visible, armor plating covering the remainder. The old paintwork along the sides of both cabs and wags was pitted and scarred where it was still visible. Camou had been painted over most of the rest. There were also a number of scores and scorch marks that made the friends wonder once more about how they had been "acquired."

These wags had only blasterports in the cabs. Although they would be hard to damage in themselves, their length and lack of slits made them vulnerable to blind-spot attack. That was probably why they sat in the middle of the convoy, flanked by two wags that carried the rest of the cargo. These were armored, with blasterports and slits. They had been converted, and both Ryan and J.B. could only admire the work that had gone into them. They looked to be solid vehicles, but they weren't big. If the cabs on the refrigerated wags could hold two people, these only held three or four, tops. Maximum of twelve crew.

The armored wag out front was more impressive. Again, it wasn't just the size, although it was a heavy-duty predark military wag, dark and heavy in color, albeit a little chipped and faded by combat. It was squat, with tires at front and a caterpillar track at the rear. It had bubble-mounted machine blasters, ob slits, shielded surveillance tech and two large mounted cannon. It could do some serious damage to anything that dared to go up against it.

"How much of the tech in that still work?" J.B. asked.

Eula answered. "Most of the surveillance tech, some of

the weapons systems. Much of it was fixable, but it's a little erratic."

J.B. looked over his shoulder. "You don't find that a problem?" he questioned, remembering how Trader had stripped much of the comp work out of War Wag One, preferring total reliability at the expense of some tech.

She shrugged. "It hasn't failed yet."

"But what about the tech that needed satellite shit? That can't be working," he added.

"I said some, not all," she snapped, taking it as though it was personal criticism.

By this time they had reached the armored wag, and the trader was running a loving hand over it.

"Hasn't seen me wrong yet," he said quietly. "This is it, guys. The convoy. Used to be two motorbikes, but they got wasted in our little, uh, *contretemps,*" he said, trying to brush past the matter.

"What?" Jak asked.

"An old word, dear boy, not English. I believe he is referring to the firefight he mentioned earlier," Doc said softly.

"Should fuckin' say so," Jak murmured.

"How many people you carry?" Ryan asked. He had noted a look of anger flash across the trader's face, and he wanted to move things on.

"This takes five people. A full complement of sec, drivers, workers comes to seventeen on a trip."

"Yeah, and how many you carrying now?" Ryan pressed.

The trader grimaced. "That's the thing. We lost eight in the firefight."

"You lost half your people, and you don't think that was a little careless?" Mildred questioned, unable to contain herself.

"Two went at the back. The bike riders are always the first to cop it," the trader mused, seeming to ponder her question deeply. "We did salvage the bikes, though," he added with some pride. "As for the other six… We had a direct hit on one wag that took out three people, two straight away and one after a day. The wags are good and strong, but it was the concussion of the blast that did it for them. Stupe thing is that they were chilled by their own weapons going off in the wag. Pathetic. Two sec bought the farm trying to protect the refrigerators. You can see those bastards are blind, and they had to get out of the cabs. I think we learned something from that. And they did. Just a shame it was too late."

He paused, seemingly lost in thought.

"And the last one?" Doc prompted. "So far you have mentioned only five casualties."

The trader shook his head, pensive. "Penn. Best quartermaster I've ever had. Just a little too protective of his post, that was all. He saw a group of coldhearts from the other convoy trying to bust into one of the wags and saw red. He was traveling with us, and was out of there before anyone had a chance to stop him. He was shouting at them to stop, firing off without aiming, and they just picked him off. One shot. Bang. Took the poor stupe bastard's head off. Swear his body kept running for a yard before he went down."

If Ryan hadn't believed a word the man had said before this, then now he certainly had no faith. The story was crap.

Just like the rest of it. No one who served time on a convoy would be so stupe. Just as no one who had served time would get chilled by their own weapons when their wag got hit. Why were they drawn when they were inside, and unnecessary?

Whatever had really happened, it hadn't been what the trader wanted them to believe.

For so many reasons, it seemed like a triple stupe thing to do, but for so many other reasons, it was their only option. Ryan found himself saying, "Okay, we'll join you. But if we're gonna work together, what do we call you?"

A number of things sprung to mind, but the trader's answer was, "LaGuerre. Armand LaGuerre." He stuck out his hand. "But you can call me 'boss.' No, only kidding," he added hurriedly, on seeing the stony looks that elicited.

Saying nothing more, Ryan took his hand, then looked at his people with an expression that communicated his own reservations were as deep as theirs.

At least they had transport out of here.

Chapter Four

Say what you like about LaGuerre, Mildred mused, he's not as big a fool as you'd take him for. He didn't survive as a trader by being stupid, and if—as they suspected—the firefight that had deprived him of nearly half his crew had less to do with being attacked than with being the attacker, then he wasn't the complete idiot he seemed. No, it seemed to her that he had a certain cunning, a certain base instinct that could kick in and override the tendency to let his mouth run away with him. A garrulous yet cunning fool. It was a combination that was volatile, and could only end one way.

The question was, when?

In the meantime, he had been smart enough to keep the friends apart. He had something he wanted from them, and he had found a way to get it without allowing them the space and time to confer, to make plans of their own and put them into action. Did he realize that they didn't trust him? Or did he just assume that no one trusted him, and in their turn were to be trusted themselves?

Ultimately, she figured that it didn't matter. The result was the same, no matter what you may surmise. The friends had been divided among the wags of the convoy, and the salvaged bikes had been put to use. It made sense

from a sec point of view to use a newly recruited group of
proved fighters in such a manner. Hell, she would have
done it that way herself. But there was something…
Maybe it was just that she didn't trust LaGuerre. No, screw
that, there really was something about the man that suggested he knew this was a good move for him as much as
for the convoy. Keep them apart, and they couldn't conspire.

So it was that Ryan and Jak rode the motorbikes at the
back of the convoy—the leader and the most dangerous
and quick of the fighters. A coincidence? She didn't think
so. It made sense for the two of them to ride at the rear of
the convoy as they were the best suited to combat and the
demands of instant response from such a position. But
still, it seemed too convenient.

Krysty and herself were now riding shotgun in the refrigerated wags. Doc rode the wag at the rear of the convoy.
One of LaGuerre's men had been shifted from the armored
wag to the one directly behind. The purpose of that had
been to allow J.B. to ride the armored, lead wag, which was
suspicious in itself. At least, it seemed so to Mildred. If
they had replaced sec at the rear of the convoy, and in all
the other wags, then why not put J.B. in the wag directly
behind the armored leader? That would have been consistent. The action that LaGuerre had taken was anything
but.

Mildred couldn't help wondering if this last course of
action was due to LaGuerre, or at the prompting of Eula.
For now J.B. was in the wag with her, which would give
her plenty of time to… Well, to what? What was her link
to John; in what way were they connected? Mildred knew

John well enough. When he had said that he had no idea who the young woman was, or why she knew so much about him, Mildred had believed him.

So who was she? What did she want? And how would that affect J.B. and the companions?

Whatever the outcome, it was impossible to do anything while they were separated. Come to that, it was proving impossible to get anything in the way of sense out of her current companion. Reese, the driver of the refrigerated wag, was a large woman. Probably 250 pounds of her was crammed behind the wheel of the big rig. Not an ounce of it fat. Her knees looked cramped, even in the space of the cab, as she was over six feet tall. She was dark and heavyset, with crude tattoos on her upper arms and multiple piercings in her upper lip, brow and ears. Hell, she probably had her nipples pierced, but Mildred wasn't about to ask.

That piercing in her upper lip should have gone through both, sealing her mouth shut. Might as well, for all that Mildred had gotten out of her. When they had first been introduced, and Mildred had clambered up into the cab, Reese had shown her the weapons bay under the dash area and explained tersely that her duty was to keep her eyes open and her trigger finger ready. That was all. Anything to do with the rig itself she was to leave to Reese. The woman made that clear with a proprietorial tone that left nothing to doubt.

And since then, silence. Mildred had tried to ask a few questions—nothing too deep, just general conversation about the convoy and the way in which they usually traveled; would there be rest stops, and when did they generally occur? This last was the kind of question any newcomer to convoy sec would ask, leaving aside Mildred's real reason of wanting to know when she would be able to communicate with the others.

"Not anyone's business. Happens when it happens."

Reese wasn't hostile. Just so taciturn as to make John seem like that old buzzard Tanner, Mildred thought. Reese kept her eyes firmly fixed on the wag ahead, and on the road ahead of that. Anything else she seemed to view as an irritating distraction.

Mildred noted that the cab was fitted with comm tech, and was in touch with all wags on the convoy. Not that you would know it so far, as it seemed that radio contact was kept to a minimum.

She wondered if the bikes were also fitted with this tech.

RYAN AND JAK RODE the edges of the road, trying to avoid the backwash of dust and dirt as much as possible. A five-wag convoy kicked up a hell of a cloud in a land like this, and it would have choked them to kick in too close to the end of the line. They had masks and goggles, but even these only cut down, rather than eliminated, the problem. Most important was their breathing and their sight. Without those, they would have been chilled either by suffocation, by riding too fast into the back of a wag in front, or by riding themselves into the treacherous blacktop.

The other problem, once you'd solved the simple matter of staying alive, was to do your job. If you couldn't see jackshit, then how could you expect to see any incoming? In this territory, where wild riders skirted the ribbon in favor of the dense-packed dirt off-road, you had to keep your vision as clear as possible for a 360-degree sweep. So you didn't just hang in behind—you kept out of the dust cloud that hung over and around the convoy, and you veered off in complex figures that would enable you to double back, get a look behind, and get back into line without hitting a pothole, a crevice, or each other.

Both Jak and Ryan wore headsets that would keep them in touch with the armored wag on point. Trouble was, it was so bastard noisy on the bikes, with the roar of their engines, the rush of the air, and the noise of the five heavy wags, that each man had little hope of hearing any message that may come his way.

They carried on their maneuvers, kept up their guard, each isolated in his own bubble of dust and noise. The only way they'd know if the convoy stopped was by overshooting it.

KRYSTY HAD THE OPPOSITE trouble to Mildred. While Reese was the strong, silent type, the driver of Krysty's wag was an emaciated old man called Ray. Short, skinny and anywhere between the age of forty and eighty for all that his wrinkled skin could tell her, he was stronger than he looked. It seemed as if she could blow on the old man and knock him down, yet he handled the heavy steering with an ease that was shown in the way he ignored the road and looked squarely at the red-haired woman, speaking in a long stream of consciousness that hardly allowed her the chance to ask him anything. He was obviously relishing the chance to speak to someone again, as the twinkling brown eyes beneath the battered baseball cap betrayed.

If only what he was saying had any real value…

"You come from the east, babe? I used to spend a lot of time in the east. That was back before I joined this crew, mind you. I always say that you can't beat a real friendly team, and I'll be frank with you, this ain't a real friendly team. Not that they're bad people, mind you. Not at all. I'll say that for them. Really loyal to Armand. And he does treat us well in return, you have to give him that. But I miss the days when I'd be driving and I was with people who didn't mind a chat. You ever hear that old word, babe? It means a talk. A talk about nothing. Least ways, a talk about stuff that most people don't think is really important. See, I use to love being in the east 'cause there were a lot of villes there that still had some of the old tech working in some way. That's what I will say for Armand, he gets that old tech working. Real good for me as I can have old music and stuff. I love all that. You don't get that out here so much. The old tech that still works like that, I mean. See, that was good about being back east. Old movies. Gee, it was a different life back then, wasn't it? But what am I saying, you might not have seen any of that stuff. Ah, you don't know what you've missed. All those old songs. I loved it when they had tech that could still play all that old stuff. I've got this real good memory for that sort of thing, and I like to sing while I'm driving. It kinda helps to speed the road along a little, and gives me something to think about…" He began to sing in a cracked tenor.

Krysty was beginning to get a headache.

DOC WAS GETTING along just fine. He was in the wag at the rear of the convoy. If he looked out of the ob slit at the back of the wag he could just about see Ryan and Jak as they weaved in and out of the dust.

"I did not know that young Jak was such an accomplished rider," he said to himself, "though I would imagine he's a wow on one of those—dammit, what were they called... Ah! Skateboards. Yes."

When he turned back to face the interior of the wag, he took in both the view and the warm fug of people forced to live close together. Too close. There were two other inhabitants, one of whom was currently trying to sleep. Her name was Raven, and when he had expressed surprise at her being a redhead, and not jet-black, she had looked at him as though he were insane. Doc, of course, was used to this, and let it slip over him. As of yet, he did not know from whence she had derived that charming name, but no doubt he would elicit this information sooner or later. When her temper improved.

"She's not normally like this," said the other inhabitant of the wag, eyes fixed on the road ahead. "It's just that we're not really letting her sleep. Tarran, the guy you replaced, he was real quiet. Never used to talk to me much at all, which was a pain in the ass as it gets real lonely and dull on some of these drives. We used to have an old tech disk player, and I'd play some old tunes from before skydark. She used to moan about that, too, so I gave it to Ray in the end. You'd like Ray. Not just 'cause he's old, like you. But 'cause he never shuts up. Talks kinda odd, like you."

"Yeah, like you don't," Raven moaned from the bunk. "You don't get me talking nonstop when you're trying to sleep."

"No, you had other things on your mind..." The driver spun to face Doc briefly, so that she could lock eyes, convince him of her veracity, before turning back to the road. Her name was Ramona, and she was dark where Raven was pale. "I tell you what, Doc, her moaning used to wake me up. Sometimes she'd let Tarran play with her pussy while she was driving. Damn near could have driven us off the road. Worse, the bitch used to let him drive sometimes, swapping while the wag was still in motion, and suck his dick while he was driving. Damn unsafe."

"You wouldn't have said that, you saw the size of his dick." Raven giggled, her anger subsiding. "No way something that small could have caused any accidents."

Doc was beginning to get used to the girls. They obviously liked to bicker. Perhaps it passed the long hours on the road. They had both slept, and changed shift, in the time that Doc had been in the wag. And both had questioned him on the connection between Eula and J.B. Both being equally disappointed when he had been unable to offer even the slightest of theories.

"Both begin with an *R*," he said by way of nothing. "That's interesting. Does LaGuerre do that on purpose, I wonder? In the same way that most of his convoy crew are women?"

"Ya know, I take it back," Ramona replied. "Doc, you're way crazier than Ray. 'Begin with an *R*,'" she said, imitating his tones badly. "What kind of a question is that? You wanna know something about Armand, baby, then you just ask outright."

"Very perceptive, I must say," Doc said, amused. "But nonetheless, it was a genuine question. Is it something to do with the way his mind works that he places in the same wags operatives who have identical initials?"

"Man, how many ways and how many words can you use in that question?"

"Whoa—okay, keep talking, this is sending me to sleep all right," Raven added.

Their words may have been harsh, but their tone was not, and Doc pressed the matter.

"It's all to do with psychology, madam. Are you familiar with that term?"

"Not as familiar as I hope to be with you, you old hunk o' man, you, sweet talking me like that," Ramona mocked. "Si-wha'? Listen up, the only reason we're both on this wag is because we've been with Armand the longest, and this is the wag with the jack. He trusts us."

Doc eyed the interior of the wag once more. There was one seat up front, for the driver. Another at the rear, for the sec man, which he occupied. The bunk on which Raven lay was along one wall, with a makeshift kitchen area—no more than a hotplate and a small icebox—at the foot. A small comm unit and some tech reception equipment was on the wall opposite. An old safe with a combination lock was beside it. The rest of the space in the narrow wag, apart from an even more narrow channel they all used to negotiate the interior, was taken up with the stock that could not have been fitted into the front wag.

"It's a combination safe," Doc noted. "You may not know the combination."

"Yeah, we do," Raven said, obviously not as bored into slumber as she had made out. "Someone got to know it other than Armand, in case he buys the farm before we get to destination. He changes it every time. Don't know how he does that, though. Guess he trusts us, but not that much. Must do some, otherwise we could just take the bastard and blow it with plas ex."

"A fair point," Doc conceded. "LaGuerre seems to be a

deeper thinker than perhaps—if you will excuse me—he appears."

Both women laughed.

"Armand ain't exactly what you'd call sharp in some ways," Ramona mused, "but in others he is, kinda. Guess he's like all of us, he's good at some shit, and, well, shit at other shit."

"His secret, seemingly, is that he knows the dividing line," Doc suggested.

Ramona thought about that for a moment, pausing only to swear at a particularly deep fissure in the road that she nearly missed. Then she said, "I guess you could say that about anyone, honey. And ya know, you're right. Most of the driving crew have always been women. 'Cept Ray, but I kinda don't know about him, sometimes. Quartermaster and sec have always been male. Quartermaster, couldn't say why. Sec, I guess it makes sense. Most guys are stronger like that. I know I couldn't have beaten Tarran in a fight of any kind, and Raven there always got herself pinned down… But mebbe that was different. Anyways, Armand does like to use women more than most traders I've seen. Course, as we're all so grateful for work and jack, and it does mean the boy has pussy on tap…."

It gave Doc a mental image that was far from her intent, and for a moment he was transported into a world of surrealism. But Doc was feeling sharp at the moment, and was determined to stay as such. Shaking this from his head, he asked, "And that would include the young woman Eula?"

Both Raven and Ramona laughed at that, the former so hard that she almost fell from the bunk, cursing as she caught herself in time.

"You have got to be shittin' me, Doc, baby," Ramona wheezed between gasps of laughter. "Think if he dared to pull it out near that one she'd damn near whip it off with her knife. Mebbe not right off, just leave him something as a reminder of what a bad boy he'd been."

"Something about her that is real scary, though," Raven said quietly. "Tell you, Doc, me and her over there have been together in this convoy for some time now, and we get on okay. Hellfire, everyone in here gets on okay with one another, really. That's what Armand likes. A happy crew does good work, he says. What the sneaky fuck means is that a happy crew ain't gonna slit his throat and run off with his jack. Anyway up, Eula comes in, and things ain't quite the same anymore. She don't talk none."

"I would suppose that would make you distrust her, as you all seem to be a little on the garrulous side," Doc murmured.

"Honey, I dunno what that word means, but it ain't nice, I can tell," Ramona said. "Ain't true, either, if it means what I think. 'Cause you ain't met Reese. She don't say more than five words a year, and mostly that's to tell you to fuck off."

"Reese?"

"Big muscle fucker, traveling with the sister." Ramona sniffed. "Lucky her… No, Reese is okay, just a little quiet. And scary. But openly. Unlike our gal Eula. She's too damn quiet in the wrong way. It's like she's always brooding on something. Something to hide. She looks at you like you're shit on her shoes, like she's got some little list in her head where she's adding up the good and bad." She snapped her fingers. "I know what it's like—it's like when Armand adds up the jack and stock he's got and that's he's got rid of, see if it balances. That's what she's doing. She got something on her back that's weighing her down, and some fucker's gonna get it big when she finds out who it is."

Doc was concerned by that. "And you think it may be my friend?"

"We dunno, do we?" Raven muttered sleepily from the bunk. "But she sure as shit seems to know him. Even if he don't know her. Think he does and he's not letting on to you, Doc? No offence, like, but are you sure?"

"I have known John Barrymore for some time now," Doc said stiffly, "and in times of emergency, the man has always been straight." His tone then softened as he bit his lip. "No, if he does know anything about her, he is truly unaware of it. It may be a mistake on her part. There was certainly no mistaking the bemusement on his face. Our good Armorer cannot hide certain things. He is controlled, and can mask emotion in combat. But he can be caught on the quick, and this was such a time. Tell me, ladies, what do you know of this Eula?"

"'Bout as much as you, hon," Ramona answered. "She says she comes from the east, and sure we picked her up there. But she don't say where, or how she learned so much about blasters and shit. Don't say much about nothing. Tell you, don't think even Armand knows much about her. Tell you something else, though—he thinks she's powerful medicine, and he trusts her judgment."

"And you do not?" Doc asked, sensing that in her tone.

Ramona gave a guttural laugh. "Hon, I'd trust that bitch even less than I could throw her scrawny ass."

Raven stirred on her bunk. "See, thing is, we ain't really got no secrets from each other, any of us. Can't do if you travel like we do, and for as long as we have. Secrets you'd like to have sometimes, sure, but it don't work that way. That's part of being a team, right? Sooner or later it comes out, or you walk. Now, you take Eula. That bitch is so tight it even pains her to piss. But no matter how hard she wants to keep it in, sooner or later it's gonna come out. And she ain't the type to walk if even the wildest guess comes close. And that's what we're kinda afraid of, right, Ramona?"

"Damn straight," the driver replied with an emphatic nod.

Doc kept his own counsel for once. He suspected Eula's secret was inextricably tied to the Armorer. And two taciturn people in the same wag would be oppressive to the point where the pressure would blow.

The only questions were when and how.

THE ARMORED WAG at the front of convoy was the only one to have a clear path ahead of it. Those in its wake were forever driving into a cloud of dust.

Zarir, the silent driver of the armored wag was, however, even more diligent than those who followed him. He was gripped by a paranoia that riders would come out of nowhere and attempt to outrun him. Maybe they wouldn't even bother with that. Maybe they would just ram into him, hoping they could deflect him from the smoothest of courses, running the wag into a crevice, a ditch, or even a trap. He was a good driver. No, he was the best. But there was always someone out to take that away from you. Well, he'd decided they wouldn't take that away from him. No. So he stayed tight-lipped, grim and silent as he concentrated on the road ahead with an intensity that made his head pound and ache. That was okay. A snort of something strong when they stopped cleared his head and kept alert for the next stretch. Sure, he hadn't slept for eight days, but at the end of the run Armand would let him sleep for a week, maybe even more if he needed. Armand was good to him.

Armand LaGuerre didn't give a shit. As long as Zarir drove fast and true, that was good. As long he stayed silent, it was even better. The rest of the trade crew were garrulous, and there was a time when LaGuerre welcomed that. Hell, even looked for it. And he was still cool with it as long as it was kept to the other wags. But since he'd taken Eula on board, he wanted some silence in his wag. The girl was quiet, and didn't react well to noise, conversation or questions. Especially the latter. So the chance to get rid of Cody, a talkative bastard at the best of times, into the next wag had been more than welcome. At the girl's request, the man Dix had replaced Cody instead of riding shotgun in the second wag. LaGuerre was confused by that. Okay, so Eula had really wanted to take the newbies aboard—in truth it had been more her idea to stop for them than his—and she was adamant that she wanted Dix to travel with them. But Cody was a tech man, not a sec fighter. Second wag was safest, but even so...

LaGuerre did not argue with Eula. He hadn't argued with her since the moment she had joined them. She had found them a little over eighteen months earlier, searching him out in a ville called Evermore, on the eastern fringes of the central badlands. He was in a gaudy house, busy enjoying himself with three gaudies, two of whom were putting on a show while the third made use of the pleasure he was showing at their performance. She had walked in as if she owned the place, asking him if he was LaGuerre and where he was headed.

Most times, if someone did that to him, he would have blown the person's head off. But there was something about this one—the way she completely ignored the surroundings, not from embarrassment but because she was too focused to notice. There was a kind of calm menace about her. When he asked her why him, she had replied that he was a trader, he was about to leave and she needed to get away quickly.

His first thought was that she had pissed off Baron Chandler, head of Evermore, and taking her on would lead to a firefight with the baron's sec. She had to have sensed that because she was quick to tell him that her problem was with another ville. She had already traveled a hundred klicks, but she knew she was being followed, and she needed the cover of a convoy to hide her tracks.

It would have sounded bullshit, and dangerous at that, if he'd heard it from anyone else. But from her it was different. It was the way she spoke, the way she carried herself, the serious hardware that was draped around her in a way that wasn't usual for anyone, let alone a young woman who looked barely old enough to handle a blaster.

Like all good traders, LaGuerre had a nose for a good deal. He may not have been the best trader, but he was better than a lot. She had that air of a rare stash about her. She was something a bit special, and could lead him to a higher level. It got his sense of greed tingling. So he agreed to take her on.

There was one other thing, too. It was on a much baser level, but all things were as one to Armand LaGuerre. It was the way she had looked at his dick when the gaudy slut took it out of her mouth.

He hadn't had Eula's pussy. Not yet. But it was only a matter of time.

Meanwhile, he just sat and watched. Watched the two of them sit, stand, walk around the interior of the wag, and say nothing to each other even though the very air around them crackled with tension. Eula had been insistent that Dix travel with them, and for his part the skinny guy with the glasses and hat had seemed pleased by that. LaGuerre couldn't make him out. When he said that he didn't know her, he seemed to be on the level. Yet the way he kept looking at her from the corner of his eye; the way the few words he said were guarded, almost to the point of being cryptic; the body language as he stiffened and pulled back every time she got close. All of that suggested that he had suspicions of where they may have met.

LaGuerre would love to know that. She had never enlarged on her initial statement to him. A ville about a hundred klicks from Evermore, going east. That could have been any number of villes. Part of the area to the east was fucked—completely uninhabited. Okay, scratch that. Maybe there were a few settlements in the contaminated area, but they weren't anywhere he or any other trader particularly cared to go. That still left a number of small villes ruled by desperado barons. Not many traders cared to go there, either. Not much jack, not much to barter. So he didn't know squat about any of them. If she was telling him the truth—bitch was too self-contained and sure of herself to do anything else—then it had to have been one of those.

He'd moved on quickly, and hadn't been back that way in the year and a half since she'd joined, so there hadn't been the chance to check out her story. But he knew one thing—the only trader to really make use of those areas had been Trader himself. The man was legend. He'd got richer than anyone, had more of a stash than anyone, done more business than anyone because he'd worked harder. Yeah, and where had it got him? Sometimes you just had to kick back a little and enjoy the fruits of your labors. LaGuerre realized he was wandering. The point of his train of thought was… Hell, what was it again? Yeah, that was it. If this guy Dix had ridden with Trader, along with the one-eyed guy, then he had to have been to some of those villes in the east. Probably the one that Eula came from, the one where she had gotten into some trouble and had to run.

So maybe Dix knew her secret. And, given that she had wanted to search those guys out, and was interested more in him than in any of the others, maybe she knew his.

That would explain why she was even quieter than usual, and he was like a mutie cat on a sun-fried wag roof.

WHILE THIS HAD BEEN going through LaGuerre's head, Eula had been guiding J.B. through the armory and associated tech held by the convoy. She had explained to him in few words the condition of the armory when she had joined, and the steps she had taken to both improve the quality of what was there, and to add to the inventory, making them stronger. Each blaster she detailed at length, telling him things he already knew, but seeming to tell him these things for a reason.

For the life of him, J.B. could not work out what the code behind her words may be. She was demonstrating her knowledge to impress him. But why? Why would she want to impress a man she claimed to know, but who had no recollection of her?

J.B. was not a man for subterfuge. He could stay impassive when needed—indeed, there were those who would argue that it was a natural state for both himself and Jak—but an outright lie was something he found hard, even in extreme danger. Why bother? If people didn't like the truth, then fuck 'em. Equally, he didn't respond well to situations where people were evasive, trying to tempt you into playing their games. Life was shit, hard and way too short for games. Especially games like that.

He had tried to keep his distance from her. Tried to rack his memory and remember her. Tried to even guess what the connection could be. But there was nothing except a nagging feeling of danger deep in his gut. And a growing curiosity over the fact that she had chosen the vocation of armorer. She was impressing this upon him, as though it would somehow open the floodgates of memory.

Well, if that was what she had hoped, then it was a bad call—not even a trickle.

She was in the middle of showing him the comm tech that she had managed to get up and running after they salvaged it from some ruined ex-military wags—carefully avoiding an explanation of how they had come to be wrecked, he noted—when J.B. decided that he could take no more.

"You're good," he said simply, stopping her in midflow, "and I want to know where you learned all this. 'Specially so young. Took me years on the road with Trader to amass the kind of knowledge you've got. Had some before I joined, but it was only hitting the road and finding shit that helped it build. But you must have grown up with someone who knew this stuff."

"I did," she said simply.

LaGuerre's ears pricked. Ask her more, Dix, he thought.

"So who taught you?" J.B. pushed.

Eula shook her head. "In time, John Barrymore. In time. I don't give anything away for free. I want from you, in return."

"What?"

"That'll have to wait. You need to do some thinking. Think about this, John Barrymore—remember a place called Hollowstar?"

J.B.'s face stayed impassive, but his mind jolted.

Yeah. He remembered Hollowstar....

Chapter Five

The Past

It took a month—no more—for J.B. to settle in to Trader's way of life, to stop being the new kid, and to start being just J.B. Such was his skill and knowledge, given room to grow by the ordnance that Trader's people collected on the way, that he became more than "that new guy the armorer," but became known as the Armorer, just as Trader was Trader. They were the definitive article—their positions used as names, spoken as though there were none other than they fit to carry such a name.

Not that it came easily. Poet knew how good the kid was from the beginning. After all, he was the one who had been sent to look at J.B., assess his skills, then fake the work to test them.

Hunnaker was hostile. She was always hostile to anything new. A loyal and trusted fighter, with a ruthless streak a mile wide, who could always be trusted in times of battle, yet she had a spiky, difficult temperament in her. She was insecure of her position in the convoy, which she prized highly. She measured herself by her standing with Trader, as the convoy was the only family she had, and despite her seeming ability to act and live independently of anyone or anything, there was a little hollow inside of her that craved the familial security of the convoy. Everything revolved around that, and when it changed, then she bristled, and lashed out.

It was a dangerous way to live, especially on a convoy where every day brought the chance for someone to buy the farm, and change was an unspoken constant. Which, perhaps, explained why there were days when all everyone wanted to do—even Trader—was stay the hell out of Hunn's way.

And she kind of liked it that way. It gave her status in the convoy. Except that J.B. walked in and acted like that was nothing. He didn't challenge her. That she could take, she could face down, she could do something about. No, he did something far worse—he ignored her. He acted like her moods didn't happen, like there weren't days that people edged around her rather than get into a fight. He just didn't notice.

So she loathed him for some time. It became a subject of discussion among the convoy, and the subject of a book run by Poet on how long until they had a fight, and who would win. Virtually everyone put jack on it—even Trader—and it was a keenly awaited event. Given Hunn's temperament, and the taciturn and phlegmatic new man, it was only a matter of time, and not much of that.

The fact that it never happened was, as Abe had put it, "jus' one of the weird shit things happen around here."

They were up north, where the temperatures drop, and any potential combat had to be undertaken with the added encumbrance of furs and padded clothing. Movement was difficult, threw off timing. Worse, it led to blasters screwing up in the extremes of temperature, which is exactly what happened to Hunn, and how she nearly got herself chilled in the cold.

It was an ambush by a bunch of desperate coldhearts who had been waiting for convoys to raid for too long. They were crazed with cold and hunger, giving them the desperation and madness to take on the convoy in what seemed to be a stupe position. Which was why, maybe, they nearly got away with it. Desperate measures sometimes brought the element of surprise that can turn a firefight. So it was that a steep, rocky pass covered in snow nearly became the graveyard that marked Trader's passing.

There was no other way through the narrow channel. No signs of life, but still not ideal. If not man, then nature could bite hard. An avalanche could trap or bury them; maybe both. But with no other way through, it was heads down and run for the other side, keeping noise to a minimum. Anything could trigger a rock fall.

Anyone with any sense wouldn't have started loosing off blaster fire, lobbing grens. But these desperadoes did exactly that. A hole in the track ahead of them from one gren made it impossible to proceed until they could get out and fill in the gap, which was too deep for War Wag One itself to traverse, let alone the other wags in the convoy.

They had to get out and fight, seeking whatever cover they could in the rocks and ice, climbing to where the mad bastard coldhearts were firing on them. The only break they had was that there couldn't be too many of the opposition, as they weren't spread along the ridge at the top of the climb.

Hunn was one of the best in situations like this. She was a good fighter, and when she was pissed off she was virtually unstoppable. And she was pissed off right now. She thought it was bad enough being this far up north, where it was cold enough to freeze her tits off; now they were being fired on by a bunch of stupe bastards who might just bury the convoy and not get what they were after. And what was the fuckin' point of that?

As she climbed, exchanging fire at intervals, she got more and more pissed, the anger building in her until it reached the point where she could see nothing but red mist. She was cold, she was aching because the rocks were battering her through the padding and the furs every time she took evasive action, and she was convinced that she was going to have to walk out of the pass as these stupes were going to bring down the rock walls on the convoy below.

Hunn in a real fighting anger was both a good and bad thing: good because she became a chilling machine, stopping at nothing. Bad for the very same reason. She paid no heed to danger and rushed headlong into it. It made her a spearhead and a liability at the same time. So far she had always been the former, simply because she always came out on top. But one day she would be the latter because she would screw up.

Like this day.

The ascent was hard, but she didn't care once the anger took hold, blinding rage, blotting out every other feeling, every other concern. She didn't even register that she had reached the top of the ridge, had picked her way along to the enclave where the bunch of coldhearts this side of the pass had ensconced themselves, didn't even register as she raised the Uzi, sighted the bastards, squeezed on the trigger.

Her weapon jammed, and Hunn cursed, making the

coldhearts aware of her presence, making them turn and sight on her. She realized that her luck had run out.

Knowing there was no time to take cover—there was none on top of the ridge anyway—she had closed her eyes and prepared to buy the farm. Then the air was filled with blasterfire.

Hunn realized that she was still alive and opened her eyes to see the Armorer standing over the bodies of the cold-hearts, the barrel of his mini-Uzi still smoking—or was that her imagination?—as he stepped over them and came to her.

"Cold and heat make the fuckers jam. Need to keep them so that the temperature is as constant as possible. Under your coat when you climb next time, okay?"

He didn't say anything else, taking the Uzi from her and checking it as he spoke, then handing it back to her.

They were lucky enough to get the hell out of the pass without a rock fall trapping them, some serious digging when the other group of coldhearts had been flushed out enabling them to fill the pit in the road enough to pass over it with some degree of ease. The Armorer never said anything to anyone about what had happened up on the ridge. Hunn certainly wasn't going to, if he wasn't. And she appreciated that he made no big deal of it.

No one knew why, but from that day all bets were off. It wasn't as though there was any sign of friendship, but the bristling atmosphere that she had exuded every time she was near J.B. vanished. There was a respect, grudging at first, then growing into a mutual admiration society that had bets being returned, much to Poet's disgust.

Abe had watched this from a distance. Trader's right-hand man, if not for a bout of dysentery when they had sampled the crap food in Guthrie, he would have fulfilled the tasks allotted to Poet in recruiting the Armorer. But in a way he was glad, as it gave him a chance to assess the newbie from a distance. He was just about the only man in the convoy who hadn't placed a bet, but had never said why. Who would have believed him from the evidence before their eyes, except maybe Trader.

Abe saw that J.B. and Hunn had more in common than was obvious. Both had their defense mechanisms in place—her spikiness, his taciturnity—to keep people at bay until they chose. Both were dedicated to their work. Both had something in their pasts that they wanted to remain that way, and both would open up only when they were ready. That was why they had butted heads: like attracted like, but also caused suspicion as—even on an unconscious level—recognizing like made a person wary.

Time went on, and Abe watched as they got each other's backs in situations of danger. He wasn't surprised. He once said to Trader: "You know, long as we've got those two on the team, then there isn't any way anyone's going to come through us. Long as we got them, then we've always got the backbone of a strong team. They might be loners, but they know how to bat for the team."

Trader could sometimes wish that Abe didn't have that old baseball card collection they'd found in a redoubt. He talked like people still played sports—like they still had time to take out from the harsh need to exist—and expected people to understand. But once you worked out what he was talking about, the thoughts if not the words made sense.

Trader had made many finds over the years that he could call good. He was coming to consider that one of the best hadn't been in finding any goods or jack, but in finding a man.

John Barrymore Dix.

So it was that the Armorer settled in, became a fixture such that no one could remember a time before he was there. But it was only a year.

Only a year before Trader returned to Hollowstar.

"WHY ARE WE GOING to this dead and alive pesthole?" J.B. asked as War Wag One rumbled along a rut-filled highway, the convoy the only vehicles on a four-lane road that headed away from the mutie growth of trees, creepers and plants that thrived in the chem-laden rains of the region, and toward a sparser, clearer region where the bleached-out and burned remains of civilization showed how the nuke damage stood as monument to skydark.

"Because it is," Trader replied cryptically. He enjoyed the look of puzzlement in J.B.'s eyes, mirrored by his spectacles.

"And that's an answer?" he said finally. "More like a fucking puzzle."

Trader smiled enigmatically. "You work it out, son. It isn't difficult."

It had been an easy ride. There were only a few isolated settlements—most too small to even be called villes—out in this stretch. The poisonous nature of the soil made it hard to farm. The equally poisonous flora of the region was also little incentive. And if that wasn't enough, the few examples of fauna that could thrive in such conditions made for a new definition of the term *hostile*. Good for travelers as it also dictated that any marauding bands of coldhearts in the region wouldn't get far before the local environment claimed them. Bad for travelers as it meant they had to get through the region as quickly and as easily as possible.

Farther east there was very little: beyond the rad-blasted mutations of this region were the hotspots where the nukes had hit, and the land was virtually waste. Nonetheless, there were a few settlements, bands of survivors who had managed to make a life rather than buy the farm in the aftermath of nuclear winter, and had adapted to their conditions before birthing those who would be their descendants.

And they all had a need to trade.

Abe explained it to J.B., seeing the young man's still puzzled expression.

"Boy, how d'you think you hooked up with us? How many convoys had come through that pesthole you found yourself in? Not many, I'd guess. But Trader, see, he pays attention to detail. There are little places like Guthrie, like Hollowstar and the lands beyond, where there are people who want to buy. They got something to sell, too. It might not be much, but if you only go once a year or so, then it makes the trip worthwhile for us. And they're desperate for what we've got, willing to pay. 'Cause no one else can be bothered."

J.B. nodded. In the year that he'd been with them, they had headed for the big settlements, the larger villes, the areas where there was a large population. And they'd made good trade, that was for sure. But always with other traders there just before or just after, people whining about how little they'd gotten, or how much they were going to get. It figured that if there were places that were hard to get to, then few would bother. Except Trader. J.B. had been with him more than long enough to know that attention to detail was what made him the best.

So he wasn't alarmed when Hunn took War Wag One off the highway at a turn-off that led to a place called "Ne J rsey," according to the sign that hung precariously over the narrower ribbon of road. The vibration of the convoy on the ruined road made the metal posts supporting the sign shake, the once-strong metal now wasted and eaten by the environment, looking as though it could crash down on any of the wags in train.

"Always looks that way. Puts people off, but never comes down." Abe sniffed. "Least ways, not yet."

"Why not stick to the main roadway?" J.B. asked. "Looks safer."

Trader grinned. "Everyone comes this way the first time thinks that. Hell, even got caught that way ourselves first time out."

Abe chuckled. "Shoulda heard the cursing when we had to turn back. Only found this turn-off because he—" he pointed at Trader "—was so stubborn he didn't want a totally wasted journey."

Seeing J.B.'s questioning look between them, Trader elaborated. "You carry on down the highway, all you get is it ending in a big fuck-off landslide where part of the old county got a hit. Must've been some kind of quake thing going on, as you can see nothing but this big, empty hole for what seems like forever. The other side is… Well, shit, I dunno, but I'd bet not much can live over there."

That would be a no, then. J.B. knew that Trader was no gambling man.

Easing into his theme, Trader continued. "So, like Abe

said, we were all pissed—not just me." He glanced to his number two, who returned it with a grin. "Anyway, as we came back I saw this road, and thought 'fuck it, nothing's going to be alive in this bastard region.' But then it occurred to me that every fucker must think like that. So, for the sake of a few gallons of fuel, why not have a look-see? We had enough spare with us.

"And there, at the end of the line, was Hollowstar. A poor little place, but managing to get by because of where it was."

"I must be triple stupe, 'cause I don't get that," J.B. murmured.

Trader's face split into a broad grin. "Course you don't. No one does till they've been there. I sure as shit didn't—"

"And you won't hear him say that often," Abe interrupted.

"Fuck you," Trader said lightly. "See, there were a few survivors in this region, but the villes they made could only exist if they put them on a road that survived. Well, the big fucker didn't, but this smaller one did. They used to call it the New Jersey Turnpike, or so they say around here. There are a few villes, some places too small to call that, and they ribbon out along the road until it just kinda ends. Hollowstar is the richest, Baron Emmerton the smartest. And lucky."

"Why lucky?" J.B. asked, knowing that Trader was warming to his theme, and enjoying the rare chance to kick back and chew the fat while they rode a road that presented little in the way of danger.

Trader's grin widened to the point where it looked like

it might split his face. "Whoever built Hollowstar used buildings around the old toll booths for the road, and they still work. To pass through on either side you have to pay the baron. The smart thing is that whoever started the ville wasn't greedy, so in the long run they've had a steady stream of jack coming in both ways. There aren't many who pass through, but they have to pay in and out, so that's two for one. It isn't much compared to villes out there where there are more folks, but that's the word, isn't it? *Compared.* Makes Emmerton and all those who came before him richer and more powerful than any other baron in the region. Smart boy…"

Hunn, who had so far been ignoring the conversation, chipped in. "You do realize that every poor fucker who joins us and lasts this long gets exactly the same speech when we come here, almost word for word? I know the fuckin' thing by heart. I swear, I could say it in my fuckin' sleep. Probably do, for all I know."

"Fuck you, bitch," Trader said with good humor, "next time I'll make you say it, just to see."

"Yeah, well, we'll see about that. Meantime, you should all stop yakking, as we're there."

J.B. looked out of an ob port. The foliage that had covered the side of the old highway had now thinned out and changed. The vines and creepers had vanished, replaced by sparse grass under trees that were still twisted and stunted in places, but had a healthier look than the looming green giants that lined the highway. The remains of some old buildings could be seen—low-level blocks that had once been shops and warehouses, but were now split by trees that had grown through and broken the line of the structure. There were no houses in this section. If there had been, they had long since been swallowed by nature, reclaiming its damaged stock. The road they were now on had narrowed, and was two-lane gray asphalt shot through with weeds, the sidewalk a similar hue, the weeds now more prevalent in places than the original stone.

J.B. had seen places like this before, even though he had never ventured this far east as of yet. There were old industrial and residential areas around cities like this all over what was left of the old United States. They differed in detail, but in essence they were the same. J.B. came from a ville that was the remains of an old small town. Most of the places he'd drifted into before hooking up with Trader had been based around old small towns, or had been built up from scratch. He'd never really been on any of the convoy trade routes. Now he knew what the Deathlands looked like, knew how the old cities had mutated like the flora and fauna that had begun to reclaim them since skydark, the people reduced to living on the fringes, trying to regain a foothold.

All those footholds were the same. The edges of dead cities reclaimed and recycled. And beyond this one? A real wasteland, one that was so rad-blasted that it seemed as though it were the beginning of never.

If the way in which Hollowstar sat in the middle of this semiwilderness was common to many villes he had seen, then so would be the people. They didn't change in essence, no matter where you went. They had different customs and ways that you had to get used to, lest they chill you for insulting them in some manner of which you weren't even aware. But that was just surface shit, J.B.

knew. Deep down they were as brave, scared, greedy, lustful, sharing, good or evil in one place as they were in another. You just had to take them as they come, size them up, and then treat them accordingly.

It was a simple way, and one that had kept him alive so far. That put him ahead of the game as far as many were concerned. There were too many who didn't live this way, and had long since bought the farm as a result.

These were the thoughts that went through his head every time that he entered somewhere new. It was as if he was preparing himself for whatever he was about to face, reminding himself to keep a close watch until he'd understood the ways of the ville.

But this time it was stronger than he'd ever known it. As if there was something nagging at him. J.B. didn't believe in that doomie shit; not unless you were some kind of mutie, which he knew damn sure he wasn't. Nonetheless, as Hunn slowed War Wag One, signaling their approach to the old toll gates, he knew that something was going to happen here that would change things for him. Good or bad? That was the bastard thing—he couldn't tell.

Chapter Six

"Welcome back to Hollowstar, Trader. How long has it been?"

Trader eyed the sweating, grossly fat man in front of him and figured that it had been too long. Baron Emmerton was not his favorite ville leader by a long way, but he was basically harmless. It was just that there was something about him that made Trader's skin crawl. Maybe it was because his wife was so young, and there always seemed to be a new one every time he passed this way. Sure, a lot of barons had a taste for young flesh, but it seemed as though Emmerton made an art form of it. And there was something in the way that his eyes shifted uneasily across your gaze, unwilling to meet it....

But all things considered, he was a man to keep sweet. Trader was a thorough man in all ways. That was why his haul was so big, why he was the best. No one else on the trail could be bothered to check out these far-flung villes, and because of its location on the old turnpike, Hollowstar was a key ville. There was no other way to access the villes that lay beyond, so Emmerton had power. So far, his relationship with Trader had been cordial, and that was just the way that Trader intended it to stay.

So, instead of his first thought, he said, "It's been too long, friend." He took the outstretched, sweaty paw and tried not to grimace as Emmerton pumped it in his slimy grasp.

"Things haven't changed much around here," Emmerton said slyly, "except that mebbe we're running low on some things. We weren't expecting you to be so long, and so we didn't mebbe plan so well."

Trader knew only too well what that meant—the cost of going through to the villes beyond would be higher than last time, with each part of the increase carefully explained and accounted for. Shit, it was an occupational hazard to be lied to and cheated. It was just that he didn't want to have to sit around listening to the bullshit explanation.

So he said, "I'm sure we can come to some agreement. Have to say, for my part I would have been back this way sooner, but we've had a few firefights along the way with parties who wanted to make trouble. You know me, Baron, I don't like trouble. But when it happens, you have to deal with it. Anyway, we lost a few people along the way, picked up some newbies. Things go on, no matter how tough it gets."

He studied the baron's face to see if the message had hit its intended target. The way in which Emmerton licked his lips, his eyes flickering more than before, suggested that it had. Good.

"I'm sure our ville will give you ample time to rest before moving on," Emmerton said hesitantly, "and I hope that you'll take advantage of our hospitality both before and after your trip down the road."

Emmerton was referring to the one highway that linked the rad-blasted east with the lands west of his ville. It was the convoy's custom to rest a few days on either side of their trip into these lands. It gave the crew a chance to enjoy themselves before they hit the road once more, and—more importantly from Trader's point of view—it meant that his crew spent some jack in Hollowstar, making Emmerton and his sec men that bit sweeter when it was time to come around again.

Trader left Emmerton in his baronial house. The baron had been flanked by his personal sec men, Laker and Farmer. Trader had taken Abe and Poet with him, as they had traveled this way the longest and so were the most familiar with the sweating baron. As they left, Abe murmured, "Nice to see the baron's fitness plan is working so well."

Trader almost kept the smirk from his face, but figured what the hell, seeing as they were out in the open. He took the chance to look around the ville, and reflected once more on how, even by the whacko standards of some of the places they'd done business, Hollowstar was a weird one.

For a start, despite operating as a toll gate on the road that split the ville, it had been built some distance from the old toll booths. A brick construction fulfilled their function, built just beyond the last of the houses in the ville, a scaffolding gantry across the top of the road mounting armed guard. This was completely at odds with the way that the rest of the ville appeared.

If Trader had to take a guess, he would have said that whoever founded the ville had a definite idea of what they wanted—a show ville that idealized the way they wanted the country to develop again. The problem being that they had to use what they had, so it turned out kind of wrong. Trader had seen some old vids of what used to be called "smalltown 'Merica," as he understood it, and Hollowstar was modeled very much on those lines.

He figured that they had chosen here, away from the old toll booths, as those were surrounded by the remains of old industrial and retail areas. This was an empty space of land, and it looked to him as though they had painstakingly taken some of the low-level houses in the area and transported them to rebuild here. Others had been built from using salvaged materials, shaped to fit the overall plan with some odd results. Storefronts lined a main square that had a bandstand, although in all the times he had visited here he had never seen a band in there; and the square was grassed over, if it could be dignified with that term. Trader had seen pictures of how green-lawned squares like this had looked before the nukecaust. The square achieved that look only if one applied a high degree of imagination. In truth, it was a square of dry dirt, with creeping weeds choking the brown stunted grass that struggled with the toxins in the soil.

But still, it had one big asset, and he was going to enjoy that asset meeting the Armorer. Yes indeed, that would be one to watch.

"WHATEVER YOU WANT, the answer is no. I'm too busy. I don't have what you want. I don't want to have what you want. I don't care. Just go away."

J.B. raised an eyebrow at Trader. "Friendly bastard," he said mildly.

Trader shook his head. "You know, the seasons come and go, but some things just stay the same." In a louder voice, he yelled, "Luke. Get your ass out here before I take my custom elsewhere."

"Elsewhere my ass. No way you're gonna find anywhere else around here that can do what I can. Figure it that you're not gonna find anywhere else anyone that can…" The owner of the voice wandered into the storefront from a back room as he spoke. Without missing a beat or changing tone, he added, "Still, it's good to see you back, Trader. Always give me good business, and it's nice to hear a voice that doesn't talk about the same small ville shit that everyone else never shuts up about."

"Yeah, it's good to see you, Luke," Trader said with a grin. It hadn't been as fulsome a greeting as that of the baron, but it was infinitely more sincere. "But I'm figuring that you've got some competition that you didn't count on. Meet John Barrymore Dix, my new armorer, and probably the only man I've ever met who could give you a run for your jack."

Luke eyed the slight figure of J.B. with a mixture of suspicion and disbelief before extending his hand, withdrawing it hastily to wipe the gun oil off and onto the stained apron he wore, then extending it again.

"John," he said with a curt nod as the Armorer met his firm grip.

"J.B.," he corrected.

"Whatever." Luke shrugged. "So you know a bit about blasters, do you? Trader here told you how good you are? Pity if he has, as he doesn't know enough to cover his own ass, so he may have sorely misled you."

"I don't figure," J.B. replied in a noncommittal tone. "I was doing the same kind of thing as you do here before I met Trader."

"You were, huh?"

Trader was enjoying every moment. The two men were circling each other like hungry dogs, sizing each other up before plunging in for the chill, establishing who was best. Except they were too much alike as men to go for the jugular. No, they'd do it the long way around.

J.B. sniffed and looked around at the storefront. Coffee-sub boiled on a stove, there were a couple of tables and chairs in the floor space in front of the counter, and the back room was shielded by a long drape.

"Of course," he said at length, "I didn't have to run a coffee stall, as well as work on blasters. I was able to devote the whole of my time to the real work."

Luke snorted, half derision, half laugh. "This is no coffee stall, my friend." He gestured at the pot. "This is just for those who wait for me to get my work done."

J.B. nodded slowly. He knew Trader well enough to know that the man was enjoying the encounter, but also that he wouldn't do it just for sport. If Trader said Luke was good, then he was. No sense in letting him know that just yet, of course. J.B. looked him up and down. He was a big, powerful man. Around six feet, broad-shouldered, with maybe the very beginnings of a gut where he spent too long sitting working at a bench. He was wearing a plaid shirt and torn denim jeans under the apron, which was of thick, polished hide. His face was dark complected, his eyes in darker hollows framing a sharp nose. He was wearing a tattered ball cap turned backward, and his demeanor spoke of someone who didn't like to waste time.

And he was thinking that maybe this was wasting his time.

"So?" Luke said, tired of waiting for J.B., maybe even

tired of being sized up. "Do you have any work for me?" he directed to Trader. "Or has wonder boy here seen to it all?"

"I've tidied up anything that Trader needs," J.B. answered, drawing the attention back to himself. "So mebbe he's brought me here so that I can help you out."

Luke looked as though he might explode in anger. A simmering, slow burn came over him, and he said softly, "Ever tried to fit a stock on a Sharps that some damn fool has tried to recalibrate?"

"Can't say I have. You rebored it?"

"Got the lathe, just in the middle of it. Care to, uh, give me your expert opinion on what I've done?" he asked with some sarcasm.

J.B. smiled wryly. "I could try."

Luke lifted the flap of the counter, allowing the Armorer to pass through. He raised a questioning eyebrow at Trader, who shook his head. Without a word, Luke let the flap drop and followed the Armorer into the back room.

"Long time since I saw one of those," Trader heard J.B. say. He didn't know what he was talking about, and he didn't much care. He had the feeling that they'd lose him after a few minutes, anyway.

His mission here was done. Get the boys acquainted. Get them past their own spiky natures, and when they were ready, get them to look over his ordnance and anything they might pick up on the outbound journey.

Chapter Seven

The Present

Attack came sooner than any of them would have hoped. The only good thing was that, out in the dustbowl environment they traversed, there was no way that any kind of attack could be a surprise. There was no place to hide or shelter when under attack, but equally there was nowhere for any potential attackers to lie in wait. You could see the coldhearted bastards coming for miles.

That was scant consolation when a person was on a motorbike, unable to hear the comm tech from the rest of the convoy, and more exposed than any of your fellow fighters. Come to that, more than any of your enemies.

Ryan and Jak were the first to be in the firing line, and the last to see what was coming. No wonder, then, that their journey was almost over before it had begun.

KRYSTY HAD LONG SINCE ceased to pay any attention to what Ray was saying. He was a nice enough old guy, she supposed, but the fact that he never shut up meant that only one word in ten was worth listening to; and after a while, you couldn't even summon the energy to try to catch anything. But that was okay, seeing as the old man didn't seem to care whether she was listening. She guessed that he was used to people zoning out on him after a while, and was just grateful for a passive audience that let him believe he was doing something other than just talk to himself.

She looked at him, past him, and occasionally shifted on the padded seat to look the other way, at least in a token attempt at surveillance. But the truth was that his voice became kind of hypnotic after a while, and she could feel herself start to glaze over. While he talked about LaGuerre and the others in the convoy, old vids and old music, even singing snatches of old tunes in a quavery tenor, she found that she was becoming more confused. Who had been on the convoy, and who was some old vid actor from predark days? Had there been an actor called Tarran? Had there been sec men called Seagal and VanDamme? It became a little blurry around the edges.

Which was exactly how she was feeling. A little blurry. Slipping into that daydream reverie that led to sleep.

And that was why she nearly missed it. It was only when he repeated himself that she realized it was something important. He hadn't repeated himself once up to this point. More than that, when he did, the even tenor of his voice had changed, and he spoke more slowly. But still the words didn't make sense for a moment.

"Said that there are bandits on the horizon, and ain't it about time someone said something about it? Hellfire, missy, if I can see them, then it's sure as shit that someone else in the convoy will have. This is the problem, see, no one talks to each other anymore, do they?"

Krysty snapped to attention as the words began to be more than a collection of syllables delivered in that sing-song tone and took on meaning. She looked past the old man, out beyond the road and the dustbowl. They had been driving nonstop for nearly eighteen hours at a steady pace, and she was sure that she had to have dropped into some kind of sleep when it was dark, but for the most part she had been awake. It was now almost the middle of the day after they had joined the convoy, and the sun beating down on the arid land had thrown up that weird heat haze again, limiting the horizon.

Which meant that the wags she could see in the distance weren't as distant as she could have hoped. They were low-level, obscured by the clouds of dust that they were throwing up in their wake. There were at least six vehicles, maybe more but hard to tell at this stage as the formation and the clouds of dust made it hard to distinguish at distance. They didn't seem to be gaining at a great pace, which suggested that they might be at a greater distance than she had first thought. Or they were slower than she had estimated in her first, shocked, glance.

None of that mattered too much—they were hostile, and they were coming. That was all that counted.

She snatched the comm mic from the unit that rested between herself and Ray.

"Enemy approaching from the southwest, mebbe six wags. Anyone else seen them yet?"

Despite the high level of technology, the unit's age and the rad count in the atmosphere meant that it still crackled like the most primitive of radios. So when Mildred's voice came back, it was distorted and barely understood.

"I see them, Krysty. Figure we should assume that we can see six, but there may be more in train. It's better to be safe. You and me only have hardware to fight close-up. What about the other wags?"

Krysty thought about that. Why hadn't the others said anything about the incoming? Then it hit her—the other wags may be better equipped, but they were lower. The cabs of the refrigerated wags were raised much higher, and rode above the clouds of dust and wag exhaust raised by the convoy. The lower level wags that came between the trader's lead wag and the refrigerated wags would be enveloped in the clouds they raised. Then she thought about the bikes riding shotgun at the rear of the convoy. How the hell did LaGuerre expect Ryan and Jak to function with any degree of… She stopped that train of thought. If anyone could look after themselves and cope with the most adverse of conditions, it was would be Ryan and Jak. They could handle the situation.

Meanwhile, it was up to Mildred and herself to make sure the odds were as level as possible.

"I don't think they can see them because they're obscured by the convoy's own dust. I hope the bastards are listening in."

"Sure as shit am," broke in a peevish, whining voice. "Would've said something else if you damn women would shut your yaps once in a while."

"Cody, you shut your bastard mouth. You're worse than the rest of us put together," Ramona's voice cut across. "Let the sister speak, you damn fool. You're not in Armand's wag now. We need their intel."

Krysty, despite the severity of the situation, found it hard to suppress a sigh. Arguing among themselves, never shutting the hell up… It was nothing short of a miracle that they'd gotten this far. No wonder they'd lost so many the last time they'd been in a firefight. Then she remembered that, if the friends' suspicions were correct, they'd acquired the refrigerated wags as a result of that firefight. Maybe they weren't that bad, then, if they could stop the arguing and pull together.

While this had been running through part of her mind, she had also been surveying the approaching attack party. The convoy had either slowed, or the attackers had picked up speed. Whatever the reason, they were now gaining, moving from a diagonal line of approach to a straighter line, aided by the slight bend of the old highway. Even through the clouds of their own dust, it was easy to see that the initial estimate of six, maybe eight, had been too optimistic. There were two rows, one running almost exactly behind the other.

Twelve wags.

Shit, Krysty thought. They had three armed wags, two men on bikes and two big cabs that carried a minimum of ordnance. If the attack party knew what they were doing, they could flank and divide the fire of the convoy, giving them openings to pierce the defenses. They couldn't allow them to get that close.

Of course, being wild riders in the dustbowl region, the bastards might just be out of their brains on jolt, and up for a firefight rather than a concerted attempt to raid the convoy. That would make them easier to deal with, as they would be reckless and triple stupe because of the drug. Yeah, she hoped that was the scenario. They could just pick off the bastards one by one.

But they couldn't take that chance.

"Doc, J.B.," she said urgently, "you hearing this?"

"I am indeed, dear girl." Doc's tones were clear and

ringing, even with the static. "I am assuming that we want to eliminate the risk before it becomes too close?"

"Got that right," Krysty agreed.

"We've got cannon fire capacity in this wag," J.B.'s voice said. "Eula tells me that you got that, too, Cody. And it's in your wag, Doc."

"Hell, yeah," Cody said.

"I am told this is true," Doc confirmed.

"Okay," J.B. said slowly. Even from just the one word, those who knew him could tell that the Armorer's brain was working overtime, playing out scenarios in his head, assessing every possibility as he estimated the best move for all concerned parties. "We haven't heard from Jak or Ryan yet. Figure they can hear us?"

Cody was blunt. "No way. Stupe idea giving them the comm shit. Guys who bought the farm last time told me they couldn't hear us, and just acted according to what they saw."

It was as J.B. had suspected—whatever tactics they planned and relayed to each other, they would have to assume that Ryan and Jak would be acting independently. So they'd have to give them space, and not end up helping them buy the farm by accident.

"We have to keep triple-red alert for them. Soon as they see the enemy, they'll head for combat. So we need to hit as hard as we can, and now. Millie, Krysty, you've only got ordnance for close-range combat, so it's up to me, Doc and Cody to knock the bastards out. Lay down a barrage and get their range."

"My dear John Barrymore, it'll be a pleasure." Doc cackled.

"Yeah, let's hope it's that easy," J.B. said wryly.

"DOC, YOU SURE you used one of these before?" Raven asked as Doc seated himself behind the rocket launcher that had been mounted and bolted into an ob slit in the wag.

"Not this particular model," he said with assurance, though ruined the effect by adding, "at least, I think not," in an undertone, and thus undermined the confidence he wished to instill in Raven and Ramona.

"Yeah, that's cool. We let the old guy loose with a honkin' big piece of hardware that he doesn't know squat about," Ramona said dryly, without taking her eyes off the road ahead, squinting through the wash of dust that billowed from the refrigerated wag in front of her. "You see where these jokers are, Rave? 'Cause I can hardly see Ray's ass in front of me."

"That ain't a pleasant thought, babe," Raven answered, distracted, as she kept one eye on the approaching attack party and the other on Doc. "But, yeah, I can see them. And they're about to hit our range," she added to Doc, hoping he would take the cue.

Doc, studying the rocket launcher and mentally comparing it to previous weapons he had fired, was only too quick to comply.

"You are going to like this. Not a lot, but you are going to like it." He whooped with glee as he loosed off the first blast. A few seconds later, the bloom of the explosion rose from the left of the onrushing group. A couple of the wags veered, but no damage was done. The actual sound of the explosion was lost in the noise of the wag convoy.

Doc's face fell. "Heavens, what a waste of ammo. John Barrymore would be fearfully annoyed at such waste. I must endeavor to find my range a little more easily. Like this, perhaps," he added, sighting and firing once more. In the interim, another bloom had sprung to the other side of the attack party, as one of the other wags had fired and missed. Not J.B., Doc would wager.

No, that one was dear John Barrymore, he added to himself as a blast hit dead center of the attack party, followed moments later by another that hit at the fringes. That latter was his, he was sure, and he gained more satisfaction from the fact that it hit just where some of the attack party were veering to avoid the damage of the center-aimed hit.

The clouds of dust and smoke from the approach, hits and damage of the first rocket assault meant that it was now almost impossible to see how much damage had been caused.

"Hold fire," J.B. said over the comm. "Wait till we can see the bastards."

"Indubitably," Doc agreed.

Ramona shook her head. "Man, speak our language."

"Right on, uh, man," Doc said with a grin.

BOTH KRYSTY and Mildred felt helpless. At this point there was little that either of them could do, sealed in the cabs of the refrigerated wags with little in the way of hardware that would be of use for anything other than the most up-close of combat. And, in truth, close fighting with a bunch of coldhearts who outnumbered them was the last thing they wanted. Nonetheless, it seemed to them that they had been reduced to mere spectators, and that wasn't a good feeling. They worked as a team, and if their companions were in danger, then they wanted to join the fray. To be sidelined was a frustration that both women could do without—although, seeing the first rocket strikes, it didn't look as if J.B., Doc and Cody would need much help.

Their trucks were several feet higher than the dust and exhaust cloud that surrounded the lower level wags of the convoy on the old highway, so they were able to observe the results of the attack with a little more clarity. At first, the attacking party was lost in its own dirt, with the rocket damage adding to the obscuring screen of smoke and dust. But, as that began to clear, it revealed localized black columns that bespoke of hits.

There were three columns of dissipating smoke from the rockets hits, with craters at their base. Of the twelve wags, three were nothing more than smoking wrecks with their own columns of smoke from the wag fuel that rose high into the air, flames at their base. Another two were entangled together, having crashed into each other during evasive maneuvers to escape the rockets. As the women, in their respective cabs that seemed to be hermetically sealed from the outside world, looked on, the two entangled wags exploded, one after the other rather than simultaneously, in a ball of flame that spread wide.

If the rest of the attack party had still been in the vicinity, then this could have caused further damage. Unfortunately, the initial strike had done nothing more than spur them on, and they were bearing down on the convoy with even greater speed.

Mildred spoke into the comm mic. "Five down, John, seven bearing down."

J.B. LISTENED TO Mildred's words as he squinted through the ob port, trying to make out the lines of the attackers through the backwash of dust that rose from the wheels beneath the port.

"Dark night, LaGuerre, how the hell do you expect us to mount a defense when you make it this hard to see the enemy? We need to stop and meet them head-on."

He looked at the trader. LaGuerre was sweating heavily, his eyes wide with fear.

"No way. I only fight when the odds are stacked on us winning. There are too many of the bastards, man. We can't stop, can't slow down. That way lies buying the farm."

"Bullshit. We can't see the enemy, we can't hit them, we buy the farm." J.B. spit.

"Fuck that," LaGuerre snapped back. "I'm trader here, and this is my convoy. Do it my way or not at all."

J.B. knew that arguing with a terrified man was useless. Especially a terrified man who had power. Especially when there was no time. He cursed to himself and turned back to the ob port. During the few seconds he had been arguing with LaGuerre, the dust had cleared a little, and it was easier to see. Maybe it was also easier to see because the seven wags left were gaining at speed.

"Why didn't you say?" he directed at Eula. The woman had been watching all the while, and had said nothing to alert him.

She shrugged. "You're in charge. It's your job, and you're supposed to be good at it."

J.B. stared at her, openmouthed. Fuck… What the hell was the matter with these people? It didn't matter. There were more important things to think about right now. Not least of which was the fact that Ryan and Jak had left the rear of the convoy and were headed for the attackers.

Within seconds they would be too close to risk another rocket attack.

"Cody, Doc, hold fire on the attackers," J.B. snapped into the comm mic. "Ryan, Jak, what are you doing? Answer, dammit."

His answer was a silence broken only by static.

RYAN AND JAK had been operating almost in isolation since the journey had begun. Their only contact with one another was as they passed by each other on their recce maneuvers. Even then, it was impossible because of the heavy protective goggles and the dust to make anything remotely approaching eye contact. Each had, individually, wondered how the hell he was supposed to communicate with the other in a time of emergency; by the same token, each had decided individually that the only way to face this was to just tackle the problem should the need arise.

Ryan caught sight of the attackers before Jak. It was inevitable, as the albino youth's sharpest senses were dulled by what was surrounding him.

It was at the farthest reach of a patrolling arc that he saw the wags on the horizon, breaking through the shimmering heat haze. He wondered if the convoy had seen them, thought about barking his sighting into the comm mic that was by his cheek, then figured it would be next to useless. He hadn't been able to hear them, didn't even know if the bastard thing was working. There was no sign of the approaching wags being attacked, but there was no way they were in range of any ordnance carried by the convoy. Ryan figured that the best he could do right now was to make Jak aware of the approach, so that both of them would be ready to act.

As they passed on their complex circuit, he tried to yell. Even as he did so, he realized the futility of it. He couldn't hear himself, no way would Jak be able to hear him. He would have to find another way.

The two riders had fallen into a pattern, passing each other on a circuit that only their close knowledge of each other—an almost telepathic empathy built up among all the companions by their times of standing shoulder to shoulder in combat—would enable them to execute without fear of collision.

Ryan changed his pattern, taking two circuits to fall in beside Jak. The albino teen had been perplexed by Ryan's change, though no sign of this had crossed his impassive, scarred visage. Not wanting to second guess the one-eyed man, Jak had stayed in his circuit, operating as a holding pattern for Ryan to orbit until his own new pattern had been established.

Once Ryan was riding parallel to Jak, the two men looked across at each other. Ryan raised one hand, pointing in the direction of the attackers and signaling Jak to follow him. With the albino in train, Ryan led them out of the wake of the convoy, the new circuit taking them beyond the lip of the old highway and into clearer air, where it was easy to see the approaching wags. Turning so they now ran at an angle to the rear of the convoy, and keeping a line that enabled to them to recce the attackers, they saw the first rocket from Doc miss its mark, followed, to their gratification, by the following strikes.

The two riders stayed their hand until the smoke and dust had cleared enough for them to be able to fully assess the situation. Seven wags were left running, and closing on the convoy so fast that it wouldn't be long before the long-distance weapons would be too dangerous to the convoy itself at such a shortened range.

There were no other strikes, and the convoy kept moving at its current pace.

What the hell was going on? Both riders knew that J.B.'s tactics would be to bring the convoy to a halt. Sure, it made them a sitting rather than moving target, but chances were that this was a raid for jack and supplies, not a drive-by for sport. In which case, direct hits weren't in the opposition's game plan. It was a risk, but the Armorer played the odds. From a standing position they could be far more effective as a strike force while defending ground.

So J.B. would have the convoy stop. Yet still it rolled on, neither increasing nor slackening pace. LaGuerre— both Ryan and Jak had marked the trader as a slippery, tricky bastard, but neither one had thought he could be a stupe or a coward. He was either or both.

Unable to communicate with anyone else—or even each other in anything more than the most rudimentary terms—the two riders knew that they would have to take action without recourse to J.B. or any other companions. They would just have to trust that they would be seen and not become the victims of friendly fire.

Because the defensive fire had stopped, and the attackers were closing fast.

Ryan indicated to Jak that they should move out. The albino nodded and followed his leader as Ryan guided the bike onto a course that would take them in to engage with the enemy. Going through both riders' minds was the fact that the seven wags hadn't yet fired a single shot. It was reasonable to assume that this was because they needed to be closer to engage, and the only logical reason for that was that their ordnance could only be used up close. Handblasters, short-range SMGs or rifles. Grens, maybe, but only propelled manually or through attachments to the shorter range hardware.

If it was a reasonable assessment of what they would face, then they knew that to keep moving, and fast, would make them hard to pick off while the attackers were also on the move. It was a fighting chance, and that's all that Jak or Ryan would ever ask. Especially as they were now close enough to have come within range of this assumed ordnance.

The primary aim was to prevent the oncoming attackers from engaging the convoy. Because of the limited ordnance that Jak and Ryan carried, they knew that their best course of action would be to separate the seven wags in the attack. If they could pull apart any formation that the attackers had, then it would be easier for the moving convoy weapons to pick them off. And, along the way, there was the chance that a piece of good shooting from the back of the bikes would also help to achieve this aim.

Which was okay as plans went, but was a hell of a lot harder to put into practice when you were down on the dustbowl, dirt-packed ground.

Ryan and Jak were encountering the same problems. The off-road ground was smoother than the shattered highway for a short distance, as the old shoulder of the road had remained flattened and hard-packed. But go beyond this, and the ground became treacherous. Ridges of dirt and rock, holes caused by burrowing rodents, patches of dirt that clogged and covered potholes and cracks in the surface area: all of these could be easily negotiated on foot, and wouldn't cause anyone to stumble. But driven over at speed by the tires on a bike—tires that were bald, with little or no grip, and in sore need of pumping—these small contusions in the earth suddenly became traps that could maim or chill.

The bikes bucked and roared as they hit the uneven surface. If they could gain enough speed, then they could ride over the irregularities, gain enough momentum to make the uneven surface blur into regularity. The problem with that idea was that the bikes weren't quite powerful enough to do that and still retain maneuverability. The only way they could build up this momentum was to run in a straight line…and be an easy target.

So both riders opted to zigzag, trying at the same time to keep up as much speed as possible while avoiding the worst of the uneven ground. It meant that the attackers who chose to fire on them were finding their shots run high and wide. The downside was that it meant that their progress toward their target wags was hindered by bone-shaking encounters with uneven ground that threatened to unseat them from the bikes at any given moment. That, combined with the clouds of dust that were swirling almost as though they were part of the very air, meant that visibility was reduced in range, and any notion of judgment regarding distance was, at best, nominal.

It was a far from ideal situation. Unable to communicate by sign anymore, each rider had to hope that the other would know by some kind of instinct where the other sat.

Their heads were filled with the roar of the bikes and the rush of blood that accompanied each bone-shaking jolt. Their vision was obscured by the dust that swirled around them, and the dirt and flies that gathered on their goggles. The oncoming wags would be fixed in the center of their vision, only to be shot out of the side or the top by a jolt that caused the stomach to try to force its way through the craw.

How the hell they were supposed to fire was a mystery: a matter of instinct and luck, rather than any kind of judgment.

Not that it stopped them. Handblasters were all that they had, and to try to grip and fire while riding one-handed was asking to be thrown. Nonetheless, it was all they could do.

The crack of their handblasters was lost to them in the scream of bike engines tortured by the surface they were forced to ride. They couldn't tell if they were hitting their targets. Dirt swirled around them as the return fire kicked up traces. Nothing seemed to hit: the bikes didn't buck and rear from tire or engine damage, and there was no searing pain or numbing sensation from a slug ripping home.

In truth, it was hard to know what was going on. In the middle of this engagement, it was impossible to know if their tactics were working, or if circumstance had diverted them.

The true pattern could only be seen from the outside.

J.B. WAS WATCHING the maneuver with mounting apprehension. He would have much preferred to bring the convoy to a halt, adopt a defensive formation and then bring the attackers into an area where the armament he carried could blast the living hell out of them. But LaGuerre had scuppered any chance of that. J.B. knew that Ryan and Jak would expect him to do this, and wondered if part of their pulling away from the convoy was to act as bait to the attackers, drawing them into an attack that didn't exist.

The convoy hadn't deviated from its path. It followed the line of the highway, as simple as that. The attacking wags had come from a diagonal, deviating only when the rocket attack had put paid to nearly half their number. They had pulled an almost 180-degree turn, and seemed to be going back on themselves. Their aim soon became clear—they were moving to cut ahead of the convoy. Instead of coming from the side, and risking another blast from the rocket launchers, they had opted to cut back to try to meet the road so that they could turn and meet the convoy head-on.

And now Ryan and Jak were entering the fray, leaving their posts at the rear and heading across at another angle to cut in front.

J.B. figured that he knew what they would do, if they could—divide the enemy, make it easy for convoy blasters to pick them off. No way they could do much damage themselves. Looking at the way they were ducking and weaving across the dustbowl, he doubted very much if they would be able to risk any shots of their own.

And they had no communication. He couldn't raise them, and so he was damn sure that they couldn't raise each other. So friendly fire was a real and present danger.

Dark night, he could punch out LaGuerre's lights for making this difficult. Seven wags, none of which looked that heavily armed. It should have been piss easy. Instead, he was watching Ryan and Jak on their erratic course, wondering how the hell he could fire on the attacking wags without taking out the riders.

One thing for sure—whether they knew it or not, Ryan and Jak were serving the convoy well. Their sudden appearance, and the path they were carving across the land, meant that the attacking wags had been forced to modify their course, both to meet the new threat with attack, and also to avoid a collision that would have suited neither party.

Now, instead of running a course that would see them hit the road ahead of the convoy, they had been diverted into one that saw them running parallel to the highway, the bikes running interference between them. The seven wags were currently devoting their attention to the bikes, SMG fire raking the ground around the weaving path of both Jak and Ryan. The riders had avoided being hit thus far, but in truth it was only a matter of time before probability dictated such a hit.

The good thing for the convoy was that fire was being taken away from them. Without their attention being taken up by the need to respond, it gave J.B. vital seconds to plan and act, rather than being forced to react.

"Cody, Doc, listen carefully," J.B. said in calm and measured tones that were far from reflecting how he felt. "We can't talk to the bikes, and they can't talk to us. I want to avoid hitting them. But the truth is that we can't tell what Jak and Ryan are going to do. They're keeping the wags from firing on us, but that won't last long. We've got SMG capability, and we're going to use that and not the rocket launchers. I want each of you to pick a target area and stick to it. Don't try to follow the wags, just aim at those that come in a hundred-degree angle. Make that the firing area."

"Okay, you're the boss…" Cody's voice was strained. The convoy rider was having trouble grasping J.B.'s concerns—it figured, as the bike riders weren't his people, and he would have just blasted the hell out of anything in his field of vision. Would he do that anyway? J.B. hadn't had the time to form an opinion; he could only hope.

Doc's voice, when it came, was far more reassuring. "My dear boy, I completely agree. Spare the rod and pass the ammo, I say."

A fleeting grin crossed the Armorer's face. He had no idea what the hell Doc was talking about—much like usual—but he knew that he could rely on the old man.

"Okay. Pick your targets and fire at will," J.B. commanded crisply.

There was no further dialogue between the convoy wags. J.B. settled in behind the SMG post to fire at the attacking wags, and knew that his order had been successfully understood by Cody when a burst that could only have come from the second-in-line wag ripped into a clearing space between Ryan and Jak, hitting home and causing one of the attack wags to spin off course, a plume of smoke rising from a gas tank that had caught fire. The wag veered erratically away from its companions, the crew jumping to avoid being consumed by a fire that spread rapidly. Their flight was in vain. At the speed they were going, it was likely that bones would crack and internal organs tear on impact. That was assuming they could escape the blast that ripped the wag apart. The gas tank caught fully and exploded, triggering a chain reaction in the ordnance they carried. The sound of the explosion was loud enough even to be heard above the steady roar of the convoy engines, sounding a second after the flash of the explosion assailed their eyes.

"Good shooting, Cody," J.B. said into his mic, wanting to keep the man sharp and on his side with due praise.

As he spoke, he took aim for a wag that had come into his field of vision. It drew level with the LaGuerre's armored wag, then used its lighter weight and comparatively stronger horsepower to pull ahead, starting to alter course, so that it was moving out of parallel and into an orbit that would take it in front of them. Jak and Ryan were farther back, engaged in weaving between the five wags that still moved straight.

"Nice try, but no way," the Armorer murmured to himself. He admired the boldness of the move, figuring that it was probably how he would play it under such circumstances. Which was exactly why he knew it needed to be snuffed out before it became a threat.

Pulling clear of the melee at their rear, the attack wag crew knew that they were opening themselves up to attack, which was why they laid down some fire of their own. Chattering SMG fire was echoed by the dull clanging of the shells hitting the armorplate of LaGuerre's wag. If they thought such ordnance would have an effect on the wag, they were soon disabused of the notion. J.B. knew it was now time to see what else they carried with them. If it was heavy and could cause damage, then he didn't want to see it. So he had to act swiftly.

The attack wag was pulling forward and across, making any angle of fire from the leading wag more and more difficult to attain with accuracy. If they could pull out and come straight on to LaGuerre's wag, they would hit a blind spot. There was a cannon mounted for firing ahead, but the Armorer knew from its design that it was a long-distance weapon. Sighting it for close in firing would be difficult if not impossible. Further, if the attack wag was heavily armed, then blowing the bastard out of the road could lead to damage from the blast.

The narrow window of time that he had available to him was closing rapidly. J.B. switched to the rocket launcher, using the sighting device to try to get a closer look at the wag. It was far from perfect—the imaging was intended for heat-seeking and so it was like trying to unscramble a diffused, negative picture. There was a mounted SMG, and something else that looked like an adapted gren launcher…maybe a mortar of some kind. Whatever it was, it was a piece of hardware that could do them some damage if the men in the wag decided to use it.

He couldn't give them the opportunity. They were pulling ahead quickly, their wag engine obviously tuned to a finer degree than many J.B. had seen. The heavy trader's wag was fast, but the attack vehicle was lighter in construction and carrying much less weight.

The Armorer's mind raced as he made the mental calculation to allow for that. He had to get this shot right. The sighting equipment was for heat-seeking, but he didn't want to rely on it and then find it wasn't in full working order. He'd do it by eye alone. He trusted himself, if nothing else.

It had to be now. J.B. fired the rocket and heard the whoop of the watching trader even before he registered that he had hit the wag. A blinding flash, followed by a dull crump that registered above the noise of the armored wag's engine told him that he had succeeded. This was followed by a shock wave that made the wag veer momentarily from its path before the impassive Zarir righted the course, almost as though he hadn't even noticed the deviation.

Dark night, that wag had been carrying some serious shit to cause a wave like that, J.B. thought. So was that just a primary attack vehicle, or did the remaining five have a similar ordnance? It was unlikely. The other wags that had blown had been fired with less power.

"Excellent shot, my dear John Barrymore—" Doc's voice broke his reverie "—but may I suggest that we attend to the remaining vehicles. I fear our friends are running out of time."

J.B. turned his attention to the battle that was running parallel. The bikes were still weaving, but as they got closer to the five wags, their attempts to draw them out and apart seemed to be doing the opposite. The lines proscribed by their paths seemed to do little more than ensnare them, the dirt around their wheels pocked by blasterfire that came closer and closer to taking them out.

So while it was imperative that the convoy take out the wags first, the very proximity of the bikes made this a harder task than at any other point.

"Doc, Cody, we've got no choices here. Keep firing like before, but keep the blasts tight. Short bursts only, and be triple careful."

"Shit, man. If the wags blow, then they could blast those guys off the bikes," Cody stated.

"I know," J.B. said tautly, "but we've got no other option. They're being drawn in too close."

"It is as Ryan would want it. Young Jak, too," Doc said

calmly. J.B. knew Doc was right, and he was glad that the old man would voice such an opinion to back him up.

More than that, Doc fired a short burst, the tracer of which was dangerously close to taking off the top of Jak's head. Yet while nearly chilling him, it also saved his life, for it hit home on the torso of a skinny, toothless attacker who was standing behind his mounted SMG in a semicrouch, laughing maniacally as he tried to swing the long barrel around to bring it to bear on the albino. It was a laugh cut short as the blast from Doc's SMG sparked off the stanchion of the mounting, arcing across the wag and strafing ragged red holes in his flesh, leaving little more than his splintered spine to hold him together as he flopped over the wildly swinging SMG.

Jak didn't see the result of the shot: instead, with the finely honed instinct of a hunter sensing a weakness in his prey, he pulled away a fraction, using just the one hand to guide the bike while the other leveled the Colt Python at the head of the wag driver. Through the dirt that smeared and streaked his goggles, Jak could see clearly enough the look of surprise and shock on the man's face as he turned to stare down the barrel of the Magnum blaster. He was slack-jawed, but was reduced to no jaw at all as Jak fired, the heavy slug taking away the lower half of his face and a chunk out of his shoulder.

The albino youth had to adjust the bike to the bite of the blaster as it kicked back at him. His attention was diverted, the need to focus on keeping the bike upright meaning that he missed the aftermath of his action. Veering wildly as the chilled driver's grip loosed on one side marginally before the other—the result of losing most of his shoulder joint from the Python slug—the wag careened into the side of a wag that was pulling ahead. Catching the rear end, it caused the second wag to go into a spin. As it spun, it clipped the underneath of the first wag, which had tilted up into a flip at the impact.

The wags became entangled as the underneath of each chassis became exposed. The occupants—those who had not bought the farm—found themselves being thrown from the wag and onto hard, unyielding and unforgiving earth. The lucky ones were knocked unconscious. Those who were not so lucky were conscious as the divergent directions of the two wags acted upon each other, the stresses of the opposing forces being too much for the metal to take, rending the bodies of the wags, sparking into fuel tanks that had been ruptured.

The two wags became a spreading ball of fire that engulfed those beneath, those thrown yards away and the land between. Jak threw his bike into a turn that took it away from the fireball, throttle opening wide to outrun the wave of heat and fire that threatened to engulf him. He could feel it at his back, feel the metal beneath him heating up. The front wheel of the bike bucked up under him as he gave it all the power he could.

Somehow—and he wasn't sure how—the dirt beneath him hit a harder, denser packed patch, allowing his tires to grip as the front wheel hit a surface again. The bike picked up speed and he felt the heat recede at his back.

"BY THE THREE KENNEDYS, the lad's a marvel," Doc breathed as he watched Jak escape by something less than the skin of his teeth. Doc had been convinced that the albino was chilled meat, even given his remarkable skills.

"Truly, whatever may govern this universe is looking down upon him on this day."

"Doc, honey, stop yakking and fire the fucking thing," Ramona yelled from the driver's seat.

Doc allowed himself the most indulgent of grins. "Of course, my dear, you are quite correct." He fired off a couple of carefully aimed bursts before adding, "The lad is a marvel because he has made it easier for us as much as for his own exploits."

Doc was right. J.B. was thinking the same thing, and he nodded to himself as he heard Doc's voice on the comm receiver. The two wags crashing together had left just the three to contend with. Further, the way in which they had collided and then blown had caused the remaining vehicles to scatter, breaking formation to escape the worst of the fireball. The enemy scattered, separated and was much easier to pick off. It was almost a bonus that Ryan and Jak were now distanced enough not to impede their compatriots' lines of fire.

"Cody, Doc—one each, guys. Let's take the bastards out once and for all," J.B. snapped.

"A pleasure," Doc purred.

"Sure thing," Cody murmured, an equal pleasure evident in his tone.

It was like shooting fish in a barrel—or would have been, if any other than Doc had a notion of what the old phrase meant. The idea of keeping fish in a barrel to shoot would have drawn blank looks of sheer incomprehension if mentioned at all. This almost irrelevant but amusing thought crossed Doc's mind as he took aim with the SMG at the wag that was within his angle of fire. A long burst drew up short of the target, which maintained distance knowing that it was safe while the crew tried to work out what to do next.

No way was the old man going to let them get away. He switched to the rocket launcher, sighted and fired. The wag was engulfed in the explosion of a direct hit.

"Way to go, sugar," Raven purred in his ear. "Good shooting."

Doc allowed himself a shrug. "One tries," he said elliptically.

Meanwhile, Cody's wag of choice had come within range, and the marksman in the second convoy wag hit a long burst on the SMG that ripped along the side of the attackers' wag, puncturing the bodywork and the bodies of the inhabitants with equal impunity. The wag careened across the dirt-packed land before the spilling fuel and the sparking metal detonated all within.

One remained, in J.B.'s area, and just right for him. Ryan was ahead of it, drawing it in toward the convoy as it chased him, SMG fire ripping up around his wheels. The guys in the wag were consumed by fury and bloodlust, not thinking about what they were doing.

That just made it easier. J.B. held his fire until Ryan had passed through his sights; then, as the wag came into the center of his vision, he let rip a long burst of SMG fire that hit the wag head-on. The windshield shattered, the driver became a red blur of blood and bone, and as the wag swerved under the sudden lack of guidance, the sweep of fire took out the side and the men within. One shell had to have hit a gren, as the wag exploded with a sudden violence that took the Armorer by surprise.

And then it was over, almost anticlimactic.

The convoy rolled on, Zarir almost seeming to have not noticed the mayhem that had just occurred. The other wags following in his wake, unable or unwilling to slow. Ryan and Jak fell in at the rear, unable to communicate with the others, waiting for such time as LaGuerre decreed a rest stop before being able to ask questions about what had occurred and why. They were exhausted, but forced to continue.

The Armorer looked at LaGuerre.

The trader seemed unconcerned by what had just happened.

The Armorer looked at Eula.

The young woman regarded him impassively, as though the events of the firefight had not occurred, as though she were examining him in minute detail, trying to get inside his head, unconcerned by what had just happened.

J.B.'s sense of unease welled up with renewed vigor. There was something odd about the whole situation, something that could spell danger not just for him, but for all the companions.

Something for which only he could find an answer to: if he could figure out what the question was....

Chapter Eight

The Past

"I've got to hand it to you, Trader. I don't know where you got that boy from, but him and Luke are like blood brothers. I'm feared that when one leaves, the other will want to follow. And we really couldn't have that. Unless of course your boy wants to stay. Now that may be a different matter entirely."

Baron Emmerton's grin was broad but didn't reach as far as his eyes. Beady, dark and glittering, they were sizing up Trader's reaction.

The grizzled veteran of too many psychological games wasn't likely to fall for anyone as blatant as Emmerton. The man was a fat fool, and a dangerous one because of the power he had, but a fool nonetheless.

Trader returned the grin; his, however, went up to the eyes. "I don't think you've got too many worries there, Emmerton. Luke wouldn't leave this place. Can you see him doing anything but moan about having to move his tools, pack and unpack all the time? And J.B.… Well, J.B.'s just J.B. Boy likes to keep on the move, and it isn't my business to ask why."

"So there's no chance you'd try and filch Luke?"

"Luke's one of the best, mebbe even the best. You know that as well as I do. But he's not the traveling type, and I've got an Armorer who can match him. Least ways, that's how I see it. And the thing he has over Luke for me is that he wants to travel, doesn't want to settle down. In fact, he'd have a shit fit if I even so much as suggested a thing. And when that boy goes… Well, he's quiet, but when those type go, they go in a big way. I've seen some scary shit, Emmerton, but I'd rather face that than J.B. when he's really pissed."

Trader had chosen his words with care. To a casual outsider, he may have seemed to have been overstating the case. Would a trader heading a convoy really let his armorer—a subordinate—behave in such a way? Not if he was going to stay a leader for any length of time. In truth, Trader would no more have stood for such behavior than he would for being short-changed in a deal. But he was more than willing to exaggerate if it would get his point across to the baron, who sat gross and sweating in front of him.

It was the worst part of having to use Hollowstar. To make the tolls worthwhile on the way through, it was best to try to do some trade with the baron and his people, which, in terms of goods and jack was passable. Hollowstar was far from rich, but its position meant that there was always something to be picked up from the tolls imposed on those who had passed before. And it had Luke: the ordnance expert was legend in this part of the country, and before recruiting J.B. it had been the chance to use Luke's skills that had added to the appeal.

But the downside was that Emmerton always insisted on entertaining his guests. Trader had a pretty strong stomach in many ways, but Emmerton's idea of entertainment was enough to make you puke in more ways than one. First, you had to sit through the banquet: seven courses of meat, sweetmeat and rich sweets. The baron loved his meat to be fatty, his side dishes to be made with starchy, stodgy consistencies and strong spices. The sweetmeats were sticky and cloying, so sugary and thick in molasses that just looking at them made you feel as though you were stuck to your seat. If you could eat all seven courses without puking at least once, then you were lucky. Poet had once told Trader about a really ancient predark warrior race called the Roaming—presumably because they ruled half the old earth—and the things they had called vomitoriums. What that meant, Poet couldn't tell him. All he knew was that these Roamings would eat until they wanted to puke, go to the vomitorium and puke their guts up, then come back and start again.

A stupe way of wasting precious food, but it was no mere chance that Poet had told him this after the first time they had been to Emmerton's banquet. It sure as hell explained why the bastard baron was so fat. Ever since, Abe had attended the banquets with Trader, Poet refusing and claiming his gut would suffer too much. Abe was made of sterner stuff, and even though Trader gagged frequently, the skinny Abe seemed able to stomach the food. Trader didn't like to think what it did to his insides.

But that was nothing compared to the other way in which the fat baron's banquet could turn your gut.

Emmerton was obsessed with young women. It was something that Trader knew, disliked, but preferred to ignore in the greater interest of survival and trade. Trouble was, Emmerton had no shame about his depraved taste, and thought nothing of flaunting it. It was as if he believed every man shared in it. So it was that the food was served to them by scantily dressed, very young servant girls. It was sickening, but Trader rationalized it by figuring that he'd seen people slice shit out of each other, and that was bad, too. It was kind of harder to ignore when the wandering fingers of the baron's fat paws reached out and clawed idly at the girls.

And, always assuming that you could get past the sight of that without heaving, there was the floor show, which was way worse. It was amazing what some people called entertainment.

The strange thing about Hollowstar was that it was modeled after the kind of predark towns where everything was supposed to be perfect and "nice." It was a word Trader knew from old books and vids, but there was nothing in this world that qualified for the word, as far as he understood it. The rest of Hollowstar made an effort to attain it, but their best efforts were blown out of the water by the excesses of the baron. From the outside, his house was only a little larger than the others in the ville, and it was painted in the same manner.

From the inside, it was different: the rooms had been knocked into one, with engraved columns holding up those areas where supporting walls had previously stood. The columns were engraved with figures in various stages of undress. The walls and ceiling were painted with scenes depicting similar nude scenes, and those areas that were unpainted were covered with rich drapes and hangings in heavy, dark-dyed fabrics. The baron's sleeping area was cordoned off by railed drapes, the bed beyond large and soft when seen through the gap. The most recent of his wives was sleeping there while they ate and talked, oblivious to what was going on. Doped out of her head, Trader guessed from past experience. The rest of the room was cluttered with ornaments from as many predark eras as could be pillaged; desks, tables and bureaux covered with papers, jack and valuables of all kinds. Couches and chaise longues were gathered around a central, tiled area.

That was where the entertainment would take place.

Trader steeled himself for this moment, and when Emmerton beckoned that he and Abe seat themselves for a good view, he consoled his turning stomach and equally rebelling conscience with the notion that he was putting up with this because it allowed his people safe passage. Besides, it would have gone on, whoever was present. Himself, or some other trader. Probably had.

Yeah, maybe…that didn't stop him feeling soiled every time he witnessed it and had to walk away without cutting the sick bastard's throat. After the second time, Poet having refused to attend and Abe taking his place, Trader had asked the skinny man how he could stand it. Abe had shrugged and said that there were sick bastards everywhere. As long as you weren't one, and did what you could when you could, then screw it. What was wrong with the sec men who hung around with the fat prick every day? Why didn't they do something? They had more chance. In the end, you zone out and just let the shit wash over it without swallowing any.

Emmerton kept returning to the subject of J.B. and Luke. He was a sly bastard at the best of times. The way he was talking about it, hunting around the edge of the subject, trying to sound out Trader's own views all the time before voicing his own… It was hard for Trader to know whether the fat man was worried about Luke wanting to join Trader because of the way he and J.B. had bonded, or whether he wanted to snatch J.B. from Trader and join the two of them together as a product that could be exploited for greater gain.

Either way, the baron had noticed how close the two men had become, and although it hadn't really entered Trader's mind up to this point, he began to dwell on it as he and Abe made their way back to the convoy, dismissed by the sec men after the baron had passed out from drinking too much. He'd become used to having the quiet man around, and with his skills he'd forged for himself an invaluable place in the convoy. He'd be more than missed.

On the other hand, they hadn't seen that much of him for the few days they'd been in Hollowstar. In Luke, he'd found a kindred spirit. Maybe the ville would appeal to a man who had never put down roots. Not everyone was a natural nomad like Trader and the majority of his crew. He'd assumed that J.B. was one of them in that respect.

What if he was wrong?

"AND I'M TELLING YOU, if you machine tool the bore on something that old, you're going to turn it into a piece of shit. Is that really what you want?"

"I'm paying you to do a job, and I'm telling you—"

"You're telling me you don't know your ass from your elbow, and you're talking out of both." Luke took off his battered baseball cap, which rarely left his head, scratched vigorously, and then jammed it back into place with a firmness that echoed his tone.

"Listen, bub, you might think you're the hottest piece of shit this side of a stickie's turd, but I'm still giving you good jack to do a job, and I expect you to do it."

The man was small and fat, but he was quivering with rage. And he had a Smith & Wesson snubbie tucked into the waistband of his tattered pants, while Luke had nothing but the overwhelming force of his personality. Odd thing that J.B. had noticed about him—for a man who loved ordnance so much, Luke never actually carried any kind of blaster himself.

So that was one hell of a lot of lead against nothing but harsh words. A few men were gathered in the old storefront, playing cards and drinking coffee-sub. They gathered there every morning, it seemed, and Luke let them stay even though they had no business for him, and he barely acknowledged their presence. Right now, they weren't even watching the argument.

The fat little man was flexing his fingers as he stared up, red-faced, into Luke's impassive visage.

Calmly, Luke almost whispered, "I don't give a rat's fuck about your stupe jack, Howie. You can stuff it up your ass for all I care. Might even stop you talking such shit all the time. I am not—repeat, am not—going to try and machine tool an old piece of hardware like that. It was made with loving care, hand-crafted by men who didn't know there was shit like this on the horizon, and who just wanted to do the best job they could. They loved their work, and I respect that. I love my work, and I'm not going to sully my reputation by carrying out an order—that I know to be stupe and wrong—just because some asshole thinks he knows better. Why, Howie, why, if you know how this piece of work should be done, have you even bothered coming here in the first place? How fucking stupe is that?"

The little fat man blustered. "You…you…you shit-stained piece of rag. You always talk to me like that—"

"Yeah, and you always come back, asshole," Luke interjected.

"Fuck you. Just do the fucking job and give me my blaster back in working order, right now," Howie yelped, his voice rising higher and higher as his anger grew.

And as his hand crept closer and closer to the Smith & Wesson in his belt. J.B. noted that, and decided to take a hand himself.

"Listen, Luke isn't shitting you on this," he said quietly, sliding himself between the two men and using the soft tone he always used to calm Hunnaker when she was going ballistic on everyone's ass. He figured that any kind of anger that would make a man squeal like a woman was somewhere near the kind of rage he'd seen from her.

Maybe he was right. Howie looked at him blankly, trying to comprehend what was being said to him, his face almost purple with rage but his eyes starting to get a puzzled light in them. Yeah, J.B. had seen this kind of thing before.

More assured now, he continued. "Luke may be telling you bluntly, Howie, but he's right, See, this is a nice blaster," he continued, reaching out behind him and flexing his fingers for Luke to hand him the old rifle that was the bone of contention. An apt phrase, as the cool, dry metal felt like a bleached and fossilized bone in his grasp. "It's a really nice piece of work. Think about it—it's lasted more than a hundred years, through skydark to now, and it was made before men even had the machines to make blasters. This had to be done by hand. It's a different kind of metal from blasters made by machine."

"But metal is metal," Howie blurted. He was still mad, but there was an uncertain edge to his voice, now. The Armorer's calm tones and love of the craft was beginning to soothe him.

"No, Howie, that's a mistake a lot of people make. The metals used in blasters changed from time to time, as the process of making them changed. See, if you look inside the barrel of this beauty, you can see that the bore markings aren't as exact as those on a machine-tooled blaster of the same type. Now, if you put it in a machine like the ones Luke has out back and try to rebore it, you'll do nothing more than ruin what's there and probably screw up the true line of the barrel, as the metal is softer than that the machines are made for. You see what I'm saying, Howie?"

The little fat man looked at him with an odd mix of awe and complete lack of understanding on his face. He nodded, though he didn't know why. J.B.'s tone had been both comforting, soothing and authoritative at the same time. Anyone from Trader's convoy other than Hunn would have been astounded to hear the Armorer wax lyrical, and at such length. He was known as a man of few words. Yet, once he was on his favorite subject, it was sometimes hard to shut him up. The same was true of Luke, and no one who had heard them over the last few days and had prior knowledge of their personalities would have believed what they were hearing.

But what the hell. It had worked on Howie, who said, "Well…well why didn't Luke just say that in the first place?"

"He was trying to," J.B. said. That was a bare-faced lie, and the Armorer barely kept the grin off his face. "Anyway, the only way he can do this blaster by hand, which means you'll have to leave it here. Can't be done while you wait. Long job," he added, just to make sure the little man got the point.

Howie sniffed, peered over J.B.'s shoulder at Luke, who glowered at him.

"Well, if some people would just say what they mean in the first place. I'll call for it tomorrow. That okay?"

Luke gave the briefest and most condescending of nods. Howie sniffed hard again, returned the nod and left the old storefront. J.B. turned to Luke, the blaster still in his hand and a quizzical look on his face.

"Dude, you spoiled my fun," Luke said gently.

"Mad little fucker looked like he was about to chill you," J.B. murmured.

Luke's face split into a grin. "Howie? Hell, no… I just like riding the little shit is all. He likes it, too. Gets his kicks from arguing with me."

"His hand was getting a little too close to that Smith & Wesson."

"Always does. Howie hasn't so much as shot a mutie rabbit in years. He runs the dry-goods store across the road, and his wife does all the shooting if anyone tries to get away without paying. Oh, man, she's the scary one. Twice his size up and half across. Face like an ax that's been splintering redwoods all season. You know, that's why he comes in here. Gets rid of all his aggression and anger. I've argued with him and rebored that rifle at least five times. Doesn't really need it. You look."

J.B. examined the blaster in greater detail. Luke was right. The bore showed signs of manual reworking, and with great dexterity. Recent, too. J.B. switched his attention to Luke, who was still grinning. Even when they had been deep in discussion about ordnance, it was rare that the big man's face had cracked. Now, it was like watching someone else in Luke's face.

Catching J.B.'s thoughts from his expression, Luke shrugged. "So I supply a public service, dude. It's not only about the hardware, just mostly. And besides, it livens up the day sometimes."

With which he turned and walked past the tattered drape and into the back room, leaving J.B. with the ancient but rebored rifle in his hand. Looking around, he saw that old guys playing cards had completely ignored the exchanges that had just taken place. Maybe it was just that it was all part of the order of the ville. Everyone knew about, but didn't feel the need to explain unless an outsider tried to intervene.

He shrugged. Maybe most villes worked this way, and he'd just never noticed it before. Reading people as well as he could read blasters was something he felt he needed to improve upon. Maybe Luke was good at it, as he'd obviously been around. The big man had never talked about where he had come from, just as he had never asked J.B. about himself. But it was clear he didn't come from around here. The reference to chopping redwoods gave it away. J.B. had heard of the giant trees, knew that there were some left still standing after the nuke winters of skydark, but they were on the other side of the continent. Luke had referred to them in the casual manner of someone who knew from experience what he was talking about.

So maybe he had some buried secrets. Maybe he was even more like the Armorer than either man suspected.

J.B. was somehow warmed by the thought.

EVEN J.B. HAD TO DO SOME work for Trader at some time during their stay. It had been several days stretching toward a week since they had arrived. Usually, the convoy was only in Hollowstar for a couple of days each side of their trek into the desolate lands beyond. Time enough to do a little trade and lessen the cost of the toll raised by the baron for using the only road to the east. Time enough for the crew of the convoy to have some downtime: drink brew, go to gaudy houses, rest up and have some fun before the arduous wastes that lay in wait for them.

This time was different. Trader kept only Abe and Poet in close counsel with him. For the rest of the crew he had a policy of strictly need-to-know. When things became relevant, that was the time to be open. They were loyal to him; many of them had traveled with him since their formative years, and Trader had a good eye for character. But it was also because of this that he knew he couldn't tell them everything all the time. People were fallible. They got drunk and said too much, sometimes without realizing it. Enemies didn't always need intelligence laid out on a plate in front of them. A sober, alert crew knew that. When drunk, the lines of judgment became blurred. The same was true of what a man or woman said in the throes of lust. Hell, Trader knew that he couldn't trust himself one hundred percent, let alone anyone else. Poet and Abe had to know shit, in case something happened to Trader. But even then, it was still a risk.

So he had stayed silent to all except his two trusted lieu-tenants about the manner in which Baron Emmerton had been cagey about tolls and trade, delaying decisions and asking questions in and around the subject of Luke and J.B. It was starting to irritate Trader. He wished the fat bastard would just come out and say what he meant, so that they could deal with it. Trader wanted J.B. to stay with him and had no designs on Luke. But he figured that wasn't what Emmerton thought. And he was pretty sure he knew what Emmerton wanted, the more he pondered it. Well, the greasy bastard wasn't going to get it.

Which would mean nothing but trouble. Meantime, all that he could do was keep his people occupied, stop them getting into too many fights, and hope that Emmerton would come out into the open pretty damn quick.

"DARK NIGHT, how many more times are you going to have me doing this?" J.B. mumbled and grumbled as Trader took him through an inventory of every piece of ordnance carried by the convoy, both for their own use and for use as trade.

"As many time as I want, son. I'm the boss here, remember?"

J.B. shrugged. "I know, but I haven't seen you this itchy before, and I'm figuring there's a reason."

Trader weighed up the slight, bespectacled figure in front of him. J.B. was shrewd, and he'd figure it out, more or less, if given time. Best to take a calculated risk and let him know at least part of the story.

"You're no stupe, J.B. You must have realized from what the others have said that we don't usually spend that long here before moving out." When J.B. nodded, he continued. "Truth of the matter is that I'm having trouble with Emmerton over the tolls this time out. I'm not sure why, but the fucker is being cagier than a pen full of mutie pumas. So we're stuck here, and you know what some of us are like when we get cabin fever, or too much time and too much jack to spend."

J.B. nodded once more. From the look on his face, it hadn't occurred to him that Trader could have meant the Armorer himself. More likely he was thinking of Hunnaker, who had the capacity to go triple crazy with little or no provocation. It was a fair enough guess, as Trader did have some concerns in that corner. Nonetheless...

"Okay, well, you know the best way to stop that happening is to keep people busy. Keep them somewhere that they can't raise hell and get themselves blasted from here to the farm, and leave us in the shit."

J.B. shrugged. "Guess so," he said in a slow drawl, "but shit, all I was gonna do was spend some more time with Luke. Could learn a lot off a man like that. And there won't be that much time, as we'll be on our way soon enough," he added.

Trader was glad to hear that last sentiment, but he masked his satisfaction well. "True enough. But I got something else I need you to do for me, J.B. Y'all got some downtime tonight, and I know that Hunn is going to want to go and get wasted on the local brew. She always does it when we're here, tries to fuck anything that'll have her, and gets real feisty if something or someone gets in her way."

Trader let the last words die away without feeling the

need to elaborate. From the look on J.B.'s face—a slowly dawning, pained expression—he knew that the Armorer had drawn the conclusion he wanted.

"Shit, no. I've got to bodyguard her all night and make sure nothing happens and no one buys the farm?"

Trader grinned. "Got it in one."

"Fuck. I'll do anything. Take the whole armory apart, grease it and reassemble it. Clean the shit off all the latrines. Hell, I'll even let Abe try to explain the comm system to me again. But not that…"

Trader clapped a hand on J.B.'s shoulder. "I knew you'd understand, J.B. You and her get on better than anyone. Shit, I know enough to know that no fucker on the face of this rad-blasted earth can control her, but you've got a better chance of keeping her under wraps than anyone else on the convoy. It's the shitty end of the stick, but sometimes that's all there is to grab hold of and haul yourself out."

"And that's supposed to make me feel better?" J.B. mused.

Trader shook his head. "Tell you what. It sure as hell makes me feel better."

As J.B. went back to his task, cursing under his breath for what he knew was to follow that evening, Trader congratulated himself on his double score. Not only had he kept Luke and J.B. apart for a while, to give Emmerton something to think about, he had also got the ever-present problem of Hunnaker under control for the moment.

It seemed such a simple solution. How could it go wrong?

"FUCK'S SAKE, I don't need to be wet-nursed like a baby," Hunn grumbled as she entered the bar with J.B. at her elbow.

"Who says it's that?" J.B. queried in reply. "Mebbe I just want to have a few brews with—"

"Aw, bullshit, J.B.," Hunn interrupted. "How many kinds of stupe d'you think I am? If you had your way, you'd be boring about bore with that lump of rock, Luke."

"He didn't want to fuck you, eh?" J.B. asked with a fleeting smile.

She waved dismissively as they approached the bar. "I didn't want the big lunk anyway. Only thing that'd get him hard is a kind of blaster he hasn't seen before… Not," she added hastily, "that I'm saying the same thing about you, but—"

"I didn't think you were," J.B. replied, "at least, not until you mentioned it. Just for that, it's your jack on the bar tonight."

Even though it was still daylight outside, the bar was already in a twilight gloom. Like most of the storefronts that surrounded the sparse green of the ville square, it was lit by tallow lamps. Fuel for generators was always at a premium, and carefully conserved. Unlike most of the storefronts, the bar had a smoked glass that had been fitted where the others had clear. It had originally been taken from a building with a much smaller window space, as the frame of the front window had been extended by boarding to house the glass. From what he'd been told, the smoked glass had been in place for some time and had never yet been cracked or broken in any way. So he could only assume that the inhabitants of Hollowstar had some serious sec enforcement when it came to their bars. And that Hunn had never yet run amok.

Hunnaker and the Armorer seated themselves at the old bar stools that were metal framed and bolted to the floor. Looking around, J.B. could see that the tables and seats in the rest of the bar had been taken from an old predark diner, and were similarly bolted down. Well, that explained at least in part why the glass had stayed in place so long.

The bar was more or less empty. It was still early, and most of the people in Hollowstar were going about their business. Everyone in Hollowstar had business— manufacture and repair of small goods, small holdings on the edge of the ville, education in trades for the children. The only people who had any kind of excuse to be in the bar at this time of day were those whose work kept them busy at night. Now was their time to take some rest and recuperation, before beginning the evening and night-shifts that ensured the ville worked 24/7. Emmerton and his predecessors had instilled in the community a strong work ethic.

Some may have asked why a community should work itself so hard for seemingly so little reward. Riches were not there to be had this far east, but, by the same token, a crushing poverty that could have wiped out the community was only a spit away. The work ethic, and the organization that it brought to the community, were what kept them afloat. The price of their freedom—of their very lives—was eternal diligence.

Women worked in this ville; however, many of them worked not in occupations but as wives and mothers. Children were important to keeping the machine that was

Hollowstar in motion, a new generation replacing the elderly—those that lived that long—at regular intervals. Despite the seemingly sedate pace of life that echoed the old vids on which the ville was modeled, there was a restless urgency lurking beneath the surface that was born of the high-tension wire on which their lives were balanced.

There had to be some release. And so those women who were not wives and mothers found themselves, at some time or another, doing service in the gaudy houses that lay on the outskirts of the ville, hidden behind the facade but common enough knowledge for the traveler to find them with ease. After all, they oiled the wheels of the local economy as much as they provided relief.

So what did these women do in their downtime? They drank in the bars of whatever ville they worked. Maybe to blot it out, maybe because they liked it, maybe… J.B. didn't know, and could only guess. The reasons didn't really matter to him. He just knew that this was what they did. Here as much as they did anywhere else. And they drank alone.

That was why he thought she was a gaudy house slut when he saw her in there. It wasn't the first time that he'd seen her. When he was in the center of Hollowstar, either going to or from Luke's, or even when he had been on some task for Trader, he had seen her often over the past few days. For this reason, if nothing else, it entered his head that she had to work the gaudy house mostly at night. Once he had seen her leaving Luke's when he had been on his way there. What the big guy got up to was no business of J.B.'s, and he hadn't asked. Neither had Luke said anything.

She was always alone, which was another reason he figured she worked in a gaudy house. She was never with anyone. Most of the women who didn't work the houses could be seen with a man or with kid at some point. It was that kind of a regimented ville.

Each time he'd seen her, their eyes met and he'd seen some kind of spark in there, a light that seemed to be smiling at him, even though her face said nothing. Hell, he didn't even know what her name was. Maybe if he did, he could have found where she worked and paid for a few hours. Maybe not. In a way it would ruin the illusion.

J.B. was no romantic, but this thing that he could feel within him was like nothing he had ever felt before. Hunn sat next to him, a bristling ball of energy. Even when she was still, the nervous tension that powered her had a kineticism that made her seem to be in perpetual motion, even when she was still. Normally, he took no notice. Now, it seemed to irritate the hell out of him, a constant reminder that she was there when he wanted to be alone, so that the woman across the bar would talk to him.

So that when she did, he could be certain she was looking at him, not at Hunn, or at both of them when he heard her voice for the first time.

"You gonna sit there, or you gonna buy me a drink?"

Chapter Nine

The Present

"DARK NIGHT, when the fuck are you going to stop?" J.B. asked of LaGuerre. The trader had kept his convoy rolling for hours after the skirmish, and even though dusk was descending, he showed no signs of calling a temporary halt to their insistent progress.

"Don't see no reason to stop, man," LaGuerre replied in a lazy drawl. "Shit, we've already been attacked once. Don't want it to happen again, right?"

The Armorer was furious, but he tried to keep his anger in check. The battle had been easy for those in the convoy, but for Ryan and Jak it had been strenuous. The two riders had to be exhausted and in need of a break. Instead of which, they had been trailing in the wake of the convoy as the heat of the afternoon began to fade, and the wall of heat haze was replaced by the wall of twilight.

"Riders are supposed to be tough," Eula added. "Every rider we've ever had has been hard."

"And how many have you had, just in the time you've been with this convoy?" J.B. questioned.

She shrugged. "Dunno. Six, mebbe eight or nine."

"In less than two years, and you're not even sure how many." The Armorer spit. "You ever stop to think why?"

"Those are the risks." LaGuerre shrugged.

"Bullshit. You run a good convoy, then you look after the people you run. Good working and a good profit comes from taking care of the pieces that make the whole. That means people as much as wags and ordnance. Keep the same personnel and you get a better-run convoy."

"Those words of wisdom from your precious Trader?" LaGuerre sneered. "And where is he now?"

J.B. left his post and crossed the cramped interior of the wag. Before LaGuerre had a chance to react, the Armorer had his hands around his throat, pinning him back against the wall. The trader still had his aviator shades on—they never seemed to leave his face—and so J.B. couldn't see into his eyes. But his breathing had become short, gasping, and was an indicator of his level of fear.

"What happened to Trader isn't anyone's business but his," J.B. said softly, his voice hard-edged. "I'll tell you something else, too—it wasn't the way he ran his convoy that gave him grief. Might just be that way for you, though."

Even as he spoke, he felt the cold, hard muzzle of a blaster nudge gently at the base of his skull. The soft click of a hammer being pulled back sounded loud in his ear, the vibration reverberating in his skull.

"Easy, John Barrymore Dix. You wouldn't want to do anything too stupe, would you?"

For a moment the world seemed to stand still. J.B. could feel everything around him as though the detail were heightened, his senses taking in every scrap of information as though it would be the last thing he would ever know. He was aware of LaGuerre's breath, hot and stinking of garlic, and the breathy wheeze that accompanied every fetid gust as the man's chest tightened. He could feel the vibration of the blacktop beneath his feet as it rattled the suspension of the armored wag. He could feel the sweat as it began to gather around the rim of his fedora, soaking the line of hair around the hat band. Farther down his body, a small, cold pool was gathering in the hollow of his back as he unconsciously arched his spine away from the source of danger.

Bizarrely, it struck him that he could feel nothing of Zarir's presence. The jolt-wired wag jockey was oblivious to anything except the road ahead of him and the controls at his fingertips. Perhaps he was even oblivious to his own self. Certainly, he seemed to have no notion of the drama being played out to his rear.

Most of all, J.B. was aware of the blaster muzzle at his neck. He was aware that Eula was holding it steady. So steady that it was firm against the neck muscle, without the slightest tremor. He hadn't noticed that she had a handblaster. It wasn't like him to miss that, unless she had it well concealed. Okay, that didn't matter right now, but if she didn't just blow his head off, then it would be worth remembering.

He figured it was an old revolver as that had definitely been a hammer click and not just a round chambering. And it must have a pretty long barrel, too, as she was some distance away. He couldn't feel the heat of her body up close, or feel her hot breath on him. Long barrel and she was at arm's length—that made it difficult for him to risk a sweep back to try to deflect her aim.

Maybe it was a .357 or a .44. It didn't really matter, but while he let it play through his mind it allowed him to try to mentally step back. The girl had wanted him with them in the lead wag, and she'd been studying him the way Jak studied prey. Whatever reason she had for wanting him there, it wasn't a burning admiration. But she had a purpose. She wanted him there for the long haul, so it was unlikely that she would just take his head off for the sake of it.

"Okay, listen carefully," he said slowly. "I'm going to let go of this bastard, and I'm going to step back slowly. I'm telling you this so you don't get twitchy."

"Does it feel like I get twitchy?" she asked deadpan.

"No, it doesn't. But I like to be sure," he replied, thinking all the while that she was way beyond triple dangerous. Anyone that sure that he could read her calm was worth treating with caution. He added, "I can't move until you stop trying to push that blaster through the back of my neck."

"Okay. I'm going to move back slowly, too. But not so slow that you could try anything and get away with it."

"I can believe that," he said simply. As he spoke, he felt the pressure ease on the back of his neck, fading as the muzzle moved away from his skin, and only the tingling after-impression was left. Equally slowly, he loosened his grip at LaGuerre's throat and stepped back.

"That's cool," LaGuerre said, gingerly feeling the skin beneath his beard, his voice roughened by the pressure. "We'll say no more about this, okay? It was a disagreement in the heat of the moment. You're not so stupe as to carry this forward, and neither am I."

J.B. raised an eyebrow and said nothing for a moment. At length, he said simply, "If that's what you think, I'll go with that."

The Armorer turned to Eula. She still had the blaster in her hand. The part of him that was always the Armorer was pleased to note that his guess of a Colt .44 had been correct. The other part of him—J. B. Dix the man—had other things occupying his mind.

"You going to put that thing away, or you want me to admire the job you've done on it?"

She let the hammer down gently, put the blaster back in a holster concealed in the thigh of her combat pants. The old blaster was nearly the length of her thigh, and learning to walk without revealing the hiding place had to have taken a lot of practice—another sign of her dedication to her task. Whatever that might ultimately be… Her eyes hadn't left his the whole time, and it was still as though she was scoping his very soul. There was something about her that was familiar, but he still couldn't place it.

"Good to see you're so dedicated to your friends," she said. "Man who'd risk his skin for others is a rare enough commodity these days. Wonder if you were always like that." Her tone was flat, but there was something about the way she chose her words that told him he was missing out on something important.

"Not for me to say," he answered in as noncommittal a voice as he could. "You're not so bad like that yourself, are you?"

She shrugged. "Man pays my jack, figure he has a right to me covering his ass."

J.B. nodded. "Fair point."

He turned to LaGuerre. "Still think you're a triple shit rat fuck to not stop."

The trader shrugged. "Hey, you can't please everyone. I told you when I picked you people up that I wanted to make a straight run without stopping. You've seen why— you get scumfuckers like that attacking all the way across this pesthole."

"True enough," the Armorer replied, "but we saw them off, and there's little chance of another attack so soon. Any muties and coldhearts out here are going to be pretty spread out. Ryan and Jak need to rest up, at least get a break so they can sleep. Fuck it, man, they'll be crashing the bikes because they're falling asleep on them if you don't give them the chance to rest. We don't need them to be trailing behind as much as we need them alert and ready to fight. Least you can do is let them stash the bikes and catch some sleep in one of the wags while we ride. Everyone else gets a chance to rest."

"Zarir doesn't," the trader pointed out.

J.B. looked at the wag jockey. The man was staring ahead at the road, muscles set like high-tension wire around stone. He didn't seem to have heard his name mentioned, even to have registered what had just occurred at his back.

"Man, that boy is so hyped on jolt he's not sleeping or waking. He's more like a machine than this wag."

LaGuerre smiled, almost to himself. "Yeah, guess you got a point about that. Still don't want to stop."

"So you want to lose two good men and their bikes for the sake of pursuing this nonstop stupe plan? It's playing the odds, man. We stop now, make a quick switch and we can be on our way before any fucker has a chance to catch up with us. Check what's around. There's jackshit."

The trader stroked his beard. He looked at Eula, though his eyes were still hidden by his shades, and it was only the inclination of his head that signaled his question.

Without a word, the young woman went to the ob ports on either side of the wag and looked out into the twilight. J.B. could see over her shoulder that the land was empty as far as could be seen.

"I guess Dix is right," she said almost absently, as though absorbed in her own thoughts.

"You bet I am," J.B. said softly. The look she shot him was unreadable, but the one thing he knew for sure was that it wasn't undying admiration.

"I think he's right," she told the trader. "Makes sense, and there's not going to be a better time."

LaGuerre paused for a moment. Finally he said, "Okay, let's do it. But no fucking around. This is going to be quick."

J.B. nodded shortly and crossed to the comm mic. How to make Ryan and Jak aware of the convoy coming to a halt when the comm transmissions were inaudible to them? He would have to slow the convoy so that they were able to see that it was coming to a halt.

"Millie, Doc, Cody, we need to bring in Jak and Ryan before they drop. Get your wag drivers to slow their speed so that they can see. We stop suddenly and they'll smash into the back of us."

"A good point, my dear John Barrymore," came Doc's voice. "Such an unnecessary accident must surely be avoided."

MILDRED LOOKED at Reese, but the giant woman was impassive. She had said no more than a few words in all the time that Mildred had traveled with her, and it was unlikely that she was about to start now.

"So how much do you have to slow, and how quickly?" she asked. Reese shrugged. Mildred waited, but nothing more was forthcoming. "Well," she continued, trying to keep the irritation from her voice, "I'm not just asking you out of idle curiosity. I'm assuming that you have some kind of procedure that you use when you get such an order."

Reese tore her eyes from the road and bore them on Mildred. But rather than the hostility that Mildred expected, there was puzzlement in them. "A what?" she asked simply.

"A procedure."

"What's that?"

"The thing that you usually do when you get such an order."

"Uh…" Reese nodded slowly, as though it now made sense. "Never had an order like that before."

"What do you mean, you've never had an order like that before?" Mildred was keeping her temper, but only just, and she was sure that the repressed rage was coming out in her tone.

"Just what I say. Never done a run like this before, never had an order like that before. So got no pro-see-der."

Mildred put her hands to her face, massaging her temples. "Then what," she said slowly, "do you intend to do?"

Reese gave the slightest of shrugs. "See what they do in front, then follow them."

LaGuerre seemed to be the only one who could get through to Zarir. The wag jockey still stared straight ahead, seemingly unseeing and uncomprehending, but steering straight and true.

The trader stood and crossed the interior of the wag until he was by Zarir's side. He leaned over him, arm around his shoulders, whispering something into his ear. The wag jockey's head moved. It was the smallest of movements, noticeable only because he was otherwise so still. LaGuerre smiled, patting him on the shoulder before returning to his seat. The wag began to slow, almost imperceptibly at first but gaining a backward momentum as the distance grew longer.

So the convoy was going to pull up gradually, giving the incommunicado rear riders a chance to assimilate what was happening. That was good.

What was, perhaps, not so good—what was worrying the Armorer—was the way in which the trader had a hold over the wag jockey. Was it just jolt, or was it something else? He'd seen mutie psi-powers over the years; hell, he'd even seen good old-fashioned hypnotism. If it was something like this that the trader was using to keep Zarir under control and awake for such long periods—not just shit like jolt—then there was no way of knowing how much control he had over the rest of the convoy crew. Maybe that would explain Eula's strange attitude. Maybe not.

The Armorer didn't have the doomie sense, but he hadn't got this far by ignoring alarm bells when they went off in his head.

And this time they were deafening.

DOC LOOKED across at Raven, who had expertly slid into the driver's seat to replace Ramona while the wag was still in motion.

"It would appear, my dear, that your immaculately performed maneuver was unnecessary, as we shall shortly be stopping, albeit possibly briefly."

"Boy, you love those big words, hon," Ramona muttered sleepily from the bunk, where she lay stretched out with her eyes still closed.

"Then allow me to be a little more succinct—"

"Still too big, hon," she interrupted.

"Oh, yeah, and you wish you could say those words more often," Raven said to her, barely keeping the laughter from her voice.

"Woo, yeah," Ramona replied, in a tone that belied the expression. "Listen, Docky-babe, we don't usually do the long haul like this, but there have been plenty of times on long stretches where we've had to swap over for one reason or another. The big wag drivers, like Ray and Reese and the ones before them, they use jolt and shit to stay awake. I'm not overly fond of that shit, and neither is my girl here."

"Yeah, look at what it does to you… Why the hell you think they usually drive alone," Raven pointed out.

"A fair point," Doc conceded. He was still a little nonplussed at being called "Docky-babe," but didn't wish to press the matter. Instead he asked, "And so we slow down gradually before coming to a halt?"

"Well, how the hell else are we going to do it if we don't want to have those riders smush themselves into the wag's ass?" Raven demanded.

"That was my point," Doc replied mildly. "No one has told you by what levels and over what time scale to decrease your speed. There seems to be no way in which you have an operational structure for this."

Ramona sighed. "There you go again, Docky. Making everything more complicated than it has to be. We look at the wag in front and adjust according to what it's doing. Armand baby just leads the way, and we just let him."

Doc said nothing, but his mind was whirring. He was no expert on the etiquette of trading convoy operation: he would be the first to admit that, and gladly. All the same, it struck him that there was something a little lax about the way they seemed to do things, and to place their trust blindly in a man like LaGuerre. Faith in a leader was a good thing. The example of himself and his friends when it came to Ryan Cawdor was the example that leaped out at him. Yet, at the same time, they had a structure to their group. People knew what was expected of them in an emergency.

That did not seem to exist here, which raised the question of how they had managed to get this far in one piece. And the further question of what would happen to them if a real challenge presented itself.

Doc itched to share this concern. He suspected that he was not alone in having it. Ryan and Jak would probably be unaware of this as yet, having been so isolated.

It would be good to have them back aboard, then, for more than just their own need of rest.

CODY SAID NOTHING in the second wag. The humiliation of being turfed out of the lead wag just so the guy with glasses could ride with Armand and his piece was still fresh. But he harbored nothing against the glasses guy after that firefight. He had handled it well, and the fact that he had been quick to involve Cody and praise him for his shooting had gone a long way toward soothing those pains.

The stringy, mean-looking shooter was not a man to

harbor finer feelings toward any of his fellows, and in a way he saw no reason why they should stop and endanger themselves for the sake of picking up the bike riders. But—and this was where he prided himself on his ability to be a tactical thinker—he had seen how well they had performed in the firefight, as well. Whoever the fuck these people were that LaGuerre had picked up at Eula's behest, they were shit hot. And the convoy was low on numbers.

Cody figured that it was playing one lot of odds off against another to stop and pick the good fighters up on the chance that their skills would be needed again, rather than risk losing them to fatigue because of fear of attack once motion ceased. He knew which ones he'd go for under the circumstances, and they were the same ones that the glasses guy had persuaded LaGuerre to take.

Suited him. He had no desire to end up chilled for the sake of a few minutes' delay and lack of motion. Maybe that was all it was, in the end, that made him figure that the glasses guy was right. They shared the same kind of self-preservation instinct.

"Slow this fucker up, and don't let that asshole behind crash into us," he said simply.

The wag driver nodded and began to decrease speed gradually.

"WELL, THAT'S ONE FOR THE BOOKS, like they used to say. We're supposed to be stopping and Armand said right at the beginning that we wouldn't be, so it must be something real important to make him change his mind. Either that or your friend with the glasses is real persuasive. Mind you, Eula seems to have taken a real shine to him; what with persuading Armand to make Cody ride in the second wag, 'cause he's been with Armand since the beginning. Hell, even longer than I have, which is saying something, I guess. But then, if it means we pick up your friends from the back of the convoy, then it's got to be a good thing as far as you're concerned, right? Still, it's not like him to change his mind once he's started on a course of action. We've never done a straight run without any kind of stop along the way, of course, so mebbe he's realized that's it's not quite as easy as he thought it would be. I dunno. What do you think?"

Krysty blinked and looked into Ray's questioning eyes. The small, almost wizened old man had eyes that sparkled and burned brightly. Part of that was no doubt due to the stimulants that he was popping regularly, and which stopped him nodding out at the wheel. But part of it was his personality, and the chem only brought this out. She wanted to answer him, but she realized that she had zoned out so completely that she had lost the thread of what he was saying.

"Mebbe," she said cautiously. "I couldn't say. You know LaGuerre much better than I do. Mebbe there's something I don't know that could account for it."

It was about as noncommittal as she could get, and from the look on his face, he realized that she hadn't been listening.

"Hell, I know I go on sometimes, but I kinda thought that you'd be interested, seeing as it's your people that we're stopping for."

"I'm interested in that," she replied, "it's just that I don't know why LaGuerre would want to stop for any other reason than J.B. has persuaded him that it would be a good idea to pick up the bikers rather than run them into the ground and lose that defense."

"Okay, so you were listening a little. I know I never stop talking, honey, it's just that I can't help it these days. I do it when there's no one else in the cab, too, y'know, so it's not just you."

Krysty smiled at the old wag jockey. "I know, I figured that one out. And it's not that I don't care about LaGuerre— on the contrary, the more any of us know about him the better—it's just that—"

"It's just that it becomes one long drone after a while. I know, honey, I'm only too well aware of what it sounds like. Don't you fret, you just ignore old Ray for now, as I ain't really got much else to say. I'll just slow the container down and let it all come to a halt. And I'll just play some tunes while I'm doing it, so you don't have to hear me talk."

Despite the words, there was no sign of resentment or sarcasm in the old man's tone as he turned on the ancient tape player once more. Distorted electric guitars roared out of the speaker, squealing in electric pain before a voice came in again, and his quavery tenor joined in. Something about working on a night shift.

Krysty let the sound wash over her as the container slowed its progress in direct opposition to the tempo of the music.

RYAN WAS KEEPING the bike upright only by the carefully balanced forces of motion and his own iron will. He suspected that Jak was more alert and awake than himself because he had seen the albino hunt; and when Jak did this, he seemed to switch into a state of being that was almost beyond the limits of human endurance.

But Ryan wasn't like that. He was strong and he had stamina, for sure. The firefight had, however, taken a lot out of him. His limbs felt heavy, and his muscles ached in places they usually didn't. The posture of spending so long on a bike was beginning to reach areas of his musculature that weren't often called into use for such prolonged periods. His eyes were also heavy. His vision, already blurred by the dust and grime on the goggles and in the air around him, was further blurred by fatigue, a dark tunnel closing in at the edges. Without comm transmissions, and with the white noise of the wag and bike roar to act as an isolation blanket, he could feel sleep inexorably closing on him. He shook his head to rattle his brain and waken himself, but all it succeeded in doing was unsettle his balance so that he wobbled precariously on the bike. He was still executing the patrol pattern he had established with Jak, but it was doubtful as to whether he was actually observing anything as he completed the circuit.

So it was that he failed to notice that the convoy was gradually slowing. It was as though he was in his own private hell where nothing existed but the bone-aching fatigue and the monotony of the circuit. It took Jak breaking the circuit and adjusting so that he was riding parallel to Ryan before the one-eyed man realized that something was happening. Even longer before he understood that the convoy was coming to a halt. With Jak still riding parallel, his red eyes dulled behind the goggles, white hair whipping behind him, Ryan slowed his own machine.

The sound of the massed engines grew less in volume, dropped in pitch as gears changed. Then, for the first time since the journey had begun, he was able to hear the faint voice of the Armorer in his ear. At first he thought that he might be hallucinating, hearing something that wasn't there: it was only after a few moments, such were his reactions dulled by fatigue, that he realized he was hearing the comm tech for the first time since the journey had begun.

"Stay in the center of the blacktop, keep the vantage. Repeat, Ryan, Jak, we're bringing the convoy to a halt to take you on board so that you can rest up. The wags are slowing gradually. Decrease your own speed. Soon as you can hear this transmission, use the comm mics to respond. They're open, so all you have to do is speak. When we stop for the transfer, we're going to stay in the center of the blacktop, to keep vantage. Repeat—"

Ryan heard Jak's voice, tinny and distorted in his ear over the sound of the wags and the bikes, still only barely audible.

"J.B., read you. Ryan almost out, wondering when fuckers give us break."

"Almost, but not quite," Ryan croaked, his own voice sounding alien and distant in his ear. "With Jak on this. Fireblast, I'll be glad to get some rest."

Now aware that the convoy was coming to a halt, Ryan regulated his own speed so that it came in line with that of Jak, and of the rest of the convoy. Within a few hundred yards of contact between the riders and the rest of the convoy being reestablished, the convoy eventually rolled to a halt, the sound of the wag engines dying on the twilight air, being replaced by a silence that was almost as sweet to Ryan and Jak as the still dustbowl air that they could now breathe, untainted by wag fumes, dust and dirt thrown up by the blacktop.

Krysty and Mildred jumped down from the high cabs of the refrigerated container trucks almost before their engine noise had faded on the air. Both had reason. They wanted to escape their respective wag jockeys as much as they wanted to check on Jak and Ryan. They were beaten to their target by Doc, who had been closer.

Jak managed to dismount his bike with ease. He looked tired as the goggles were removed to reveal eyes that were redder than Doc had ever seen, but he had flipped over into hunter mode, and was proving once more his ability to run on empty.

Ryan was finding it harder. He halted the bike, veered to one side, and as he flung his leg across to dismount almost overbalanced, stumbling as it seemed that the weight of the bike would pull it over on top of him. Jak let his machine fall, moving easily across the distance between Ryan and himself to catch the machine before it trapped the one-eyed man.

Machine secured, Ryan found himself saved from falling by Doc's spindly yet strong limbs.

"Easy, my friend," Doc said softly, "you have come too far to injure yourself merely by falling over."

Doc's good humor was the boost Ryan needed as he righted himself, finding strength from the old man's gesture.

"Take a lot more than that to take me out, Doc," he replied with as much of a smile as he could muster through his fatigue.

"Good, for there is much we must discuss, I think," Doc said in more of an undertone.

Krysty and Mildred had reached them as Doc's murmured imperative died away.

"Shit, Ryan, you look all in. Let me check you," Mildred said, taking over from Doc and snapping into medic mode, checking the one-eyed man's remaining orb, as well as his pulse.

"Thought you'd both have to buy the farm out here, lover, the way this coldheart drives his crew," Krysty added in a tone as low as Doc's had been. She had, by now, taken over the role of supporting Ryan while Mildred moved on to check Jak. Not that there was much need. The hardy albino was looking as though he was ready to go again, only the layer of dirt and grime and the redness of the skin around his already blood-hued orbs giving lie to this.

"Hell of a firefight," Ryan said shortly, every word seemingly an effort to overcome fatigue, "but it's been quiet since. Why didn't he stop?"

"Fool wanted to do this run nonstop, and when he said that he meant it," Mildred stated. "Makes you kind of wonder if he lost his other sec men in exactly the way he tells it."

"I would venture that nothing that issues from Armand LaGuerre's lips should be taken as entirely truthful," Doc muttered darkly. "If one was of a suspicious nature, it would be worth inquiring to one's self what those sealed containers really held."

"And what, mebbe, he's really going to be doing when we get to our destination," Krysty added.

THE ARMORER HAD BEEN on the point of leaving the armored wag and heading back to check on Ryan and Jak when he had heard Doc's voice come through the comm receiver. He turned, half his attention on the trader and half on wondering if there was a way he could chill the receiver before someone said something that would cause a problem. He'd had every intention of sharing his concerns with his friends, but only when he'd made sure that the comm mics were removed from both Jak and Ryan. The tech was so small that it was easy to forget it was there, especially as the noise of the convoy had rendered it useless for so long.

What he heard next just proved that he was too late. If Ryan and Jak had been alert enough to realize that their mics were still live, then Mildred and Krysty had just simply forgotten about them.

The words were damning. J.B. stood in the middle of the wag, watching the impassive faces of both LaGuerre and Eula.

"Good to know what your people think of me," LaGuerre said over the relayed conversation, his tone amused. "Of course, they're only agreeing with what you think, right? And they've got a point. I work my people hard, and then we play hard. That's how we get ahead and stay there. If your people don't want to take those risks, then you know what the hell you can do. But I'd say neither of us has a choice."

J.B. listened, but as he did so his attention was focused on the woman. LaGuerre was a coldheart, but he was also obvious. He had no real guile. Eula was different. She was the one who J.B.—that all of them—had real cause to watch. She had guile in plenty, and the masked motivation to drive it.

"Go and talk to them, tell them what the hell you want," LaGuerre continued. "Man, what you gonna do? Stay out in the middle of this pesthole with no transport? Or carry on with me and hope for the best?"

He was right. Their options were less than zero.

J.B. turned and left the wag, feeling Eula's eyes burning into him, making his way to the rear of the convoy. The cabs of the two large containers were empty, their drivers making the most of the opportunity to stretch their legs and piss in peace. The same was true of the crews of the other two wags, taking advantage of downtime that would be brief but welcomed for its unexpected appearance.

His approach had an urgency that made the others look up. Maybe—just maybe—it would stop anyone else from saying something they would regret. As he drew near, J.B. tapped his cheek. He was greeted by puzzled expressions until Jak reached up to his own face, touching the mic and cursing softly as he realized they had been overheard.

"Stow the bikes on the rear wag," J.B. said loudly, indicating that the mics should be removed and stored in the bikes' saddlebags. There was a silence that fell over them until this was done. And then, stepping away, Ryan said softly, "How much?"

"Everything. Clear as if you were standing in the wag with us."

"Shit." Mildred spit. "How—"

"Do not berate yourself, or any of us," Doc said calmly,

"for what is done is done. The question is, what was our trader friend's reaction?"

J.B. shook his head. "Bastard wasn't at all surprised. But that's okay. He's not the dangerous one. He wasn't going to stop, but he's just a coldheart, and one that's easy to read. It's the woman that's really dangerous. She wants me chilled, I'm sure of it. But in her own time."

"Why?" Mildred asked simply.

"If I knew that, I'd have a better idea of how to handle her," J.B. said thoughtfully. "It's not just her and me, though. She's got something on LaGuerre. Scum like that doesn't just trust a person like he does her, not unless there's something in it for them. Mebbe if I could find some way of getting her to open up about where and how she knows me…"

"Listen up," Ryan interjected hurriedly. He had seen Eula approaching from the front of the convoy, and knew there was little time. "Be triple careful, J.B. Rest of us be the same. We know what LaGuerre's capable of, but she's an unknown quantity. Got to be prepared for all possibilities."

J.B. had turned as soon as Ryan interrupted him. The one-eyed man would only do that for a reason, and it was obvious as soon as she caught his eye. He had stepped toward her, partly to block her, and spoke loudly over Ryan's last words.

"What's the hurry? Afraid we're saying nasty things that might hurt your feelings?" he almost yelled.

"Nothing you could say could hurt me, John Barrymore. Not anymore. But we've got to get moving, so get the riders into the wag, get everyone else back at their posts, and let's get moving. I don't want us getting caught because you people want to conspire among yourselves."

She turned and ran back to the armored wag, leaving J.B. to puzzle over her first words.

What had hurt her so badly? And what did it have to do with him?

Chapter Ten

The Past

His head hurt. Badly.

As J.B. opened his eyes—as slowly and carefully as was possible—the slightest hint of light made him want to close them again. The light was like needles in his eyes. Bastard stupe phrase—how did you know what needles in the eyes were like unless some coldheart had plunged them in? In which case, the light wouldn't mean anything to you anymore.

Wandering—his mind was wandering, and he needed to concentrate, so he could at least remember where the hell he was.

Well, he could remember where he had been, if nothing else. The woman who had been haunting him for the past few days, the gaudy slut… No, wait, she wasn't that. He could remember her saying something about a husband who never paid her any attention. Shit, some crazie with a blaster coming after him because his wife had been bedded by another man was all J.B. needed. Hell, he was confident he could best anyone in Hollowstar in a one-on-one showdown. The trouble was, it wouldn't stop there.

Trader would get involved, that fat bastard Baron Emmerton would stick his flabby paws in, and it could turn into a real situation.

Wait, Dix, he cautioned himself, don't get too carried away with the possibilities yet. Try and piece together what actually happened.

It came back to him, hazy at first, but starting to make sense as he was able to put pieces together. She'd asked them if they would buy her a drink.

Them?

Shit, he was supposed to be babysitting Hunn, seeing that she didn't get out of hand. Trader would have his ass for that.

It had been early, the bar hadn't been full. He could feel Hunn itching to get at the woman as she had come over. Hunn offering her whatever she wanted in a voice that made it clear she wasn't talking about brew. Hunn making no effort to show her displeasure when she was lightly rebuffed and the woman had introduced herself to J.B.

"Sorry, sugar, but when I was asking for a drink I was kinda looking at the one with the dick. I'm just not that kind of a girl. But, hey, I can't just call you the one with the dick, can I? So what does everyone else call you?"

J.B. smiled—the effort making his face hurt—as he remembered Hunn shaping some smart-ass answer before his eye caught hers.

So the Armorer had introduced himself, feeling less at ease than at any time he could remember for a long way back. That was one of the reasons he'd drunk so much. Why, when he'd faced more situations of danger than he could think of, should talking to a beautiful woman have caused him so much anxiety?

Because she was beautiful. Because she liked him. And maybe because he was aware of Hunn simmering in the background, getting more and more drunk, more and more bellicose with each round that slipped down her throat.

Her name was Laurel, and she had a voice like molasses—dark, low, slow and smoky with a sweetness laying over it all. Hell, that was about as poetic as J. B. Dix ever got, and even if it wasn't that great, she'd seemed impressed when he told it to her.

She asked him what he did, and why she'd only just noticed him. He told her, and had noticed her face change when he explained that he was Trader's armorer. He asked her what the matter was, and she replied only that it meant he wouldn't be sticking around. He hadn't known what to say to that, and she laughed in that low, smoky voice, saying that quiet men were a weakness of hers.

They talked about where he'd come from, and what he'd seen. He told her things that he hadn't even told Trader. Why, he couldn't say. Even in his inebriated state, he'd never felt the urge to unload his past onto anyone else.

She listened. Hell, she'd even been interested—or so it seemed. And yet, when he asked her about herself, she'd been less forthcoming. All she would say was that she was married to a man in the ville who had jack, but who neglected her. He was so absorbed in his work, and the little world he'd built around it, that he didn't even notice whether or not she was there. J.B. had asked her who would be that stupe, but she hadn't answered. She had remained silent, staring into his eyes, stirring up feelings within him that he wasn't sure he had ever felt before.

Then she had leaned into him, and they had kissed. He could taste the alcohol on her breath, and the urgency. He knew that she wanted him like he wanted her.

Oh, yeah, and then Hunn had started a fight. All the while he and Laurel had been talking, Hunn had been drinking, and the bar had been filling up as the night drew on. At the edges of his attention, he had been aware that Hunn had been arguing with some big guy with a port wine birthmark on his face about who was the better hunter, who was the better shooter.

He had a loud, bragging voice, and had told her that women were shit at everything except cooking and fucking. Hunn had asked him how the hell he knew, as he was too ugly to get a woman cook for him, let alone fuck him. His answer was to pull out his cock and slap it on the bar, saying she'd soon change her mind if she tasted his meat. Her answer, unsurprisingly, had been to unsheathe her knife and nearly circumcise the fool.

J.B. had seen all this on the periphery of his attention and had ignored it. Hunn always picked a fight, when she was roaring drunk, and it was exactly why Trader had sent him out to babysit her. His job was to head this kind of shit off at the pass, not to be distracted by women and let Hunn practice amateur surgery.

He remembered pushing past Laurel, putting her behind him and telling her to take cover or get the hell out, before trying to get between Hunn and the big guy, who had just pulled his dick out of the way in time, and was reaching for his blaster—with his dick still dangling—while Hunn was trying to pry her knife from the bar surface, where it had stuck when she had rammed it down. A stinging, ringing blow to the side of the head was all he got for his pains.

And then it had broken loose. The blaster had gone off into the ceiling, plunging the bar into semidarkness as some of the lamps were knocked over in the rush to escape the shot. The bar was too well contained for anyone—apart from the enraged victim of Hunn's anger—to risk letting off a blaster, it had become a battle of knives, blunt objects, fists and boots. J.B. was already too drunk to keep track of what was happening, but he did remember getting hit on the head.

So that was why he hurt so much—not just the brew. Scant consolation, but at least Trader would see that he went down trying to stop the fight.

He risked opening his eyes again and rolled over on the bunk. Hunn was beside him, covered in blood splatters that were not her own, snoring softly.

And there he had been, expecting to roll over and see Laurel. Maybe that was just as well, in the circumstances. J.B. risked pulling himself upright and was surprised, as his eyes focused properly and the room ceased to spin, to see Abe standing on the other side of rusty bars, watching him. A faint smile creased the rangy man's face.

"Lucky for you that Emmerton prefers his men to take prisoners. Lot of villes would have seen you and Hunn buying the farm for this."

"Mebbe the farm would be better than how my head feels right now," J.B. countered.

"Don't think that kinda shit will work with Trader." Abe grinned. "Wake that stupe bitch up, and let's get out of here before Emmerton changes his mind."

"Eh?" J.B. rubbed his aching head with one hand and

prodded Hunn with the other. She mumbled and moaned, but refused to awaken.

"Works like this," Abe explained. "Hollowstar is pretty small, and they're rich compared to a lot of villes because they make the most of what they've got, which means everything is stretched as far as it'll go. Emmerton starts chilling people for bar fights, like most places, he ain't gonna have much of a workforce before too long. And that'd fuck everything up. So if they step outta line, they get punished by a few days in here, stuff taken, working without jack for a while…anything to make their life harder, make them think before they do it again. Called 'restitution' or something. Ask Trader. He explained it to me once."

"I figure he may have a few other things to say to me," J.B. murmured, attempting once more to awaken Hunn.

Abe chuckled. "Yeah, you might be right at that."

Hunn had moaned like hell when he had managed to get her awake, partly because she felt like shit, partly because she knew what Trader would say when they got out of jail. But she had to face it sooner or later, and once it was done it was done.

J.B. wasn't as resigned. He knew he'd let Trader down, and as a man who prided himself on holding on to some honor in this pesthole of a world, he felt that he'd let himself down, too. The confrontation with Trader wasn't something he was looking forward to with any kind of relish.

Yet there were some consolations. The memory of how Laurel tasted when he kissed her. And, more importantly, the fact that when he left the jail building with Hunn and Abe, and made his way across the town square, he could see her. Everyone else was too wrapped up in their everyday business to notice. Anyway, why should they care? Abe didn't know who she was. And Hunn was too concerned with her aching head and the thought of having Trader rip into her.

But J.B. noticed her, standing on the sidewalk on the opposite side of the square, near the old storefront next to Luke's. She was leaning against a stanchion, and when she caught his eye she blew him a kiss and mouthed "thank you." For saving her from harm last night, he assumed. She had to have been waiting—for how long?

After that, anything Trader had to say to him wouldn't matter.

PUNISHMENT WAS NOTHING more than a few harsh words and some detail cleaning out the wag latrines. Hunn had it worse—stripped of jack and her shares on this trip. She accepted it, and she accepted that J.B.'s punishment should be the lesser.

"Trader should have known putting a lightweight like you in to cover my ass was a mistake, John Barrymore," she said with a grin as they stripped and cleaned yet another cesspool wag latrine.

"If you weren't such a stupe, it wouldn't matter," he replied.

She looked up and away from the encrusted receptacle, glad to get some fresher air into her lungs. "All the same, you want to watch that bitch."

"Why, because she prefers me to you?" J.B. questioned, with good humor.

Hunn shook her head. "Because you like her a lot. I see it all over your face, even though you're in the middle of shit and piss. But soon we'll move on, and she'll still be here. Don't want the iron man of the convoy distracted at the wrong moment. It could chill us all. Anyways, she'll still be here. She's always been here. That means she's got people here, and people that could be trouble if they don't like you messing with her."

J.B. paused in his task. "I've thought of that, don't you worry," he said softly.

And he had. There wasn't much else that had occupied his mind since he left the jail and had seen her waiting for him. Not that it was going to make a blind bit of difference. The Armorer was stubborn and single-minded when he fixed on an idea.

And he was fixed.

"I DON'T KNOW how much longer we're going to be here," J.B. said.

"Hon, it could be an hour, it could be a week. Emmerton's an asshole when it comes to getting the jack rolling in. Shit, he never pays my old man when he should, always has to chase it. That don't improve his temper none."

She rolled over to face him, propping herself up on one elbow, squinting against the ray of light that penetrated the thin drape over the window. Her hair tumbled over one eye, the other screwed up, the better to see him. She had a thin sheet over her, and he could see the line of her breast beneath it. Her arm moved beneath the sheet, her hand reaching for him and squeezing.

"Mmm, you recover quick," she said with a raise of the eyebrow. "Bet you're real popular up and down the trade route."

J.B. laughed. "You'd never believe me."

"Try me."

"I don't usually do this. Mebbe a gaudy house now and again, but never like this. Never getting distracted from work. Keeping Trader's armory in condition, building it for him, checking ordnance for trade…keeps me busy."

"Why?"

"Because there's a lot to be done."

"No, I mean why work so hard for him?"

J.B. didn't really have to consider his answer. "I owe Trader a lot. He took me out of nowhere, gave me something to live for. It's a hard world to live in, and being with Trader makes it a whole lot easier. 'Sides, I like my work. Always been fascinated by blasters and explosives. Ordnance makes the world tick. Not much survived skydark, but those little beauties did. Machinery, engineering…intricate pieces that could survive anything. Got to admire work like that. And then there's what they mean. Ordnance is power. It means you can get it, then keep it. Man with the best armory is the most secure, can run the best convoy, the best ville."

It was as close to a philosophy as J.B. had ever gotten, and from the look on her face he could see that it had an impact on her.

"Haven't heard you talk that much before now," she said, shaking her head.

"Been too busy to talk much," he countered.

"Yeah, that's true," she answered with a grin. Then her face dropped into a more serious expression. "I know why it is I like you. Why I want you."

"And that is?"

She shrugged. "You remind me of someone. We were happy once. But he was like you. The only thing that mattered was what he did for the baron. Took up all his time, all his attention. Truth is that after a while I might as well have not been there."

"That's hard to believe," J.B. said softly.

"Yeah, you say that now. But it'll come down to that in the end. It always does."

"So what does he do that keeps him away from you?"

"Aw, hon, we don't want to talk about that," she said gently, squeezing him under the sheet. "We got better things to do."

HE CONTINUED TO SEE her every day. Before Laurel, his life had been orderly. Work was everything. And since they had been in Hollowstar, his friendship with Luke had been equally as important. But now he found himself juggling time that he didn't have. He still wanted to get the work done, and spend time with the taciturn weapons master of the ville. Then again, he burned every time he thought of Laurel. Moreover, he had to keep his liaison with her secret. So he had to act normally and not call attention to himself while making time for her.

J. B. Dix was not a naturally devious man. It took Hunn no time at all to spot that something was amiss.

"Your trouble, John Barrymore, is that you're incapable of lying," she told him. And, when he demurred, she qualified, "Okay, so mebbe if it was life or death you could do it, and if it was a one-off. But a sustained lie is a harder thing to keep going. Sneaking around just isn't you. Me?

I dunno if I could do it, either. But I don't put myself in that position. And you have. And man, do you suck at it."

It made him a little more wary, but it did nothing to deter him. He was willing to take any amount of risks for her in a way that he had never considered before. J. B. Dix was a man who had weighed the odds on everything, and had never put himself or others at risk unless it was strictly necessary. Hunn had been telling him that this was now exactly what he was doing. The bizarre thing—the thing that he found it the hardest to assimilate in so many ways—was that the liberation it gave him to be acting in this way was more exhilarating that anything he had ever known.

Which was dangerous. It made him careless.

He would go about his everyday business as though in a trance. Things got done; conversations were held; the world of Hollowstar passed by his eyes. But it was all flat, in black and white. Even the heated conversations with Luke over the qualities of blasters and explosives no longer held the sparkle and fire that they had on the first meeting.

Despite that, even J.B. was living enough in the real world to realize that it wasn't one-sided. After they had been standing side by side in silence for some time, J.B. watching Luke reconvert a recovered MP-5 from gas to real ordnance, the Armorer decided to broach new territory.

"You're quiet."

"I'm always quiet. It's what I'm known for."

"Yeah, but that's with those stupes who know nothing about ordnance. Never heard you this quiet since I got here."

Luke shrugged. "Mebbe I've got things on my mind."

"Things that have nothing to do with blasters?"

"Life would be simpler if there was nothing but that. But there isn't. That's where it gets difficult."

J.B., thinking of his recent complex life, could only agree. But he said nothing of this, only, "Any shit you want to talk about?"

Luke looked at him, puzzled. "J.B., do I strike you as the kind that likes to share shit?"

The Armorer shook his head. "No, but it's what people are supposed to ask their friends, right?"

Luke's face creased into something between a smile and a frown. "Appreciate that. But it don't do no good. Not in the long run. Only action counts."

"Guess you're right there," J.B. replied at length.

The two men lapsed into silence once more, with Luke working assiduously, until J.B. checked his wrist chron.

"Shit—Trader wanted me, and I'm late."

"Never keep the boss man waiting, J.B. I'll be seeing you," Luke murmured without looking up.

J.B. nodded—to himself as Luke was still looking down—and made his way out of the workshop, past the cluster of old guys who were still in the storefront, playing cards in a concentrated silence.

When he got out onto the covered sidewalk, he didn't turn and head for the area where Trader's convoy was sequestered. He turned the opposite way, and set off for the far end of the ville. Between the goods spilling out of the storefronts, and the cluster of people going about their business, he saw her. She was standing at the farthest reach of the covered sidewalk, and it seemed to him that the crowds parted so that he could see her. Her hair blew out behind her in the breeze, dark curls tossed in the currents. A flicker of a smile played across her full lips, and her dark eyes met his with a playful sparkle.

It didn't look exactly like that to the two people who were watching J.B. as he headed toward her. What they saw was more prosaic—Laurel leaning against a stanchion, pushing the hair from her eyes as the breeze blew it across her face, a pout on her face at not looking her best as her current squeeze hurried toward her. They saw J.B. push past people, step over goods and produce, without seeming to even notice they were there. Nothing could stay him from his destination; indeed, he seemed to speed up as he approached her.

The watchers saw him lean into her, as if to kiss her. They saw her pull back and mouth something—"not here," words to that effect, it was hard to lip-read at such a distance—and then pull him down a side street on the way to wherever their assignation was to be on this day.

J.B. thought he was being discreet. He was anything but. And the woman? Who knew what was going through Laurel's head, but for one of the watchers it was obvious that this wasn't the first time she had done this. Was the other watcher aware of that, also?

The two of them remained in position for some moments after J.B. and Laurel had gone. One watcher still had their attention fixed on the empty space where the Armorer and the woman had been but a short while before. The other had switched attention from J.B. to their counterpart. Reactions would be paramount, the second watcher figured.

Luke sighed, wiped his hands on his oily apron, shook

his head and turned back to his storefront. He took a step toward the door, then paused and looked back toward his last point of observation. He paused, his face stoic and impossible to read, before seeming to make a decision, and taking a step into the shadows of the storefront, melting out of sight.

Hunn watched him go. Then she looked back to where she had seen J.B. under the spell of the woman from the bar. A few questions over the preceding days had soon settled what had been bothering her, and she had been watching the Armorer of her own volition. Now she whistled softly to herself.

"Aw fuck. If I had a fan, man, would I be throwing shit at it right now...."

Chapter Eleven

The Present

Even before the twilight had closed upon them any further, the convoy had regrouped and set on its way once more. The bikes were secured, one each, to the back of the second wag and the one that brought up the rear. For reasons of space, LaGuerre informed them, it would be necessary for the two riders to be split up. So Ryan was deputed to travel with Doc in the rear wag, while Jak had to travel with Cody and the crew of the second wag. It struck Ryan that LaGuerre's tactic was to split the two of them so that no wag contained more than two of the friends. He'd obviously decided that to separate the two riders was his best option here.

He'd got it wrong on two counts. First, he'd underestimated Doc. He appeared to figure that Tanner was just an old crazie, so it didn't matter if one of them was in a wag with him. And it was true. There were times when Doc lost it, and really was as mad as he appeared. But only those who had stood shoulder to shoulder with Doc in time of adversity would realize the mettle of the man who lay hidden beneath a sometimes fragile state.

Second mistake—putting Ryan in with Doc, instead of

Jak. The one-eyed man wasn't certain, but he was assuming that LaGuerre assessed Jak as a greater threat,
even though he wasn't the nominal leader. Okay, he was
right in that, as Jak was a chilling machine. But Jak, even
though he and Doc had a relationship that was built on the
surprising comradeship that diversity could bring, was not
a talker. Ryan was. Doc certainly was. Even under the listening ears of Raven and Ramona, it was possible for the
two of them to discuss their situation. Albeit in an elliptic
manner. It was something Jak would have found impossible, as he had little time for such language skills.

So, obviously LaGuerre liked to think of himself as a
schemer and thinker. Trouble for him was that he wasn't
as smart as he would have liked to think. Double trouble
for him was that he assumed Raven and Ramona would
keep their ears open. He liked to think his crew was as
sharp and devious as himself.

Another misjudgment, as Ryan found out within a short
time of being aboard their wag. Shortly after the convoy
began to roll, the one-eyed man crashed out on the bunk,
exhausted by his time on the bike. But his rest was disturbed, either by the adrenaline coursing through his veins
that had kept him from nodding out on the blacktop, or else
from the noise within the wag, which seemed to be only
marginally quieter than when he was in its wake.

He opened his eye to find Ramona staring down at him.
Her face loomed at him, a tight smile on her lips. Her eyes
were dark and brown, drinking him in. Her hair, long and
ringleted despite its close consistency to Mildred's plaits,
was unnaturally stiff around her head. Altogether, it gave
her something of a predatory air.

"It's okay, sugar," she said sibilantly, catching his off-guard look of surprise, "I wasn't gonna bite. Not unless you want me to."

"Ramona, leave the poor man alone. He ain't gonna be no good to you unless he's had some rest," Raven called from the driver's seat.

"Yeah, and you telling me that you wouldn't be doing exactly the same thing if you wasn't sitting where I am?" Ramona countered, without taking her eyes from Ryan's face.

"That ain't the point, babe," Raven answered, laughing so hard that she began to cough, her voice rasping.

Ryan, still partly in the throes of a disturbed sleep, was having some trouble assimilating what the two women meant. That wasn't helped when Doc's face loomed into vision. The old man's smile was strong and brilliant, his eyes sparkling. His words held an undertone that, even in his still befuddled state, Ryan was able to grasp.

"You must excuse Ramona, and indeed Raven, my dear Ryan. They mean no harm, but I fear that being so long on the road with little in the way of male company to keep them warm on a long, cold night has made them a little overkeen to assess any passing male as though he were little more than prey. They are, perhaps, the sexual equivalent of Jak when he wishes to hunt. We can only hope that such dedication to the pursuit of the priapic does not deter or distract them from their other tasks."

At this last, the old man's eyes seemed to sparkle even more brightly, and Ryan caught his meaning. The women's almost single-minded devotion to the sexual would blind them to anything else discussed, as long as it was approached in an elliptic manner.

Ryan decided to test the waters.

"Lady, you're wasting your time looking at me like that. The way I feel now, I couldn't raise it with the best gaudy on the western seaboard. Besides, I may be needed for other things."

Ramona looked him up and down, her tongue flicking over her lips—consciously or not, he couldn't tell.

"Honey," she said huskily, "there ain't much else I'd think was worth wasting you on."

"But I'm supposed to be running sec," Ryan replied, "so I'm going to need all the rest and all the strength I can."

Ramona shook her head, a laugh escaping her lips. "Honey, running sec for Armand is a shortcut to getting chilled. Make the most of things while you can."

"What do you mean?" the one-eyed man asked, propping himself up on one elbow and deciding that it was time to eschew the oblique and go for the direct approach.

"This is a run to nowhere, sugar. Some shithouse place called Jenningsville offered Armand big jack to do a run that no one else will go near. A run that we needed specialist equipment for. A run that means there are several other traders who want his ass in a sling. A run that saw most of our old sec buying the farm before we even started out. A straight run across land that most convoys would think more than twice before starting. Honey, you think any of us really has any chance of getting across here in one piece? Especially when the pack come calling?"

Ryan took this in. The woman was certainly less than guarded, and her words confirmed his earlier suspicions about LaGuerre's methods of obtaining the refrigerated wags, and the true manner in which his convoy had been reduced.

Doc was looking over her shoulder. His expression confirmed for Ryan that he had been right in his assumptions. But overriding all was something that Ramona had said at the end of her litany.

"What the fuck is the pack?" Ryan asked. "And why the fuck is it going to be so triple bad?"

Ramona sucked in her breath. "Uh-huh. So Armand never said anything about that, eh?" The look on Ryan's face confirmed this for her. She continued. "Shithead probably thought you wouldn't join up if you knew. How can you be good sec if you don't know what's ahead, though?"

"Fireblast and fuck. I'm glad you can see that, even if LaGuerre can't," Ryan murmured, his voice heavy with irony.

He was about to ask once more about "the pack," but something else superseded the need to know.

CODY COULDN'T WORK OUT Jak, try as he might. The thin, cynical convoy man thought he had seen everything since he had traveled with LaGuerre. The albino youth who lay sleeping on the bunk in the wag was something new to him. Jak had taken to being thrust upon Cody and his crew with ill-disguised bad grace.

"Tired. Let me sleep or regret," was all he had said when Cody had tried to introduce the albino to the other two members of the wag crew. Jed was the driver at present, a tall, bulky man whose muscle was turning to fat, and who spilled over the edges of the driving seat as he was beginning to spill out of his clothes. His gray hair was cropped close to his head, and the road map of scars on his skull from numerous fights shone through. Raf, who was off-duty and who had been sleeping in the bunk, was taller and rangier, his coal-black skin highlighted by pink combat scars, a shock of white in the black forest of dreads that tumbled down his shoulders giving him an immediately recognizable mien. Neither man looked like the type of road warrior that you would wish to antagonize—indeed, Cody had known them long enough to recognize that they were both more dangerous than even their looks would suggest—and yet the albino had ignored their presence as though they weren't even there.

Cody had figured that Jak was fearless, either from stupidity or because he knew that he could outfight anyone. On balance, Cody reckoned it was the latter, if only from the way that Raf seemed to sense the coiled spring of Jak's aggression, and had gladly given up the bunk to the exhausted albino, despite that fact that Jak seemed to be only half the size of the dreadlocked giant.

Jak had fallen asleep almost as soon as his head had hit the bunk, exhaustion seeming to claim him. There was much that Cody wanted to ask him, as much to satisfy his own curiosity as to dig for the nuggets of information he knew LaGuerre would expect him to mine. The convoy man had dropped in the pecking order since Eula had joined, and like most of the others in the convoy he found her attitude and the seeming fascination that she held for LaGuerre divisive to a degree that could easily become dangerous. Since her arrival, there seemed to be an agenda that LaGuerre kept from the rest of the wag crews. It was the cause of a slow but sure growth of discontent. Cody knew from his own experience on convoys he had served before joining LaGuerre how poisonous and ultimately destructive this could be. He didn't want it all turning to shit while they were stuck in the middle of this dustbowl hell, where there was no way out. And he figured that the albino and the people he traveled with held the key to what was really on LaGuerre's mind. Maybe he was wrong, but when he thought about how much that Eula had wanted these cold-hearts to join them, he couldn't help but see it any other way.

So he wanted to question Jak. In truth, he wanted to reach across and shake the albino awake.

What was stopping him? The fact that Jed and Raf had deferred to Jak. The fact that, even in the depths of slumber, the small frame held a menace that made him think more than twice. And the fact that, even in that brief period that he had been conscious, Jak had seemed to be a long way from being the talkative type.

So Cody sat and watched as the skies darkened to night and the convoy rolled on, wondering what would happen when Jak awoke. Would he then get the chance to probe? Or would he find Jak an immovable force?

ALTHOUGH JAK WAS STILL and silent on the bunk, inside his head the dreams and nightmares raged. Things that had happened to him in recent times were always merged with the one thing that still haunted him—the chilling of his wife and daughter. Even though he had hunted down the cold-hearts who had perpetrated the deed and made them pay at length before they, too, bought the farm, still his family came back to accuse him every time he closed his eyes. Why wasn't he at the ranch when the coldhearts showed up? Jak, the great hunter, the great protector, had failed in his task.

Now they were being pursued by wags like those he and Ryan had engaged with just a few hours before. They were running across the hard-packed ground, his wife almost dragging the crying child in her haste to remove her from danger. The wags toyed with them, circling, coming in close to taunt and tease before pulling away again. The men in the wags leered and laughed, their faces twisted from human into grotesque mutie shapes that echoed animals.

And where was he when this was happening? Nowhere and everywhere. He could see what was happening from every angle, could see the expressions of fear and of cruel relish; could see from close or from far away. Yet despite this he could take no action, as if there was a wall between him and what was going on.

Finally, his wife could run no longer. Her ankle caught on a rut in the hardened dirt, she tumbled and fell, dragging the child with her. The circle of wags closed in on her.

And then they were no longer wags. The metal twisted and distorted like the faces, becoming flesh-covered in hide that was dark, short fur pockmarked by open sores. Faces and heads became completely animal, with dark eyes the color of congealed blood. Exultant voices yelping human glee and lust became coarsened even more, turning from words to incoherent yowls and barks of bloodlust and hunger.

Skeletal mutie cattle and dogs, what little muscle there was clearly visible beneath almost translucently thin hide, heads raised in victory cries before those heads were lowered to feast with wet, tearing sounds as flesh was rendered from bone. Heads raised again, jaws dripping with fresh blood. The barks and yowls almost—but not quite—loud enough to hide the sounds of crying and squealing pain from the two carcasses of skin and bone that had once been human, and were now nothing more than sentient feed for the creatures that revelled in their pain.

There was something in this nightmare that was different to those that had come before. Something that, deep within the parts of Jak's unconscious that were tortured every day by his perceived failure to protect his family, began to make those nerve-endings that were powered by his instinct begin to twitch.

"SHIT!" CODY ALMOST FELL off his chair. He had been leaning over the albino, studying him hard as though the inert form would somehow yield clues as to the man. Jak had been so still, breathing so shallowly, as to be almost lifeless. The last thing the convoy man had expected was for the white face to twitch violently, the road map of pale scars writhing, as the albino's bright red eyes opened and fixed him with a stare that seemed to go right through him.

Cody's heart pounded as he leaned back, his hand involuntarily going for his blaster. He wasn't even aware of his instinct to draw and fire until he felt Raf's hand on his.

Cody looked in puzzlement at the black giant. Raf shook his head, unwilling to speak but silently imploring Cody to wait and see. Perhaps it was a fear of the unknown, perhaps it was nothing more than the respect of one warrior recognizing another. Whatever the reason, Raf knew that Cody should wait and see what Jak was doing; and Cody knew that Raf was correct.

Jak sat upright, his expression barely changing except for the eyes, which seemed to focus in on the interior of the wag, settling on Cody and Raf.

"Something coming. Animals. Shitload. Vicious fuckers, and hungry."

"The pack," Raf whispered. It was the first time Jak had heard the giant speak, and his voice was surprisingly high and gentle. But there was no mistaking the import of his simple phrase.

Whatever the pack might be, it was nothing but trouble. Jak looked from one man to the other.

"What the pack?" he said blearily, the moment of sharp focus that awoke him now fading as the aftermath of sleep hit home.

"Legend in these parts," Raf said briefly. "People talk of 'em, but we've never seen 'em. Some kind of mutie cattle and dogs. Adapted to the rad-blasted land round here, eat any kind of shit gets in their way. Plants, animals…humans."

Jak looked puzzled. He'd never known of cattle that would eat other flesh, even in desperation. But the rad-damage had made so many weird muties… Something else puzzled him.

"Dogs?"

Raf nodded. "Seems so. Don't make no sense to me why the dogs ain't eaten the cattle, but…"

"Less they ain't just roaming. Mebbe come from somewhere," Jak answered, almost to himself. That was the only thing that would make sense, and if that was so…

His reverie was interrupted by Cody.

"How can you be sure?" The man's tone wasn't accusing, but rather it was wondering, as though he wanted to believe the albino but couldn't for the life of him work out how Jak knew.

Could Jak tell him he had seen it in a dream? Not if he

wanted to be taken seriously. But then, he couldn't understand exactly why he had seen them in his dream, unless…

Jak sniffed the air, listened hard to what was around him. The smells that assailed his nostrils were those you would expect from a wag: fuel, stale sweat, exhaust fumes, old food, hot metal and plastics. But there was something else, an undertone that had been sucked in from the outside through the air-con unit. The musk of cattle, and that of dogs, but not quite as he was used to it.

The pheremones and secretions of every animal were in part dictated by its diet. That was why some creatures smelled so different from others, even though their species placed them close together. In this instance, the cattle musk was altered from the usual. Their diet was more animal protein based than he was used to—they smelled too much like the carnivorous dogs they ran with.

That was why they had eaten his wife and daughter in the dream.

He tried to dismiss this image from his mind, and think again about the smells and sounds that surrounded him. This time, the sounds…

The wag engine covered everything. But it only took certain frequencies. There were spaces above, below and around that were filled with other sounds. Ones that told stories, if a person cared to listen.

There was the humming of the air con. The breathing of the three men—Jed was wheezy, his weight making it hard for him to take in air; Cody was short and shallow, the adrenaline making him nervous; Raf was calm and measured, a warrior keeping himself in check until real effort was a necessity.

There were the creaks and groans of the metal interior and exterior of the wag, and the sound of the other convoy wags beneath this.

And then there was something more. Was it a sound, or the slightest change in vibration beneath them? A change that could only be unconsciously registered; the feel of the blacktop and wag meeting that did not correspond as there was some other disturbance? Maybe—just maybe—the faintest echo of yowling and moaning had been sucked in by the air con and had registered beneath the radar of Jak's sleeping mind.

There were many who met the small albino hunter who assumed he was a mutie. It was partly his size, the scars that distorted his face, his pale skin and red eyes, and the speed and ruthlessness with which he could act. But it was also because of the almost preternatural ability he had to detect prey, to smell out danger.

In truth, Jak was no mutie. He was just short and albino because of genetics, and not those blasted by radiation. His secret was nothing more than a desire to hunt that, from an early age, had led him to develop and heighten his senses by constant practice to a point where he was able to feel and hear with a level of ability that was in all men, but had not been used for scores of generations in that land that had become the Deathlands. He was a human animal who, rather than regressing, had simply rediscovered those senses that, allied with intelligence, had enabled man to first rise above the other animals.

But people took one look and thought he was a mutie. And no matter how much it pissed him off, he had neither the vocabulary nor the patience to explain it. So, when he took one look at the faces of Cody and Raf, he figured that he'd let them think what the hell they wanted, as long as they listened to him.

"Pack coming, then. Nor' nor'east, think. And fast."

"You sure?" Cody asked.

"He's sure," Raf answered for Jak, taking in the albino's expression.

Cody, if disinclined to trust Jak's instincts because of his inability to understand him, was nonetheless equally inclined to trust the word of the black giant, who had stood by him in countless firefights. The thin, nervous man moved over to the comm equipment and picked up the mic.

"Armand, J. B. Dix—you guys listen to this...."

Chapter Twelve

LaGuerre exchanged glances with Eula as he listened to what Cody had to say. J.B. watched both of them. He knew to trust Jak, but would they listen to him?

"This true?" LaGuerre asked simply.

"It is," J.B. stated before Eula had a chance to say anything. "So what should I know about this pack. Pack of what, for fuck's sake?"

Eula glanced at LaGuerre, who nodded. Dragging in a breath, she told J.B. exactly what Jak had been told.

"We've got wags, plenty of ordnance. Why should we be too worried about this pack?"

"Stories are just that they're vicious as fuck, and that there's a shitload of them. Enough to drive most wags off the road."

"Most wags in these parts aren't like yours," J.B. mused. "But if Jak's alarmed…" He hit the comm transmitter. "Jak, how many of these fuckers are there, and why should we be triple red?"

Jak's voice came back over the comm without pause. "Not tell how many, J.B. Just know big number. And bad. Smell like chilling. Like locusts."

Jak's comparison was enough to convince the Armorer that this was a serious threat. Jak Lauren was not a man given to exaggeration. He was about to question LaGuerre and Eula about tracking equipment in the wag when he was forestalled by Mildred's voice over the comm.

"John, I think Jak's right. Take a look out the port."

J.B. moved to the ob port that faced the direction in which Jak had heard the approaching pack. When he looked out, he sucked in his breath sharply.

"Dark night!"

In the distance, a dust cloud was thrown up against the backdrop of the moon, the pale light coloring the cloud gray against the clear dark skies. It spread over several hundred yards, and rose almost half as high. Close to the ground, they could see a number of shapes, moving and shifting together in and out of phase, an amorphous mass that, even at such a distance, oozed malevolence.

"What the hell is that?" Mildred's voice wondered over the comm receiver.

"The pack," J.B. replied. "Whatever the hell that turns out to be."

KRYSTY HAD HEARD about the approaching pack, and the legends surrounding it, from Ray. And at great length. She had been inclined to write it off as yet more of the old man's ramblings—at least, until she had seen the distant cloud. As she watched, her sentient red hair began to curl protectively around her skull and her neck. Ray noticed this as he turned to speak to her once more.

"Whoa! I didn't know you were a mutie. I remember once we were in this ville where they used to burn people they thought were muties, figuring that they were witches, like some of those old ways they had long before skydark.

Those who worshipped that guy Satan, instead of God. Though I'll tell you for what, if there's a God then he sure as shit deserted this world a long time ago. Mebbe the nukes got him at skydark? Anyway, I'm figuring that your hair going all weird like that ain't such a good thing, right?"

Krysty looked at the old man. "Right. Looks like trouble ahead. LaGuerre better have some answers."

Ray looked at her, his ingenuousness lending chilling weight to his words. "Sweetie, that's why your people are here. It ain't Armand that needs to have a plan, it's your man J.B."

They would stand or fall by J.B.'s ability to marshal a convoy ordnance that he did not fully know, assisted by an armorer with an agenda that would not, necessarily, be sympathetic to his cause.

She watched the pack get nearer, the shifting mass of shapes beginning to take a more recognizable form.

"Gaia—there are hundreds of them," she whispered.

In the rear wag, Ryan had been watching the approaching pack, along with Ramona and Doc. The three of them were at the ob ports, looking out over the empty expanse of dustbowl at the approaching cloud.

"That's one hell of a big herd," Ryan whispered. "How can they survive out here?"

"Don't matter how they survive, gorgeous," Ramona replied. "The only thing that matters is that they want our asses."

"On the contrary," Doc murmured, "I think Ryan has a very good point. We see before us a very large, and very hungry horde. I cannot imagine that there is much in the way of pickings for them along this stretch of the highway. Indeed, I find it hard to imagine that a mass even half that size could survive out here on just the occasional convoy such as ourselves."

"Especially as they'll lose numbers coming for us," Ryan added. "You thinking what I'm thinking, Doc?"

"I fear that I am, my dear boy. And if so, it puts us in a very perilous situation."

Ramona looked from one to the other. "Shit, wish you'd tell me what you're thinking then, boys, as I don't have a clue. And I'm sure my girl there doesn't, either," she added, gesturing to Raven.

"Babe, I'm trying not to think about it… Not while I've gotta keep this thing on the road," Raven replied.

Ryan and Doc looked at each other. Was this the right time to share their thoughts, or should they avoid spreading unease until the current situation had been dealt with?

They were spared from making a decision by J.B.'s voice over the comm receiver.

"Wait till they come within range, then hit the bastards with everything we've got. Rockets long range as soon as they hit the optimum. Then blast them with machine-gun fire if they come through it. This isn't the time to be tactical."

THE ARMORER HAD ONLY to think briefly about his course of action. Even the briefest recce had been enough to establish that, although the herd was big, it was only coming from the one direction. There were no pincer movements or counterattacks to consider. No ordnance had to be diverted to the flanks. The herd was moving in one direction only.

It didn't take the greatest tactical brain in the world to work out that their best course of action would be to direct fire in a concentrated stream against the onrushing mass of the herd. To deflect and damage was the sole aim.

Wipe them out? It was possible, but not likely. There was such a mass, and their approaching speed was such that it was likely that at least some of the animals would make it through any barrage to the convoy. The question then would be whether the animals were strong enough to cause damage. J.B. had seen wags that had collided with single animals the size of a cow. They had incurred some damage. Okay, so the wags they were traveling in were armored, and the refrigerated containers were huge. A single animal wouldn't cause sufficient damage to stop it. Yet a group of them may be able to deflect an armored wag from its path, and in so doing cause collisions for those in its wake. To be run off the road and damaged in this wasteland, at the mercy of even the remnants of a ravenous horde, was not a prospect he wanted to consider.

At all costs, they had to keep as many of the pack as possible from getting close.

In the three wags, the rocket launchers all had comp sighting equipment. In theory, this should have made it easy to get the range, aim and fire. In practice, it worked out a little differently. While much of the ordnance tech was in itself fine, and that which had incurred wear and damage had been replaceable or repairable, the comp equipment was another matter. Some of it worked; some of it appeared to work; and some of it was blown and would never work again. So it was always the better move to eschew the possibility of using tech as a shortcut, and to sight and aim by eye alone.

Which was okay if you were familiar with the ordnance you were using, but not so good if it was new to you. The thought crossed J.B.'s mind as he seated himself at the rocket launcher and tried to sight on the approaching pack. He was acutely aware of LaGuerre and Eula watching his every move. Normally, the Armorer would be able to block out such distractions. Now was different. Now was about what the woman and the trader were really after, and how it would affect not just himself, but his friends.

Dark night, J.B. thought, this was no time to let your mind wander. The Armorer focused his attention and his vision on the sights in front of him. The night vision scope on the sights still worked. The figures that should have given him auto direction and distance were broken up, the digital figures in the corner of the screen little more than halflines. That was okay. He was more concerned about what the rest of the screen told him.

He felt a churning in his guts as he caught his first close-up view of the pack.

There were more cattle than dogs in the herd. About four to one, he reckoned. They were several hands high and looked different from cattle he had seen in other parts of the country. High on the shoulder and narrow of breast, their forelegs were more developed than he would have expected, with the shanks more heavily muscled. They had power. That accounted for the speed with which they were approaching. More than that—their heads were abnormally long, their noses tapering into snouts that had protruding incisors. Their eyes were dark, as were their hides. Their eyes were hooded, their hides thick and scaly. For a moment, it occurred to the Armorer that these hides may be too thick for standard ammo, in which case they'd better hope that the rockets took out as many as possible. But only for a moment. There would be time enough to worry about that when it happened.

The dogs that moved between them were also different from many of the mangy creatures that he had seen across the width and breadth of the Deathlands. For a start, the manner in which they snaked between the legs of the cattle that towered over them gave them an almost serpentine grace that made them seem something other than what they were. It was astounding that, without looking down, the cattle were able to continue sure-footed without trampling, or stumbling over, the dogs. For their part, the dogs moved without looking up or pausing, continuing their slithering path without recourse to the creatures with which they ran. It was as though the two species were symbiotic in some way, and able to move as one.

The dogs were loping, almost vulpine in build, and like the cattle, heavily muscled. That meant they had to either have a ready supply of food somewhere out here, or else they were deadly efficient hunters. The thoughts that had been bothering Ryan and Doc had not entered his head— perhaps this was just as well, as it was one less problem for him to consider. And right now, the less to clutter his focus the better.

Because either way, the convoy was in trouble. The dogs, with their matted and oily fur hanging in clumps as they ran, had a look that was equally as dangerous—as blankly malevolent—as the cattle. They, too, had long snouts that ended in overhanging, sharp incisors that looked practiced in the art of ripping flesh. And, like the cattle, they, too, had dark, hooded eyes that spoke of nothing other than the lust for blood.

The more of these bastards they could take out at distance, J.B. knew, the better. No doubt about that.

J.B. judged from the size of them in the night-vision scope that they were in range. He was unfamiliar with this kind of launcher, sure, but he knew enough to make an informed guess.

"Cody, they look just right for blasting. This is your tech—you figure I'm right?"

"Hell yeah, let 'em rip," the rangy fighter replied over the open comm line.

J.B. triggered a rocket, and from the corner of the ob port saw a trail like that left by his own weapon as Cody also let fly. A cackling laugh over the open line told him that Doc had also let loose from the rear wag, an impression reinforced when a third streamer entered his line of vision.

No sooner had he the time to absorb this impression than the three rockets hit home, almost simultaneously. Because of the speed of the convoy, the explosions seemed to be at their rear, the mass of the pack already having changed direction to shadow them so that the three rockets caused damage, but nowhere near as much as the Armorer would have wished.

The noise from the pack rose to such a pitch that it was higher and louder than that produced from the convoy as it motored along the blacktop. A screeching howl of fury and pain from the cattle and dogs—pain from those scorched by the very edges of the rockets' detonation, fury from those who were not affected, but felt the loss of their fellow pack members; as though, perhaps, they were of one group mind.

The rockets had caused some damage to the whole, but had only really caught the fringes of the group. Those that were old, slow and not the most vicious and driven by the urge to chill had been taken out. These had disappeared in the cloud of explosive smoke caused by impact, which had mixed with the cloud of dust thrown up by the hooves and pads of the creatures, now tinged also with the red mist of blood and vaporized flesh and bone. As the pack moved on, pulling the cloud with them and leaving that which was in their wake to settle, so the remnants of what had once been cattle and dogs spread out behind them—strips of hide, of flesh roasted by the intense heat of the impact, of bone and while limbs and skulls left by those who had not been in direct line. The debris did little more than remind of how large the pack was—at least, would have done if the convoy could have stopped and observed.

Coming to halt was the last thing they wanted. Enraged by the attack on their corporate being, the pack had increased its pace and was beginning to gain on the convoy.

"Dark night, how fast can those bastards move?" J.B. breathed. Without a needed comp reading, but from his experienced eye alone, the Armorer could tell that the pack had dipped under the minimum range of the rockets. To unleash such explosive power now would result in an impact that would blow back on the convoy itself.

He turned to LaGuerre. "Get that boy to up the speed," he barked, indicating the still impassive and motionless Zarir.

The trader shook his head. "Can't do that. We go faster, we leave the big rigs behind. Ain't gonna do that."

J.B. turned back to the approaching animals. He knew it was only his imagination, but it seemed to him that he could smell their hot breath down his neck, could smell the reek of their hide. The former was his fear; the latter was a genuine sensory impression. It hit him that the pack was now so near, and so large in numbers, that the heat produced by their collective stampede was enough to drive the smell of their fury across the blacktop, sucked in by the air con and relayed to those who may have thought themselves safe in wags, but were now inclined to reconsider their position.

"Machine-gun fire. It's our only option, and we've got to make every shell count," he barked over the open comm mic. "Too close to risk the rockets."

"Figure you're right," Cody's voice returned. "Switching to that right now."

J.B. was glad of the backup from the convoy man. In the lead wag, Eula had watched in silence, as though waiting for the Armorer to slip up, to show a chink in his armour. For what reason he could only guess. One thing for sure, she was not helping anyone else in the convoy, and why LaGuerre was letting her do this was something he could only put on hold, to puzzle over if they got out of this in one piece.

So it was that he glad to hear Ryan's voice follow hot on the trail of Cody's.

"J.B., Doc let me take over the machine guns. Let's chill those bastards before they get the chance to do it to us."

DOC HAD BEEN DISSATISFIED as soon as he had seen the rockets hit home, even though Ramona had whooped with joy to see the pack hit by the three-pronged attack.

"Go get 'em, Docky-babe," she yelled, hugging him. "Those fuckers are nothing more than tomorrow's barbecue."

Doc had disentangled himself with some alacrity. "Madam, unhand me, I implore you. The task is barely begun, and this is no time to be wasted in premature celebration."

"Doc's right," Ryan breathed. "Look."

Ramona stopped, and followed the line of Ryan's finger as it pointed out beyond the ob port.

"Aw shit," she whispered, all joy drained from her as the smoke cleared and she could see the size of the pack that was gaining on them.

"They'll be too close to fire on with this before too long," Doc mused. "Why don't we increase speed?"

"Bet your ass J.B.'s already thought of that," Ryan murmured.

"Yeah, and he would have gotten a no for his trouble," Ramona said. "Listen, hon, these wags can go a whole lot faster than this, but those refrigerated trailers are shit heavy, and even though the cabs are powerful, they can't go much above this. Never mind the bullshit about wanting to go nonstop for the time. Fact is that if he's gonna deliver before the generators on those rigs give out and the trade is ruined, then he's got to push it nonstop."

Ryan nodded. It made sense, now. This insane desire to run nonstop had a concrete cause that lay beyond just extra jack for quick delivery. If only the slippery bastard had been more honest with them. J.B. would be counting on a speed increase, and only finding out now, when it was the worst time for the fact to be revealed…

Ryan knew how his old friend would react. Speed and efficiency was now of the essence. The one-eyed man tapped Doc on the shoulder. The old man looked up from his perch behind the ordnance mount, and instantly read the expression in Ryan's eye.

"Of course, of course," he muttered, sliding out from his seat and allowing Ryan to replace him.

Catching Ramona's questioning glance, he smiled and addressed her. "My dear lady, strange as it may seem to relate, but even with just the one eye, friend Ryan is a far better shot than I could ever hope to be. Indeed, when one comes to consider the question, does one need more than the single orb in order to effect the chilling shot?"

"Uh, I'll just have to take your word for that," Ramona stammered in a tone of voice suggesting that she wouldn't need such an explanation, given Doc's mode of expression, to believe such a thing.

It was then that Ryan, cutting everything behind him out of his focus, heard J.B.'s imprecation, and made his reply.

As the pack closed, Ryan sited on the nearest cattle and dogs to the rear wag. He'd seen Cody shoot, and trusted that the man was as good as himself or J.B., at least in a situation such as this. He'd have to be: the speed at which they were closing gave them next to no time in which to make every squeeze of the trigger count.

The smell of the pack permeated the wag, the stench making the metal shell of the wag seem to close in on them. Ryan tried to shut this out of his mind as he sighted and squeezed.

The chatter of machine-gun fire, overlapping into an echoing and overlapping rhythmic pattern, cut through the sound of the wag engines and the baying of the pack. Up so close now that he could see the dark heart of their eyes, expressionless except for the blank lust to chill, the pack stood little chance of avoiding being hit. Cattle and dogs stumbled and fell as shells ripped into their flesh, tearing at the scaly hides and biting into the lank, matted fur. Bones splintered, organs ruptured and the sudden halt or erratic change to their impetus dictated by the impact caused them to career into their fellows. The carefully orchestrated pack progress, the group mind, was broken for the briefest of moments, and it seemed as though the group would tumble into disarray as their momentum was interrupted. For that moment, it seemed as though the convoy had been victorious, and the danger was averted.

It was a false dawn. The line of cattle and dogs nearest to the convoy—those decimated by the first rounds of machine-gun fire—went down and hit the ground. The very front runners hit the hard shoulder at the side of the blacktop, bringing home how close they now were to their target. It should have been the turning of the tide.

Just as Ryan was prepared to take a deep breath before picking off the fading stragglers, the dream was shattered by the breaking through of a second rank of pack animals, trampling over the fallen, paying them no heed except to use this as a spur for a further challenge.

"Fireblast and fuck," he whispered softly. If they were this determined, then there was going to be little or no way of stopping them. And where would that lead them all?

Meantime, he had to keep firing into the onrushing pack, just as J.B. and Cody had to keep up their barrage. Even if they were unable to halt them completely, they could at least thin out their numbers so that they were fewer when they reached the convoy, and could wreak less havoc.

A steady stream of fire rained into the pack from each of the three armed wags, but seemed to make little difference to the onrushing numbers. As cattle and dogs stumbled and fell under the hail of shells, their blood making the dust beneath them churn into red mud, splattered with flying blood on the flanks of those that came in their train, so it seemed that those very creatures replacing them were part of an endless and unstoppable onslaught.

Looking down from the cabs of the refrigerated wags, armed only with small arms that were of use only in close combat, both Mildred and Krysty were appalled and yet awed by the size of the pack, and the relentless group mind with which it kept coming forward. They felt helpless, as though they were watching some old vid in which they could not take part, and in which they had no real interest. And yet, as the pack spilled off the dustbowl and the hard shoulder, and began to run parallel to the convoy on the blacktop, it became apparent that this would soon involve them in a very direct way. The thought was made real by the shuddering shock of some of the cattle hitting the wheels of the container. The screech of pain showed that those in contact had paid, possibly with their lives, for the attack. Yet it had enough force to make the container swerve and buck at the rear of the cab. Both Reese and Ray had to wrestle with the steering wheels of their wags, the old man surprising Krysty by actually ceasing to speak. The veins on his forehead stood out as he sought to keep his rig straight. More impacts at the rear made the degree of swerve increase, the swinging of the containers making the wags seem that they could jackknife at any moment.

Ryan, still grimly firing into the mass of scaled hide and matted fur that came closer with every second, wondered in some part of his mind how the pack could survive out here and grow so large. He had the suspicion that the answer was in some way significant. But not for now. It was all he could do to keep blasting into the mass as the cattle repeated their attack on the containers, spreading their attention to the wags between, using the same simple tactic.

Except that the wags in which the rest of the crew rode were closer to the ground, and lighter.

Ryan was thrown off his seat as the wag was hit by a phalanx of cattle, a staggered impact that caused the wag to veer with a bone-jarring shudder on the road. Raven swore loudly as she wrestled with the steering column, the wag zigzagging wildly as she tried to right its path, only to be met with another collision that twisted the wheel in her hand. Her wrists felt as though they'd been dislocated by the violent pull against her instigated by the wag moving contrary to the direction of the wheel.

As the one-eyed man tried to rise to his feet, Ramona leaned over to help him. Another shuddering hit threatened to knock the wag onto its side, and Ramona tumbled over the prone warrior as his own balance was thrown once more.

Doc slid into the seat behind the mounted blaster. His face set in grim determination, he angled the blaster so that it was pointed downward as far as the mount and the slit in the side of the wag would allow. Forcing it as far as he could, he rose off the seat as he commenced firing, the shells from the blaster raking almost along the side of the wag. It was a ridiculous and stupid angle. The chances of hitting anything under normal combat circumstances would be next to zero, and there was always the danger that one of the shells would actually cause damage to the wag itself. But these were far from normal circumstances, and called for desperate measures.

In this instance, Doc's gamble proved correct. The shells ate away at the wall of scaled hide that pushed against the wag, chopping some of it to the blacktop, driving the rest of it back far enough for Raven to right the steering without further impairment.

Ryan and Ramona were both back on their feet, staring out of the ob port at the trail of devastation Doc had left in their wake, and at the bodies of chilled cattle and dogs left by the other wags.

"Shit, man, how many of those nasty fuckers are there?" Ramona whispered, looking to the mass of flesh that still tracked them.

"Too many for my liking," Ryan murmured. "How come there's so many? How do they live? Unless…"

He didn't get a chance to finish. Doc's urgent cry cut short his musing.

"Ryan, they don't want to wipe us out. That's too easy. They're moving us, directing us where they want us to go."

Ryan frowned, then cast his attention to an ob port on the other side of the wag. Here, with no obstructive wall of flesh, it was easier to see exactly what Doc meant. They were moving from the middle of the road over to the hard shoulder. He could see the snaking line of the convoy ahead of them, moving inexorably to the right. LaGuerre's wag was already off the hard shoulder and into the hard-packed ground that lay beyond. It was heading into the night, clumps of cacti black against the starlight darkness. Where it was heading was a guess that Ryan did not want to make. He only knew that the pack had some purpose in sacrificing themselves in this way.

"DARK NIGHT, where are we headed?" J.B. asked, almost to himself as he looked past the still-impassive Zarir and out of the front of the wag at the dustbowl night as it engulfed them.

"You tell me," Eula replied in a neutral tone.

"And how the fuck am I supposed to know that?" he snapped.

She shrugged. "You asked first."

J.B. looked at her, and then at LaGuerre, who was still seated in the same position, his eyes unreadable behind the shades.

"You don't seem too worried," J.B. said slowly. "Could be you were expecting something like this?"

"It was always a possibility," LaGuerre replied with a shrug. "But that's why we wanted your people. It's your job to get us out of any trouble this is leading to."

J.B. shook his head. "You're one stupe fucker...or just plain crazy."

LaGuerre's face split into a grin. "You have to be, to do this," he said simply.

J.B. looked out into the night.

One way or another, it was going to be a long one.

IT SOON BECAME obvious that the pack's group mind had a simple and immovable objective: to herd the convoy as their ancestors had once been herded themselves. In the interests of preserving ammo for whatever may lay ahead,

J.B. had ordered that the pack should now only be fired on
if it encroached far enough into the convoy to present a
threat. Which was not something it showed any inclination
to do. It would appear that the pack was content with
having changed the direction of the convoy, and was gently
prodding them in exactly the direction it wished.

And so it was a bizarre sight that wound across the
dustbowl night, drawing farther and farther away at an
acute angle from the ribbon of the blacktop. The convoy
drove straight, unimpeded by the pack, which ran beside
it. Although heavily depleted, there were still more than
enough cattle and dogs to stretch out in an unbroken line
several bodies deep, discouraging the thought of trying to
break through and double back toward the road.

Similarly, the notion of turning in the opposite direction
had been dismissed by the Armorer for the simple reason
that to try to turn the big rigs on treacherous ground and
then outrun the pack would, in all probability, make a bad
situation infinitely worse. Better to conserve energy and
ammo until they reached whatever their destination may be.
That was when they would need to be on triple red.

IT WAS MILDRED, seated high in the cab of the first refrigerated container wag, who saw it before anyone else. They
had been driving into the night for more than half an hour,
with nothing but the dirt and a few patches of mutated cacti
to mark their path. The land was curving, the movement
beneath the surface in the upheaval of nuclear winter
having left this part of the land not only arid, but undulat-
ing in bizarre twists that made the curve of the earth lose
its plane and become subject to an almost random law.

Maybe this was why it seemed to loom out of nowhere. Maybe it was that the lights of the shanty ville that appeared as if from another dimension had all been extinguished, dormant until the noise of the approaching pack and convoy had alerted the residents to the new arrivals. For whatever reason, lights flickered on to reveal a settlement of a dozen huts. The flicker may have been oil lamps, or it may have been an erratically firing generator. Whatever, it now revealed that there was life where there had been none before.

And the pack was nudging them straight into the arms of whoever was waiting in those buildings.

"John, can you see that up ahead?" she almost whispered into the open comm mic. "Maybe it's just me, but I can't help think that they've been waiting for us."

"Figuring on that myself, Millie," the Armorer replied. "It sure as hell would account for why the pack is able to keep up its numbers."

"Farmed and trained to bring home prey," Mildred stated flatly.

Ryan's voice joined them on the comm. "Been wondering how come there could be so many of them when there seems to be so little out here… Is this how these coldhearts keep themselves alive? Plunder convoys using the animals they farm?"

J.B. turned to LaGuerre. "You knew this could happen." It wasn't a question. LaGuerre didn't answer. Eula did.

"There are rumors. Nothing more than that. How could there be? Anyone that gets taken isn't likely to get out alive."

"So why didn't you tell us?" J.B. demanded. "How the fuck can we be prepared for something like this if we don't know it could happen?"

Eula raised an eyebrow. As ever, she was calm, so frustratingly that J.B. could gladly have taken out his mini-Uzi and dropped her in his fury. But that would achieve nothing, even if her next words made his anger all the more acute.

"Face it," she said simply, "would you have wanted to join us so readily if you knew this was likely? Even being stuck where you were could have seemed a better prospect than this. Besides, why tell you? Your reputation suggests you can cope with anything—mebbe even better when it hits you without warning."

"Yeah, well, that ain't one of those things you want to put to the test too much," he said, turning away to look at the approaching ville. What he saw caused him to frown.

It didn't make sense.

Through the windshield of the armored wag he could see that, instead of keeping to the course they had previously maintained—one that would take them into the heart of the shanty ville—they were drifting toward the east, away from the ville itself. The deviation had been slight to begin with, but as with their previous direction changes, the angle had become incremental. As before, it was as if the pack had nudged them, the desire to keep safe distance unconsciously pushing the wag drivers onto a different course.

But why would the pack be directing them around the ville, and not into it? Had their assumption been wrong? Was the ville just a clutch of shanty huts that stood in the way of the pack, a happenstance and inconvenience? Or was it that—

"Dark night! Stop, stop the fucking wag now," the Armorer yelled at Zarir. At the same time, he whirled to the open comm mic, and repeated, "Stop! Stop all wags now. Chill those bastard engines."

"Why—" Cody's voice began.

"Ask later—just do it," J.B. barked.

Even as he spoke, he was aware that the armored wag had not decreased its speed. He turned back to the impassive and seemingly unresponsive wag jockey.

"Chill the engine, stupe. Stop the wag—"

But it was too late. The wag jockey was so wired on jolt, so focused on his primary task, and so responsive only to the voice of LaGuerre that it was doubtful J.B.'s words had even impressed themselves on what passed for his consciousness. Zarir had not slowed the wag by a single mile.

Which was why they sped across the dustbowl surface at such a speed that it took a hundred yards before the crumbling earth beneath them gave lie to the trap beneath. By then it was too late for the wag to be thrown into Reverse. Even if Zarir had been quick enough or reactive enough to do so, the weight of that portion of the wag that was now overhanging an empty space was enough to pull it forward and down.

A bastard simple trap, and one he should have seen coming. A pit, nothing more: carefully covered, and aided by the darkness of night. The pack had been not just a means to drive them there, but also a distraction—keep your eye on them, and you miss that which is right in front of you.

Dark night, J.B. thought, he'd been a stupe. The lead wag would crash into the pit, and the others would either follow, or career into one another in their haste to stop in time. Either way, it made it easier for the coldhearts of the shanty to come out and pillage.

The fact that his barked orders may have stopped those behind from repeating his mistake was little consolation as the steep incline of the wag threw him forward and into the dash with a force that knocked the breath from his body. Eula and LaGuerre followed, slamming into the dash and windshield, the trader screaming in agony as he hit the driver's seat on the way.

The interior lights of the wag went dark as the electrics cut out on impact, and J.B.'s brain followed suit as his head cracked against the reinforced glass of the windshield.

Even the pain was lost in the blackness.

Chapter Thirteen

The Past

Careless. Reckless. Just plain stupe. These were not words that Hunn thought she would ever have to use when she was talking about J. B. Dix. But all of them fitted him right now—all these and more. Not that she could talk about it. She could only think it and keep the anger bottled up inside. That was chilling her slowly. Hunnaker was not the sort of woman who could contain her anger, as a litter of the maimed and chilled that stretched across the Deathlands could attest.

But right now, she had little option. If she uttered a word of what she knew to Trader, it would be J.B.'s balls dragged across hot coals. Baron Emmerton prized his man Luke, and anything that upset the taciturn and moody bastard would bounce right back to the convoy.

She had tried to broach the subject with J.B., but the Armorer had proved oblivious to subtlety. Hunn and subtlety: another concept that was alien, but which she had been straining her tits off to achieve. And, in truth, the strain was getting too much. She didn't know what was going on between Emmerton and Trader that it was taking them so long to get the hell out of the ville, but it had better be resolved before too long. Because if Luke didn't catch on, and J.B. didn't make it even more obvious, then she sure as hell was going to explode.

J.B. CONTINUED TO HANG around at Luke's workshop, but he was starting to get the feeling that he wasn't wanted. When the two men weren't discussing the ins and outs of ordnance maintenance, then they had maintained a companionable silence while they worked, or watched each other at work. But over the last day or two, the Armorer had felt that the silences were a little strained, as though Luke didn't want him there. Of course, Luke wouldn't say anything. And J.B. was loathe to broach anything that went deeper than ordnance details. So they sat in silence, prickly and awkward, until J.B.—puzzled—could stand it no longer.

"Luke, I get the feeling that there's something that's bothering you," he said tentatively.

The taciturn man turned his head to look at J.B., pushed his backward baseball cap back and scratched his hairline. At length, he said quietly, "You reckon?"

J.B. furrowed his brow. "Yeah. I'd say so."

"And you'd not be knowing what that is?"

Luke was looking at the Armorer as though it was a question for which he would know the answer. But, J.B. mused, how was he supposed to know what was going on in Luke's head? Sure, they got on, but he'd only known him for a short time.

"No," was the only response he could muster, after some time.

Luke studied him carefully. The only time J.B. had seen the big man look like that before was when he was dismantling an ancient Gatling, trying to pry rust from the mechanism. It was a study that intense.

Why?

The Armorer's genuine puzzlement had to have been obvious, even to a man who spent more time on the study of machine than of man. Luke shook his head, snorted softly.

"This woman you've been spending time with…" He let it hang, waiting for J.B. to speak.

"Yeah, there is a woman. Her name's Laurel. Says her old man is neglecting her. Never known anyone like her…" As the words tumbled out, J.B. wondered why he was telling Luke this. He hadn't mentioned her to anyone else, and only Hunn knew that they had even met. Laurel had been adamant that he say nothing, which he hadn't, up till now. Come to that, why should Luke want to know? Was he in some way envious of losing the Armorer's company? Of sharing him? J.B. had encountered men who liked other men, but he'd never have put Luke down as one of them. Not that it mattered, it was just that—

His train of thought was interrupted. Luke said, "That's all you know? That she has some guy who she says is neglecting her? You don't know who he is, though?"

J.B. shook his head. He was aware that Luke was still staring intently at him. It was, to say the least, unnerving. Incomprehensible.

Luke gave the briefest of nods. "Yeah. That figures."

"What figures?"

Luke shrugged. "She'd have to be stupe to tell you. That way you can't think twice."

J.B. frowned. "Like I should? Is there something that I should know here? Like who this guy is? Like there's some kind of deep shitpit that she could land me—or Trader—in?"

Luke laughed, but there was little humor in it. "No, J.B., no. There's no shitpit as far as I can see. And I guess it serves this guy right."

"So you know her?"

"Yeah," Luke said slowly, "I know of her… Mebbe she's right. Guess it's not doing any harm as long as she keeps it quiet. But be careful. You never know with people."

It was Luke's last word on the subject. He returned to the weapon upon which he had been working, and said little more on anything. The atmosphere had changed. J.B. could feel it. But if anything, it had become more uncomfortable. It was not long before the Armorer had made an excuse to leave.

The feeling of unease lingered no longer than it took him to see Laurel, waiting and beckoning to him from a street corner.

He didn't see Hunn. He didn't see Luke follow him out, and watch him go.

"Aw, fuck, this isn't gonna go away, is it?" Hunn muttered to herself.

"THAT FAT BASTARD is up to something, boss," Abe said as he and Trader left their latest audience with Emmerton. "He has to be. Why the fuck else would he change overnight like that?"

Trader shook his head. "I dunno. But the greasy ratfuck son of a bitch is starting to piss me off big-time. He carries on like this and I won't be coming through his shitty little ville again. Fuck the east, Abe, it ain't worth the bother."

Abe knew that Emmerton's attitude had really gotten to Trader. It was unlike a man who had based his entire reputation and accumulation of wealth on thoroughness and a willingness to go where others wouldn't to simply dismiss a part of the lands that were neglected by other traders for no other reason than the actions of one man.

Over the last few days, the fat man had stopped trying to persuade Trader that it would be good for J. B. Dix to stay in Hollowstar and work with Luke. And, conversely, he was no longer worried about his man Luke wanting to join the convoy. If anything, he was demanding greater tithes from Trader for the dubious pleasure of passing through to the wastes beyond the toll road. Tithes that were getting so large, it would not be too long before Trader would be better off turning back.

That was if Emmerton would let him. For, along with this demand for increased payment, there was an underlying threat that Emmerton would not let the convoy pass. At times, he seemed so angered by their presence that it was almost as if he were trying to taunt Trader into a situation that would lead to combat.

Now, Abe knew that Trader would have every confidence in his people being able to wipe the very floor with anything that Emmerton had to throw at them, even granted that they were in the middle of what would rapidly become enemy territory. But there would be some casualties, and some damage. And that would cost jack, one way or another. There was no way that Trader would willingly put himself in a position where a trip would make a loss. As it was, they stood to be doing this for no profit. And that was biting at Trader. Abe could see this.

"There's something underlying everything that fat fuck is doing," Trader said as they made their way back to the convoy. "I don't know what it is, yet, but I'm gonna find out. Something has got up his fat ass and is burrowing under his skin."

"Shit, boss, I don't wanna think about that." Abe gulped. He was now cursed with a mental picture that made him want to heave.

Trader allowed himself a smile that was rare over the past few days. "Hey, I get these ideas, I don't want to be the only one to suffer," he said, his humor—at least temporarily—improved. "We've got to find out what's bugging him."

"Yeah, and how are we supposed to do that without getting him or his sec suspicious?" Abe asked as they approached the convoy.

Trader tugged at his ear. "Tell you the truth, I figure that it's too late for that. Something one of us has done, or is doing, has pissed him off. And if he's already pissed, I don't see how we can really make it worse. Besides which, if I'm right in figuring that it's something that one of us has done, then all we have to do is look among ourselves."

Abe sighed. "Yeah, and we know the first place to look, right?"

Trader nodded. "I know J.B.'s said nothing about her, but those two are tighter than a rat's ass when a randy dog comes calling."

Not for the first time, Abe was puzzled about where Trader got these sayings. Were they from the old predark shit he used to read, or did he just make them up?

Back in the bosom of the convoy, a few inquiries revealed that neither J.B. nor Hunn had been seen for some time. Trader dispatched those convoy members not engaged on routine maintenance duties to search and find. While they were still out, Hunn appeared in the fenced-in patch of land that was used as a wag park, and where the convoy was based on every trip to Hollowstar. She was alone, and seemed lost in thought.

"Hunn, where the fuck you been?" Abe asked as he approached her.

"Nowhere that's any of your damn' business," she answered, immediately on the defensive.

"Ain't mine, but it's Trader's," he replied. "Anyways, where's J.B.? He's supposed to be your shadow."

She shook her head. "That right? If only it was that simple."

"What's that supposed to mean?"

"Doesn't matter," she said dismissively.

"Better let Trader be the judge of that," Abe mused. "Go see him now. Things are really fucked up, and until he finds out exactly what you and J.B. have been up to—"

"Why would it be us? And what the fuck, exactly, does he think has been going down?"

Abe shrugged. "Don't ask me. Just go. Can't remember the last time I saw him like this."

Hunn left him with a heavy heart, echoed by her dragging feet as she approached War Wag One. It was deserted apart from Trader, who was trying but failing to enjoy a cigar. Given his love for them, and their scarcity, it was a sign of how angered and annoyed he was. This impression was only confirmed by his tone, and the gleam in his eye, as he greeted her.

"So, what the fuck you been doing now?"

"Ah, nothing… I mean, it's not me, is it… But…"

Trader looked at her, confusion written large on his face. "What the hell are you babbling on about? Shit, woman, all the time you've ridden with us, I've never known you to be like this."

She sighed, rubbed the heel of her hand over her cropped head. "Look, it's not like he knows. He wouldn't have fucked up like this if he'd had any idea. Besides, he likes the guy, so it's not like he's gonna—"

Trader sat forward. He spoke softly, but with a tone that emphasized his firmness and his barely contained anger.

"Hunn, what has J.B. been doing that he's so unaware of? Tell me. Our getting out of here in one piece could depend on it."

So Hunn began, hesitantly at first and then warming to her theme, to tell Trader about what she had observed— from the first encounter in the bar, to the last time she had seen J.B. walk out of Luke's shop and into Laurel's waiting embrace.

When she had finished, Trader sat back and whistled. "Shit, that explains why Emmerton is so pissed. If Luke stops being the armament genius he is, then that's a lot of Hollowstar's prestige and jack down the shitter. And what's gonna piss a man off more than his wife being screwed senseless by the man he calls friend?"

"Yeah, but J.B. really doesn't know."

Trader looked at her. "How can you be sure?"

Hunn sighed. "C'mon, boss, you know J.B. like I do. He ain't that sort of man. Hell, he's hardly interested in women at all, let alone the kind of pussyhound who chases other men's women. And he's a loyal friend. No—" she shook her head again "—you can bet your ass that the bitch hasn't told him who her old man is. And if Luke's anything like J.B., he's gonna suffer in silence until we go. He ain't gonna blame J.B., but it's all gonna go off big-time once we're out of here."

"Or before, if Emmerton's temper doesn't hold," Trader mused. "I can't work out what he wants. Why didn't he say something, if he knows this is going on?"

"Mebbe he thinks you know, and it's shit on your shoes that you have to clean up," Hunn offered.

Trader winced. "That's not what I wanted to hear. You're right. But it's not what I wanted to hear at all. So I'm figuring that you know where J.B. is right now?" She nodded. "And you're here because he's going to be some time, yeah?" She nodded again. Trader breathed in heavily, rubbing his hand across his brow as though trying to alleviate a headache; which, in many senses, was exactly what he was doing.

"Okay," he murmured. "Let's get this over and done with."

He was out of War Wag One and crossing the fenced-in compound before Hunn had a chance to draw breath and follow him. She had to run to catch up as he reached the gates, looking over his shoulder. He waited for her to catch up, allowing her to overtake him and lead the way.

They walked in silence through the bustle of late-afternoon Hollowstar. Around them, the inhabitants of the ville went about their everyday business as though nothing of any import was about to happen. Which, in truth, was true. It was only for Trader and his people that events about to unfurl would have any impact, either positive or negative.

Hunn knew exactly where she was going. As Trader followed her, he wondered how long she had been letting this go on. Stupe bitch should have known it would lead to trouble, he thought. And the funniest thing was, although she was loyal to the convoy, he had never known her carry a personal loyalty like she did with J. B. Dix. Hunn never stopped surprising him; but in truth she was nothing next to the bundle of shock the Armorer had turned out to be.

By this time, they were on the edge of the ville, moving out toward where the cinder-block buildings around the tollbooth were the delineating feature. There were a few dwellings scattered around these parts, but they were moving away from the main bulk of the population. Which, Trader guessed, was the point of the woman bringing J.B. here. They wouldn't be easily disturbed. It couldn't have been caution, as she didn't sound as though she'd been too careful about snaring him.

"You should have told me sooner," Trader said in an undertone as they approached a one-story house with a wood porch.

"Why? I didn't know that porky creep Emmerton knew. Shit, I still don't know how he tumbled to it. I haven't seen any of his sec."

"He doesn't need sec for this. Everyone in this pesthole pulls together. Always have done. A word here, a word there, and—"

Trader was stayed by a raised hand. With a gesture, Hunn indicated that they move forward in silence. Fair enough, Trader figured. Hunn was the hunter, the fighter. And if they wanted to catch J.B. and the bitch unawares...

He could hear them talking as he approached the window. J.B.'s voice, low and soft. He couldn't make out what the Armorer said. Then her voice in reply, higher and clearer, but with a honeyed tone that—before he even saw her—made him realize why J.B. had been so easily led.

"You know I can't, hon. There are just reasons that mean I can't leave. It's not that I don't want to, it's just—"

More low mumbling from J.B. Then Laurel replied, "I can't tell you. Not yet. mebbe not ever. But there are things that keep me here, and there's nothing that can change that. No matter what I do or don't want."

Trader looked at Hunn. She mimed putting two fingers down her throat and gagging, leaving him in no doubt as to her opinion.

He shook his head. Now was not the time. He gestured to her to go ahead. He wanted to take the Armorer by surprise, but knew that even in such moments, J.B. would never have a blaster too far from reach; more, J.B.'s reflexes were such that he wouldn't want to test them. Especially not with himself or Hunn in the front line.

Hunn approached the door, making no attempt to disguise or deaden her footsteps. Trader allowed himself a wry grin: Hunn had obviously had the same thought. Even as he smiled, he heard a muffled exclamation from the woman, and a silence that was unnatural compared to what had gone before.

Hunn banged on the door. "J.B., it's me. Stop dicking around and open the fucking door before I lose my temper and blow the fucker off its hinges." She was met with silence, and turned to Trader with an expression that was part anger, part exasperation.

"J.B., do it. She's not screwing around, and neither am I," Trader said in a level voice.

There were scuffling sounds from inside, and after a few moments the front door opened, revealing an owlishly blinking J. B. Dix, astoundingly hatless, and still attempting to dress himself. He looked hassled, which was a new one on Trader.

Hunn pushed past J.B. and into the building.

"Where the fuck is she?" she barked.

"Who?" J.B. asked. His tone of voice, however, betrayed that even he didn't think he was going to get away with that one.

Trader sighed. "Don't fuck around, son. The woman. Where is she?"

J.B. looked at Trader. Ellipitically, he mouthed, "First Luke, and now you. What is it about Laurel that's so damned important?"

Trader was about to speak when Hunn reappeared, dragging Laurel behind her. Even half upright and with her hair in Hunn's fist, Trader could see why she had captivated J.B. That look, with that voice... Hell, he couldn't blame the boy...

"What the fuck are you doing?" J.B. yelled, on seeing Laurel in Hunn's grasp. He lunged toward them, but was restrained by Trader's strong grasp.

"Easy, son, easy," Trader muttered.

J.B. looked at him, bewildered. "What has she done? Dark night, what have I done that's making you do this?"

"It's not so much what she'd done as who she is," Trader said softly. Seeing J.B.'s look of confusion deepen, he expounded. "You do know who she is, don't you?"

J.B. shook his head. "You're acting like she's important.

She told me that her old man was always too busy, so I figured he must be high up in Emmerton's command—"

He was stopped by a right from Trader that whipped across his face. The sudden force and impact stunned him, knocking him to one side, sending his glasses skidding across the floor.

J.B.'s immediate reaction was to hit back, but some instinct deep within him stayed his hand. This was Trader. If he attacked him, he knew Hunn would be compelled to fire on him, no matter how she may feel about it. And Trader wouldn't do this without a good reason.

For a few moments that seemed to stretch to an infinity, J.B. half stood, half crouched, reaching for his glasses and putting them on. As he did, it seemed that the clarity of vision that came with the lenses was echoed by a clarity within his own mind. He looked from Trader, to Hunn and Laurel, and back again.

Suddenly, and with an awful realization, he knew why Emmerton would be leaning on Trader; why Laurel was being "neglected"—as she saw it—by her husband; and why Luke's attitude to him had changed in a way that he had not been able to previously explain.

"You stupe bitch," he said softly. "Why didn't you tell me?"

"You didn't ask, hon," she said, mock wide-eyed. "'Sides which, you wouldn't have fucked me if you'd known, and I wanted you pretty bad."

"I don't get it," Hunn said, with a savage twist on Laurel's hair, making her squeal. "If Luke's neglecting you, why the fuck do you want to go for a guy that's just like him?"

"Aa-ah, mebbe, just mebbe," Laurel gasped through the pain, "I like guys who are the strong, silent type. Mebbe I just like seeing if I can tempt them away from their little hobbies."

"Sick little…" Trader shook his head. "You know how much trouble you've caused for us? For yourself?"

"Ain't caused nothing for myself, sugar," Laurel said softly. "Luke, he loves me. Like some little kid over me. So I've had some fun. Ain't the first time, probably won't be the last."

"What happened to the other men?" Hunn asked, her voice cold.

Laurel shrugged—as much as she could in her awkward position. "Emmerton don't like Luke being upset. Don't much like anyone that causes that… Figure that he'd have me chilled if he thought it'd solve the problem. 'Scept it wouldn't. Emmerton needs me because Luke does."

"And that's why you wouldn't leave. Because you put Luke first?" As he spoke, J.B. didn't know how he wanted her to answer. Part of him wanted to mean more to her than Luke, but another part of him would have felt let down for the taciturn armorer if that were so… As it was, her answer surprised him.

"It ain't about Luke, not for me. Not just him, anyways. There are other reasons."

J.B. waited, but it was clear she would not be drawn on the matter.

"If I didn't think it'd make things worse, I'd chill you myself," Trader spit.

"You'd have to beat me to it," Hunn cut in.

Trader shook his head. "You," he snapped, addressing J.B., "get back to the convoy with Hunn. No stopping, no nothing on the way. Hunn, tell Abe to meet me at Emmerton's, and get Poet to ready us to leave. We're pulling out as soon as… And as for you," he said, looking at Laurel, "I hope you rot in hell, bitch."

J.B. said nothing to Hunn as they returned to the compound. He said nothing as they prepared to leave.

In return, nothing was said when Trader returned with Abe to tell them they had safe passage to leave. Except that they were heading west.

J.B. never saw Laurel again. Never saw Luke. He didn't know what it was that kept the woman in Hollowstar.

The matter was never raised after that, not if you wanted to stop Trader exploding in anger. One thing for sure—they never headed east that way again. Not after Ryan joined. Not before the one-eyed man and J.B. went their separate way from War Wag One.

Hollowstar, Luke, Laurel—they became unspoken, buried memories. Forgotten.

But there were things that didn't want to stay that way, that had a habit of coming back to bite you in the ass.

So it was that it was more than J.B.'s head that ached when he woke up in that dustbowl ditch.

Chapter Fourteen

The Present

Dark night… For real, as well as how J.B. felt. As he swam to the surface of consciousness, breaking the wave with a feeling that he was going to puke, J.B. couldn't see a thing. The first ripple of panic said that his eyes had been damaged, and that his vision was screwed. Maybe it was because of his glasses, but that was always the first thing that came to mind, and he was quick to squash it. Particularly as his vision became accustomed to the gloom around him.

Think clearly, Dix… Night was closing in when the pack pushed you in this direction. And then there's the angle at which you lie—a pit. A simple pit trap, and because that rad-blasted wag jockey was so jolt-wired he'd driven straight into it. So that's most of the reason that it was so black in here… What about the wag's emergency electrics? In most wags this well-equipped, a backup should at least provide lighting from which the crew could continue to work. Another thing that Eula hadn't seen to properly, or anyone else in this half-assed crew. How LaGuerre had kept himself afloat so long was becoming more and more of a question for the Armorer.

Thinking of the stupe trader made him suddenly aware of the small sounds of moaning that came from the other side of the wag jockey's fixed seat.

There was some illumination in the wag, and it emanated from the emergency lighting on the dash, which lit up the array of dials around the wheel. J.B. was blocking some of this illumination himself, and the level of light improved slightly when he raised himself up. He was now able to see that the majority of this feeble lighting was blocked by the inert body of Zarir, who was slumped forward, his face touching the dash, his back bent at an angle that seemed somehow not right, propped in this manner by the opposing forces of the wheel and his seat belt. Most wag drivers didn't bother with this predark appurtenance; for Zarir, it was almost as if this held the wag jockey into his seat for the long haul.

Not that it had done him much good this time. As J.B. lifted his head, and more light streamed up around him, it was clear that the wag jockey had bought the farm. His chest had been crushed into the wheel, the belt not being tight enough to prevent the impact. Even so, it had been forceful enough for his shoulders to have been pulled from their sockets by the crash.

Zarir's face was showing expression for the first time since J.B. had stepped into the wag. Yet this was no genuine expression of feeling, but rather the rictus and shock of a sudden chill. His eyes were wide and staring, the lips drawn back from his teeth in a humorless grin. As J.B. lifted his head, the movement caused the jaws to slacken, the teeth to open, and a gout of blood poured from where it had gathered in the chilled man's mouth, splattering the dash and making the dim illumination temporarily redden.

On the other side, as J.B. let the corpse fall, he could see that LaGuerre was half on the dash, half on the windshield. He was on his back, arms at his sides. He was the source of the small noises of agony. J.B. carefully picked his way around the driver's seat, finding the odd angle of the wag hard for finding balance, and came to where the trader lay.

"This is gonna hurt, but it's the only way," he whispered before starting to check the trader's body for injury. He could feel that LaGuerre had at least three rib fractures, all on one side, and that his elbow was at an angle that was far from natural. Fracture and dislocation: painful, but it wasn't going to buy the farm. Not that you'd know it from the way the trader yelled when J.B.'s probing fingers found the weak spots.

"Shut up," J.B. said simply, "you aren't going nowhere. I'll get Mildred to look you over, and you'll soon be fine." He stopped abruptly. Mention of his lover made him realize that his reawakening and exploration had not been carried out to a background of silence. It was there, but it was distant. He figured that he had subconsciously known this, and calculated that there was no imminent danger. Priorities: check the wag crew and himself, and assess the situation. But now that he had made himself aware of it, he could hear it in the background.

The sounds of combat: blasterfire, intermittent; yells and screams, both human and animal. There was one hell of a firefight going on out there, and it sounded as though it was turning to hand-to-hand. Given that the wag gave them a degree of soundproofing, the distance still suggested that their wag had fallen down a hell of a steep pit.

"Dix, what are you doing? Why have you stopped?"

Eula's voice pulled him from his reverie. He became aware that he hadn't felt her presence while he was examining LaGuerre or Zarir. Her voice was thick, and redolent of someone coming out of sleep or unconsciousness.

How long had she been watching? And why hadn't she said anything?

J.B. scanned the interior of the wag. There were great pools of darkness where the feeble light had failed to reach, and she had to be in one of these. How come she wasn't at the front?

"Don't play stupe games, girl," J.B. snapped. "Zarir's bought the farm, LaGuerre's hurt but not bad, and I'm just fine—" he ignored the raging pain in his temple from impact, and the nausea it churned in his gut "—and it's going off out there. We should be thinking about how to get out."

"What d'you think I was doing while you were resting against the windshield," she bit back. Her voice was still muzzy, but there was no mistaking the venom. "I pulled myself up here and checked to see what was working. Fuck all, as it happens, but I'll tell you something—we're a good three yards from the top of this bastard pit, so if we're gonna get out and join the fight, we're gonna have to hurry, 'cause—"

"If it comes down to us, we're cornered," he finished for her. He glanced over at LaGuerre. "We'll have to leave him here and hope for the best. If we fight our way out of this, then he can get some attention. If not, he's fucked anyway."

"Then it's you and me, Dix. Time to see what you're really made of."

"I could say the same. You better be able to back up that

mouth." Yet, even as he said it, he knew that the young woman had an inner core that would make her fight to the last. Maybe that was what made him wary of her—that she was like him in that way. Maybe that was why she was both fascinated and scornful of him, because she, too, recognized that.

But this was not the time to try to work out such things. Now, they had to concentrate on getting out before the fight was carried to them and they were trapped.

J.B. made his way to the rear of the wag, his feet slipping on the metal floor at its obtuse angle, grabbing at any handhold he could find. It grew darker toward the rear and top of the wag, and he could only just make out her shape as she loomed from the darkness, hand extended to grip his arm and haul him to where she stood. She was using the side of the fixed armory cabinet to prop herself up and keep from tumbling back. Her grip had been firm, but when J.B. was close enough he could hear that her breathing was shallow and labored.

"Let's be honest," he said flatly. "I've had a crack on the head that's given me a mild concussion. I'm not seeing double, but I might puke any moment and I feel like some coldheart bastard is hammering on my head. There's nothing else broken, or anything other than bruised. But I can't guarantee my reflexes are a hundred percent."

"Why are you telling me this? Not gonna make me inclined to carry you, Dix."

"Cut the crap. I'm telling you because we've got to back each other up, and if we're gonna do that we need to know strengths and weaknesses."

There was a pause before she answered, reluctantly.

"Okay, guess you're right. Got a crack on the head, like you. Feel like I'm wading through fog. Not gonna puke though, got stronger guts than you. Also figure that I've cracked at least one rib as it hurts when I breathe too hard. Not so bad I can't fight through it, but it might slow me up. Also feel like I've lost most of my blood from that fucking head crack. Seemed like I was wiping it up forever."

"At least we know." J.B. shrugged. "We aren't gonna be up to that much if the others are losing, but if I know them it's gonna take more than a bunch of inbred fuckers and some mutie livestock to beat them. So mebbe we've got a chance… Best way of getting out of here?"

"Straight out the back and up. It's steep, but ain't sheer. Figure you can do it? 'Cause if we're gonna do the honest bit, I wouldn't send me up first, not with these ribs. I can cover you, but sounds like you'll be faster. Figure I can scramble up if you'll cover me from the top, but it won't be quick."

"Okay, so you're saying our way of getting out of here puts me in the front line at each end?"

In the gloom, he could just about see her shrug. "Yep. No other way to put it. No other way up, either—sides are blocked in down there," she added, indicating the front of the wag, below them.

J.B. sucked in a sharp breath, blew it out. "Dark night, if I knew it was going to be like this…"

"It's always like this, Dix. There isn't another way."

For a moment, the Armorer was taken aback. Maybe without even realizing it, Eula had summed up his life. And maybe—just maybe—he'd miss it if it wasn't there.

"Okay. Let's do it," he said softly.

Eula moved to open the rear doors of the wag, and allow him to scramble up the side of the pit. As she did, something descended into the pit, hitting the rear doors with a resounding thump, causing the back of the wag to shake. Paws scratched at the metal, a snarling sound issuing deep from within the throat of the creature outside. There was little doubt that it was one of the mutie dogs. The shape of its shaggy hide could be seen through the frosted armaglass panes that allowed what little outside light there may be to enter.

"Fuck!" J.B. exclaimed, half in surprise and half in exasperation. Their only exit was now effectively barred by the mutie beast. "Any chance of firing out at it?" he questioned.

"Looks like armaglass, and is," Eula replied. "All we'd do is get a shitload of shells ricocheting around in here. Might as well put the blaster to our heads as do that."

J.B. sighed. No one ever said life was going to be easy, but there were some days…

"Okay, wait till the bastard goes to the left door, then push this one up as far as you can and I'll just try to blast it," he whispered. But despite his attempts to keep his voice low, the animal still heard him and came sniffing around the door that lay just above their heads.

J.B. looked at Eula. Now that his vision had adjusted to the gloom, he was able to make out her eyes clearly, which meant that she could read his. He took his mini-Uzi, and with as much care as possible, flicked it to rapid fire. Then he rolled his eyes toward the door, signaling her to be ready. She nodded, carefully moving to a position that would allow her the maximum leverage. When she was in position, J.B. leaned across and tapped at the armaglass on the left-hand door with the barrel of his blaster.

As he had hoped, the beast responded to the stimulus, moving across to the left door to sniff at the area where the noise had emanated.

Taking her cue, Eula hit the lock on the door and heaved upward with all the strength she could muster. The veins popped in her head, her vision blurred with yellow and red lights that flickered, and her ribs seemed to separate and spear her in every organ.

But she got the door open. Her initial push got it to ninety degrees, and momentum carried it back until it slammed against the side of the pit and against the frame of the wag. Not that this sound was audible above the chatter of the mini-Uzi.

J.B. waited that fraction of the second after Eula's initial push before following the line of the door, arm raised above his head so that the muzzle of the blaster was first out of the trap. He squeezed as he raised his arm, so that the first blast only just cleared the edge of the right-hand door.

As he followed his arm into the open, he was assailed by the smell of cordite and warm blood, his ears filled with the incessant hammer of the blaster and the squeals and yells of the beast.

It didn't stand a chance. It was chilled from the moment that his finger tightened enough to trigger the rapid blasts. The shells, at such close range, seared into its hide, penetrating the thick clumps of matted fur and the tough, leathery skin that protected it so well under normal circumstances. Burst arteries spouted blood that hit J.B. as he emerged from the shelter of the wag. He spit out the salty yet bitter liquid as it squirted into his mouth, his glasses blurring but his eyes saved from the stinging, blinding spray. Chunks of the creature were thrown up by the chopping of the shells, and its screams faded as the life ebbed from it. Still he kept firing, until he could be sure. He was halfway out the door, having used the edge of the cabinet to propel himself, now wobbling unsteadily as Eula's cupped hands supported one foot. There was no way he was going to give the furry bastard the chance to make a last gasp lunge for him.

His ears rang as he let the pressure on the trigger ease. The lump of lifeless meat and fur opposite him, stinking from chilling, was no threat now. It had smelled rank in life, and now in its demise it smelled worse, the metal tang of spilled blood and fresh meat combining with the stench of the creature's voided bowels and bladder.

There was no time to pause, no time to take stock or to try to recover. All he could do—that they could do—was to keep moving. Ramming the mini-Uzi temporarily into the waistband of his combat pants, finger automatically flicking over the safety, he needed both hands free to get enough of a hold on the blood-and-urine-slicked metal to haul himself up, his knees skidding on the surface as he turned to reach down and help Eula up, out of the wag and onto the door.

She looked at the pile of fur and flesh that had been a threat scant seconds before.

"Remind me never to piss you off," she murmured.

"No time," J.B. said shortly. He knew that the sound of

the firing, even over the sounds of combat that raged above them, would alert at least some of the enemy to the fact that there was life in the pit, and it was on the move. Hopefully, it would alert some of their allies, as well. But you couldn't rely on that. He could only rely on himself.

J.B. looked up the incline of the pit. Eula had been right. It was steep, but not impossibly sheer. He would still need both hands free until he reached the lip, and that made him triple vulnerable. He had to trust her. Until half an hour ago, he wouldn't have. But adversity could change things.

Enough, he hoped…

"Anything puts its nose over the top of that ridge, shoot first ask later," he said.

"What if it's one of ours?" Eula questioned.

J.B. grinned. "If any of my people are triple stupe enough to do that without precautions, I'd shoot them myself."

Then, pausing only to see that she had a blaster in hand, the Armorer turned to the steep and slippery incline of the pit. The soil was dry and powdery, making it hard to find anything remotely approaching a handhold. He had to dig deep with the toes of his boots, putting in more effort than the rewarded upward movement should warrant, feeling the abrasive soil scour at his skin as he dug in his fingers—his whole hand—and pushed upward. He didn't look up, didn't want to. There was jackshit he could do about anything that might come from above his head. He just had to hope that Eula would cover him adequately, and keep moving up as swiftly as he could.

Breath came in short gasps, vision colored purple and red as the effort made his lungs ache and his temples throb.

He wanted to puke into the soil in front of him, but knew that he couldn't afford the precious seconds it would take him to stop and heave. Instead, he kept going until he reached the lip of the pit, hauling himself over the edge and onto the flat, reaching for the holstered mini-Uzi as he rolled, hoping that if anything was near enough to get him, then a moving target would present just enough of a problem to deter them until...

He rolled and pushed up, coming to his knees, starting to move 180 degrees, rising onto one foot as he did so to pivot with greater ease and speed.

He was lucky. The fight was going on away from the pit. As he scrambled to his feet and backed toward the lip of the pit, he could see that the container wags and the other armed wags had managed to pull up short of following the lead wag into the trap. It was a testament to the skill of the wag jockeys, and perhaps to the foresight of the friends who had been stationed in each wag. Now the battle was taking place heading toward the shanty ville from which the pack had diverted the convoy.

Mildred and Krysty had left the safety of the cabs on the refrigerated wags. It was a calculated risk on their part. There was little they could do unless directly attacked, and like all of those who had traveled with Ryan and J.B., they carried Trader's indirect lesson that going on the offensive was better—drive the bastards back and put them on the back foot, not you. J.B. could almost hear Trader's voice.

Jak, Ryan and Doc had left their wags and were taking the battle into the heart of the enemy, joined by Cody and the huge frame of the dreadlocked warrior Raf. While the pack was being driven back by broadsides of rockets and machine-blaster fire from the two armed wags, the warriors on foot were going for the inhabitants of the ville, who had followed in the wake of the pack.

Part of J.B.'s brain tracked the logic of what had happened. The pack had to be maintained and bred by the coldhearts who lived in the shanty ville, then let loose to corral any stragglers on the blacktop, luring them here so that they could be plundered. Maybe that was why LaGuerre wanted to run straight through with no stopping—to cut down the risk. In which case it was a bad call. But if it happened before, then this bizarre idea of the trader's was suddenly made clear.

And, looking at the coldhearts who followed in the wake of the pack, hoping to make for easy pickings, it was obvious why they should raise such a herd and use them in such a manner. The men and women—maybe children, too, except that some of the adults were so stunted as to make the difference between adult and child impossible to distinguish—were misshapen, and used trolleys and wags to aid their speed. They had good weapons, which bespoke of the quality of plunder over the years. But they had little skill, which more than evened the odds. Particularly as much of their poor marksmanship was making inroads in thinning out the pack. Moreover, with fire coming in from both directions, the creatures were becoming confused and panicked, starting to scatter rather than follow the bloodlust with which they had been trained. And as they dispersed, they became both less of an obstacle and less of a threat to the convoy crew.

All of this came to J.B.'s attention and ran through his mind in less than a flicker of an eye, but it was still long enough for Eula to yell from the pit.

"Dix…"

It was an imprecation part puzzled concern, part angry order. It served its purpose, and the Armorer directed his attention to the pit.

"You get up okay?" he called down.

"Some of your holds are still there, probably take me," she said. "I can hack it the rest of the way…mebbe not as quick as you, though."

"No present danger. Just be sure," he barked back at her.

J.B. backed up to the lip of the pit, casting regular glances behind to check both the far side of the hole, and also the woman's progress, in between keeping the mini-Uzi focused on the battle in front of them.

The combined force of the convoy crew was halting the incoming, on the verge of turning the tide. The need for speed was lessened, and he called, "Take it easy. You've got time."

"I've got minor injuries, I'm not a fucking cripple," she gasped as she pulled herself up to the edge of the pit.

"Listen, you're no good to anyone you tumble back down and really injure yourself," he said, crouching and offering her his arm for support as she hauled herself the last few feet.

"Screw you, you fu— Sweet blaze of glory!" she exclaimed as she took in, for the first time, the scene unfolding in front of them.

"Yeah, we're lucky they were on it so quick. Imagine those coldhearts on top of us…"

Without any further discussion, J.B. set off at a trot to where the main body of action was taking place. Eula was a few paces behind, having been taken aback by his turn of speed. Despite his aching head, the Armorer knew that he was fit enough to take part in the firefight, and there was no way that he would shirk his duty when he was needed. He could hear Eula at his rear, dropping farther back, her step irregular. The damage to her ribs was slowing her, and in truth the effort to get out of the pit could only have added to her discomfort. But she was willing, he had to give her that.

The fighting had become localized, and the ville inhabitants had been driven back to their dwellings by the relentless push of the convoy crew. The land between the convoy vehicles and the ville itself was littered with the stinking corpses of cattle, dogs and things that resembled people but had—with the combined force of inbreeding and rad mutation—developed into something that bore a scant resemblance to the human race.

J.B. had seen isolated villes like this all over the rad-blasted lands, and although the variety of mutation and fleshy distortion had some variety from hotspot to hotspot, from gene pool to gene pool, there was little that could shock or repulse him. Besides which, the people and animals around him had bought the farm, and were of no risk, therefore of no concern.

Maybe it was the concussion that affected him; that made him just that little bit less than a hundred percent. It was not like the Armorer to charge through a field of corpses without the due caution that some may be less chilled than others. A caution that had kept him and his friends alive where others had perished.

Maybe, just for once, J.B. had made a bad call in risk assessment. He had judged himself to be fit to fight when it was not necessary. Was he really needed? Could he not take the time to clear his head before joining the fray?

Had he really not noticed that one of the coldhearts lying on the cold dustbowl dirt wasn't as cold as the ground that surrounded him?

As J.B. charged on, one of the corpses at his rear began to move. Slowly, then with gathering speed, a legless woman bleeding from a wound in the left side raised her torso from the earth. Propped on one elbow, she produced a Glock that, with her free arm, she leveled and trained on the departing form of J. B. Dix. The wound was bleeding freely, and the arm was not as steady as it would once have been, but she had time and a target who was unaware that he was such.

Or so she thought.

Fate was a strange and fickle beast. Eula's attitude toward the Armorer had been curious but hostile for so long, before adversity had pushed them together in the need to escape and stay alive. Now she had an attitude that was, if anything, even harder to define. If J.B. had known what went through her head at the moment she saw the mutie woman raise herself and her blaster, he would have been even more confused than he had previously been. But none of that mattered in this moment. Right now, Eula, following slowly and painfully in the Armorer's wake, had to make a decision.

She chose.

"Dix…down…" she yelled, leveling her own blaster at that moment, ignoring the sharp pain in her own side as her protesting ribs scraped and moved yet again. She winced, waves of red and purple washing across her vision as the head wound and the cracked bones told her not to exert. But she had to; for reasons that she, herself, would be hard put to explain coherently.

J.B. heard her voice. Without thinking, he threw himself to the ground. He wouldn't have trusted her until that moment. Maybe it was the way in which they had worked together to get out of the trapped wag. Maybe it was something in her voice; some quality of danger, sincerity, something between the two. Whatever it was, he trusted her implicitly at that moment.

Eula and the mutie woman formed a tableau in which each echoed the other: the mutie woman, lower because she was little more than a torso, bleeding profusely from one side, supporting herself on her right arm while her left trembled under the weight of the blaster and the need to keep a steady line. Eula, higher against the night sky, her side aching from ribs that threatened to spear her vital organs unless they were strapped, bent awkwardly against the pain to try to keep steady. Her arm extended, blaster shaking from the weight and the weakness of the pain in her side and in her head, vision blurring as she felt the blood thumping in her temples, threatening to open the wound in her head once more from the pressure.

They could have been there for a second. They could have been there forever. It would seem that way to both of them as they tried to summon the energy and will, from inside the pain, to squeeze. Ahead of both of them, J.B. seemed to go to ground in slow motion. Would he be too slow?

The mutie woman tried to muster the strength to fire before he was flat to the earth, Eula, to summon the strength to fire before the other could beat her to the punch.

J.B. hit the ground with a thud that jarred his already aching head. Waves of light swarmed in clusters across his vision, and his guts felt as though they wanted to exit through his mouth. He had to give in to the urge to puke, the bile spilling from his mouth in an acrid pool around his head. In the middle of this, he heard the roar of a blaster closer to hand than the distant chatter of the firefight.

"It's okay now, Dix."

J.B. raised himself, used his shirt to wipe the mess of vomit and dust from his face, and spit the last bitter remnants onto the ground. Turning, he could see that Eula was moving forward to stand over a mutie woman who was sprawled on the ground. Unlike those around her, she was ripped to pieces by blasterfire, blood still dribbling from fresh wounds. A Glock lay a few feet from one outstretched arm.

"Careless of you, Dix," Eula said as she poked the mutie woman with her foot. The lifeless bundle of rags and flesh barely moved, and the young armorer nodded her satisfaction.

J.B. walked over to join her, casting a glance around him that was informed by the knowledge that he had screwed up.

"Figure she was the only one who hadn't rolled over and chilled," Eula said, observing him.

"Should have spotted it," he replied shortly. "That was my ass, and you had it. Thanks."

"That's okay. We all make mistakes."

"Yeah, but mistakes get us chilled. I don't make mistakes."

She leveled a gaze at him. Her eyes were shielded, but there was something there that he felt he should understand; something underneath the words she spoke.

"We all make mistakes, Dix. No one's perfect. Not even you. You've made mistakes before. It's just that you haven't had to pay for them."

"Mebbe," he said after a pause for reflection. For a moment he felt that he'd got close to figuring her out; to understanding why she had this fascination for him that teetered on hate; to knowing why she was so damn familiar and yet someone he had never met before.

But if such revelation was to come to him, it was not destined to be in a place like this. As J.B. and Eula stood, staring at each other over the bloodied corpse of the anonymous mutie woman who had unwittingly bound them together, placing the Armorer in Eula's debt, it seemed for a moment as though they were isolated from the world around them. The undercurrents that had swept between them were to surface, and her reasons for wanting the friends to join LaGuerre's convoy were to become clear.

This moment vanished in the ground-shaking blast of the main fuel store for the shanty ville going up under attack from one of the armed wags. While one had maintained guard on the refrigerated wags, to cover any attack that may be mounted as a last-ditch by the ville dwellers, the other had followed in the wake of the combat party as they forged forward. While they had decimated the population, and driven away the remnants of the pack, there was still the obstacle of the shanty ville itself to overcome.

It was true that there were now very few of the muties left, but once they had been driven back to their ville, they had the shelter of the buildings. That gave them the advantage as they had cover, and also the possibility of unknown weapons stores contained within. Meanwhile, the combat party advancing on them had no cover that they could use to counter.

It hadn't taken much for Ramona, deputed to stay behind and man the wag that she had been traveling with Raven, Doc and Ryan, to figure that out. Seeing that the pack had dispersed, and that the muties were either chilled or driven back, it didn't take much in the way of initiative to figure that she could be more use if she followed up the combat party. Taking the wag to within firing range of the ville, she had slewed the vehicle sideways-on so that the rocket launchers were dead-on to the shanty buildings.

Her plan, as she seated herself at the launcher, was to try to pick off the biggest buildings first, figuring that the muties would want to band together, and that the biggest buildings were the likeliest to house the biggest armories.

There was no way she could have expected to hit the jackpot first time. The building she chose as her first target was the fuel store for the ville, and it was obvious that they had been storing their plundered fuel for some time.

The sky was momentarily as bright as day, a wave of heat sweeping over the combat party as it approached, scorching as the shock wave accompanying it threw them to the ground. The wave was so fierce that they were pinned to the ground, unable to see the chain reaction as the blast area flattened the shanty buildings nearest, causing their own smaller supplies of fuel, explosives and ammo to go up. In turn, these smaller blasts acted as a chain, catching the buildings nearest to them. And so the whole of the shanty ville went up in smoke and flame, lighting up the skies afresh as the initial fire began to fade.

The cries and screams of those muties who had made

the cover of the shanty ville were lost to the roar and crackle of the buildings as they detonated. By the time that the combat party was able to look up, the initial bursts of light had faded, leaving only the residual glow of a ville that was now little more than a series of rapidly burning ruins.

Unlike the rest of the combat party, J.B. and Eula had been just far enough away to witness the detonation without being thrown down. Now they watched as the party began to rise from the dustbowl floor.

"Guess we won't have to check that out quite so thoroughly," Eula said to the Armorer.

J.B. looked at her. She was grinning.

"No, not likely to make a mistake on that," he returned, his own grin part relief and part exhaustion. "But I tell you something. LaGuerre's gonna be pissed that we've left him down there."

Chapter Fifteen

J.B. wasn't far wrong. With the inhabitants of the ville already beginning to bloat up in the first rays of the morning sun, and the remnants of the pack now scattered across the dustbowl to escape the smell of chilling that their less fortunate companions had left in their wake, it was a relatively simple matter for the armored wag to be pulled from the pit. Simple after the matter of pulling the trader from the pit, that was.

Although the pit was several yards deep, it had been dug in a conical pattern, so that the sides were not sheer. Sure, they were steep, but those who had engineered the trap had their own concerns in the construction. From the look of many of them as they lay scattered across the dirt, it had been difficult enough for them to move around on a flat surface, let alone cope with the climbing that may be involved in both the construction and the execution of such a trap.

As a result, it gave the convoy a relatively simple task. The rear of the armored wag presented an easy access for block and tackle, for tow ropes and for the chains that were used to secure one vehicle to another. They were also fortunate that they were in a convoy that was using the refrigerated wags and the large cabs to pull them.

Under the direction of Raven and Ryan, old Ray used his cab to pull the armored wag from the pit. Detaching the cab from the refrigerated section, the wag jockey moved to the edge of the pit while Raven and Ryan scrambled down with chains, ropes and block tackle. Taking no chances on any of the connections severing and allowing the armored wag to fall back into the pit, they evenly distributed their chains, ropes and tackle, making sure that they secured the ties while distributing the weight to avoid any one connection taking too much strain. The ties were attached to both the top and bottom of the wag, under the chassis and on the bodywork. Wherever they could find a secure spot to attach a tie, they did it until they had run out of chains, ropes and tackle.

The other end of their snaking maze of metal and rope was attached to the heavy-duty fender on the front of the wag cab. At a signal from Ryan, who was looking down into the pit, Ray began to reverse the wag cab slowly, pulling at the armored wag.

It didn't give easily. Despite the disparity in weight, it was harder to shift than any of them would have thought. Zarir's reactions had been so slow that, as he had piloted the armored wag into the pit, he had still been at full throttle. As a result, the momentum of the wag had driven its nose into the hard-packed earth, and the ground was a harsh and unforgiving medium.

Raven sat up in the cab with Ray, watching Ryan closely. She still felt as though she hardly knew the one-eyed man, but like her friend Ramona, had instinctively known that she could trust his judgment. Ray, on the other hand, she didn't trust. The old man was a less than full tank up top, and he was still babbling away to her about nothing much as he reversed his wag. At least, she figured it was nothing much. She was focusing her attention on Ryan, and Ray's words were nothing more than a blur of sound to her. As she watched the one-eyed man, she noticed his rippling muscles and the rugged handsomeness of his face. Sure he had that scar, but that only added to his macho charm. On the other hand, the red-haired bitch was his, and looked far too tough for Raven to take on. She was a feisty woman, but she knew her limits. Besides which, now was not the time.

Ray yelped as she hit him on the arm, just for emphasis, every time that she yelled at him to stop or to increase speed. He punctuated his monologue with complaints that fell on closed ears.

Raven watched Ryan, and then the lip of the pit. She saw the chains and ropes they had attached to the top of the armored wag start to slacken. They had tied them at different lengths, to allow for the discrepancy that would occur when the wag began to right itself as it hit the flat. Even so, it seemed that their necessary haste, and the need to judge it by eye alone, had been more than a little out. She only hoped that the bottom of the chassis could take the extra strain that would now be on it.

Ray, despite the constant stream of words from his mouth, had not been jockeying wags for so long without learning something along the way. Despite his seeming lack of attention, he had felt the sudden jerk of the cab when the armored wag had freed itself from the earth's grip, and so had eased off on the throttle to allow for that. Even now he was regulating his speed, actually one second ahead of the barked commands and punctuating punch of Raven.

On the lip of the pit, Ryan stared down at the wag as it was released from its prison. The ties on the top of the vehicle were slack too quickly for his liking, leaving the bottom to take the strain of the pull. The wag was strong, but it was also heavy. And while the cab had enough power to pull it out, it was a question of whether or not the wag jockey had the skill to pull it out in one piece.

The armored wag made a slow and sure ascent until it reached the lip. The rear wheels fought for purchase on the dusty, crumbling soil, seeming at times to willfully drive the earth from beneath them, leaving nothing but empty space for purchase. Ryan swore softly to himself, realizing that if he had thought about it quicker, he could have organized planking from the shanties of the ville—what was left of them—to shore up the unsafe surface and allow for greater purchase.

But it was of no matter now. All he could do was watch and pray, directing the efforts of the old wag jockey as best as he could.

The rear wheels finally gained sufficient grip to allow the wag to drag itself toward the horizontal. As the length of the wag allowed for the underneath to scrape along the surface with a squeal that made his teeth ache, it reached a point where the ties on the upper section finally came into their own, growing taut once more and pulling the body of the wag upright so that the front wheels dangled over the abyss that had been their prison.

Ryan sucked in his breath. If there was to be one moment where the wag could succumb to the tensions that were working within the structure and render it asunder, this would be that moment…

He indicated to Raven and Ray that it was the moment to put pedal to metal. Before Raven could even open her mouth or move her fist, Ray had stamped on the accelerator, the big rig moving backward with increasing speed, dragging the heavy armored wag onto the flat before it had the chance to rip itself to pieces.

Ryan heaved a sigh of relief, and he wasn't alone. In the cab of the wag, Raven, too, sighed heavily.

Ray looked at her. "Hon, I don't know why you were worried. You tie it well enough, I can shift it."

Raven looked back at him, realizing that she had been looking at Ray as some old crazie for too long. She'd forgotten why Armand kept him on for so long.

"Next time I underestimate you, hit me," she said.

Ray grinned. "Shit, I'll settle for you not hitting me anymore. My arm's numb from the shoulder down."

WHILE THIS HAD BEEN going on, LaGuerre was moaning in every sense of the word. So much so that Mildred sincerely wished that the trader had bought the farm down in the pit, and not the wag driver who, she understood from J.B., had been silent. In truth, if the miserable bastard didn't shut up soon, she'd succumb to the temptation to fill the man so full of morphine that he'd be too blissed out to speak. The only thing that had stopped her was that she really didn't like him, and the thought of the idiot suffering some pain was a pleasant, if not particularly charitable, thought.

"Man, you better hope that my wag ain't badly damaged. I need that machine, and I need for us to get on the way soonest possible, so they better not be fucking around in trying to get it out of the ground. Man, if they take as little care as they took in getting me out, then my machine ain't got shit in the way of a chance. I thought I could trust that bitch Eula, then what does she do? Leave me down there with Zarir, man, leave me down there with a fucking chill boy while she and that man of yours get to make a break for it. Thank fuck you people were able to do your job and get rid of these crazies—man, what did happen up here?— and get me out. Shit, who runs this show, man? Ow. What the fuck are you doing?" he yelped as Mildred deliberately jabbed a hypo full of antibiotic into a particularly fleshy and therefore more painful part of his rear end.

"Sorry," she murmured, realizing that her tone belied the word, but not caring. Hell, she didn't even need to do it in his ass. His arm would have done just as well, but she'd hoped that flipping him over might dull the noise. No chance. Not that LaGuerre seemed to notice any of this.

"You damn well should be," he grumbled. "This was supposed to be a straight run with you people heading off trouble at the pass. Stead of which I get left in a shallow grave while my two supposed armorers turn tail and run."

That was too much for Mildred.

"You ungrateful fuck," she gritted in his ear. "J.B. nearly bought the farm, so did Eula. Hell, we all did. We were up here fighting while you were hiding in the dark. Couple of busted ribs never stopped any of us fighting when our lives depended on it. Your people did good, and we're all alive. Including you. And if you hadn't pumped that driver of yours full of junk to keep him awake, then he might have had the sense not to drive into a fucking big hole in the ground."

LaGuerre turned onto his front, and looked at her with a quizzical expression that, in the circumstances, surprised her.

"Shit, what's your problem?" he said in a tone that, bizarrely, sounded as though he was wounded more by her words that the injuries sustained in the crash. He added, "I was only saying, that's all…"

Mildred, shook her head, openmouthed. "Just pull your pants up and shut up," was all she could say, dumbfounded as she moved on to the next patient.

Next was Cody, who had sustained a graze across the shoulder from a stray slug in the firefight. The bleeding had been staunched, and it was a matter of simply cleaning and dressing the wound to avoid infection. Despite the fact that it was raw, and still fresh, the skinny fighter didn't flinch.

"Pay no mind to Armand. He's stupe about some things 'cause we've been lucky. Hell, guy's the luckiest trader I ever run with," he mused, "which I guess is why I stick around."

Mildred shrugged. There was nothing more to say. Besides which, she had other things on her mind.

After the firefight, as the convoy had regrouped in the wake of battle, and assessed that they had no casualties of any import, with nothing more than a few superficial wounds, J.B. had sought out Mildred to speak to her. She had known J.B. for what seemed like forever; despite the short amount of time it represented in her actual life span, the nature of her life after awakening from cryogenic freezing had made every experience seem deeper. As a result, the bonds forged among the traveling companions had gone deeper than any she had known. Particularly those she shared with the Armorer.

What J.B. had said to her, and the tones in which he had

spoken, had made a deep impression on her. He told her of the way in which Eula had saved his life, and of the change in her attitude prior to that. It was clear that he was confused about what had prompted it, but felt no inclination to be anything other than convinced that her ambivalence had been resolved. He didn't know why. He only knew that in the act of saving his life when there had been compulsion, she had made her choice clear.

Well, Mildred could live with that. It was John's choice, even though she was inclined to wait and see this change for herself. What had concerned her more was what he had said next.

In the aftermath of battle, when he had thanked her for her actions, Eula had told him that she wanted to leave LaGuerre after they reached Jenningsville. What she was looking for could not be found with the trader. She wanted to travel with J.B. and his companions. With them she could find what she sought.

J.B. was puzzled but willing to take her word when he relayed this to Mildred. Her actions had been proof enough of intent for him.

But Mildred felt differently. While she was more than glad that Eula had stopped J.B. from buying the farm, she was damn sure there was another motive behind it all. There was no way that she could believe such a sudden and total about-turn in attitude. Maybe John was right. She had never known his judgment to be so flawed. But for Mildred, something was itching at her. Perhaps it was just old-fashioned jealousy.

WHILE MILDRED PONDERED this, the rest of the convoy checked out their wags while they waited for Ray to haul the lead wag from the pit. It wasn't a process that took them long. In the firefight, they had sustained little damage from blasterfire, and only some superficial damage from the impact of the pack as it had driven them onto this path.

In truth, the majority of their time had been spent combing the remains of the ville for anything that could be salvaged and put to use. It had been a mostly fruitless task. The damage incurred when the ville went up in a chain reaction had left little behind that was identifiable. The inhabitants who had retreated to their shanties had been reduced to ash and charred debris like their homes and whatever belongings they had plundered over the years. Any indication of how they had lived, how they had survived, had been eradicated in the fierce blaze. There was nothing to even suggest to the convoy what their fate may have been had they not fought so well. All that had survived the scorched earth were a couple of ramshackle barns with the remains of some feed, which had obviously been used at some point for part or all of the pack, perhaps to raise the young so that they were responsive to their masters, rather than growing completely feral.

Maybe it was better that they had no idea of what may have become of them. Better to maintain ignorance than risk nightmares.

While the members of the convoy had, for the most part, contented themselves with rummaging in the remains, so J.B. and Eula had made it their task to get LaGuerre from his wag before Ryan and Raven directed its removal.

The young woman had said nothing to Mildred while the medic had treated her for her injuries—the same injuries that had prompted Mildred's comments to LaGuerre sometime later—and this as much as anything had caused the doubt in Mildred's mind when J.B. had told her what Eula had said.

Back then, Eula had been keen to get away from the healer, and to return to her task with the Armorer. Her ribs strapped and precious morphine dulling the pain, she had joined him in scrambling down the incline, trailing ropes that were held at the top by Ryan and Raven.

They used flashlights to see their way in the interior of the wag. Although the sun was now up, the pit was deep and the angle of the wag meant that light was blocked by the solid panels of the armoring. There was, at best, a dim illumination in the interior as they picked their way past the stinking remains of the mutie dog and the still open rear door of the wag. Some of the blood and filth from the corpse had leaked and trickled into the wag, making the foul and stagnant air within worse than it would otherwise have been.

The stench of Zarir's body, decomposing already in the heat, didn't do much to help matters.

LaGuerre had been where they had left him the previous night, lying awkwardly and uncomfortably on the dash and windshield of the wag. He was semiconscious when they got to him, and was muttering to the chilled wag driver, cursing him in a patois J.B. recognized as similar to the Creole that he had heard people using in the areas where Jak originally came from.

Ignoring his ravings, the smell of decay that infested the wag and the screams of LaGuerre as they moved him and the pain cut through his delirium, J.B. and Eula made a sling in which they secured the injured man. Keeping talking to a minimum in order to keep breathing as shallow as possible and so avoid the desire to puke from the odor of chilling that permeated the air around them, J.B. signaled to Eula that he would climb back the way they had come and take the weight of the sling.

Slithering past the sticky wetness caused by the corpse on the back of the wag doors, J.B. was glad to attain the relatively fresh air of the morning, even though the scent of blood and buying the farm was starting to rise with the sun.

Cody had driven his wag almost to the lip of the pit, reversing it so that the raised bar around the roof of the vehicle could be used as a pivot to pull the sling. J.B. looked questioningly at the wound on Cody's shoulder.

"Can wait," the thin man said dismissively.

The two men attached the ropes to the bar. J.B. went to the lip of the pit, yelled down to Eula that they were ready to begin, and while she steadied the trader in the makeshift sling, the Armorer and Cody began to haul on the ropes that ran through the bar.

LaGuerre was a heavy weight to haul, surprisingly so, but the level of delirium into which he had sunk had taken the fight from him, and he dangled helplessly, unable or unwilling to help them as they pulled. It took no little effort for men who had recently been exhausted by the rigors of combat to haul the injured trader up from the pit. In return, their only reward was a mouthful of semicoherent abuse in both English and Creole patois as the trader bumped over the lip of the pit.

As LaGuerre lay on the earth, both men realized that they were too tired to carry the trader to where Mildred had established a makeshift medical station, and also to help Eula out of the pit.

Cody swore softly to himself, then yelled out in a voice that made J.B. wince. It did, however, have the desired effect, and brought Raf lumbering over. The heavily scarred, dreadlocked warrior was immensely strong, as well as big, and plucked the trader off the floor as though he weighed no more than a grain of sand.

J.B., breathing heavily with the effort of hauling LaGuerre from the wag in the pit, could only look on in a kind of admiration as Raf carried the trader off to Mildred. Then he looked at the sling on the ground, where Raf had left it.

"This should be easier," he said to Cody.

"Sure hope so," the thin man replied, wincing as he flexed his injured shoulder.

J.B. was right. Taking the sling to the lip of the pit, he called to Eula and flung it down, aiming for the open door and seeing the rope harness disappear into the darkness. There was a brief pause while she made herself secure, and then she called back to him.

Her injuries were such that climbing from the wag would have been difficult—perhaps almost impossible—without aid. Getting down there had been okay, but the reverse journey would have put too much strain on her cracked ribs, which had already suffered during her forced climb of the night previous.

Fortunately, all she needed was someone to take up the slack and bear some of her weight as she made the climb. Bracing themselves, Cody and J.B. found that they had little to do in the way of hauling. As long as they stood still, she was able for the most part to haul herself out of the wag and up the sides of the pit. It was only near the lip, where the dry soil was at its most treacherous, that they were called upon to really exert any effort.

When Eula was out of the pit, and lay gasping on the flat earth, she looked up at the two of them as they stood over her.

"Anyone asks, it wasn't this difficult, right?" she panted.

"Hey, no more than it would be for anyone with busted ribs." Cody shrugged.

"'Sides which, look at how LaGuerre took it," J.B. added.

Eula managed a grin. It was the first time Cody could ever recall her cracking her face since she had joined the convoy.

"Think he'll teach us some of those words when he feels better?" she asked. "Only, seems like some of 'em were really filthy."

Cody grimaced, flexing his injured shoulder. "Kid, we don't get on with hauling his precious wag out that pit, he'll give us a practical demonstration of 'em."

WHILE LAGUERRE WAS BEING tended to by Mildred, and the wag was being hauled out of the pit, J.B. and Eula took some downtime. Everyone else was engaged in either wag maintenance or attempting to scavenge the remains of the ville, so they were able to rest up for a few precious moments with no one to ask why they weren't engaged on another task.

J.B. wasn't used to the idea of doing nothing, and he could see from the way that she was on edge, that Eula felt the same way.

"Didn't think that you'd want to help me get out last night," he said hesitantly. "Let alone stop me getting chilled. I owe you for that."

"I might hold you to that," she said. There was a silence more of exhaustion than anything else before she added: "LaGuerre has something in mind for you, y'know."

J.B. frowned. "Like what?"

"When we get to Jenningsville. There's a reason he agreed to take this run, and it's not because of the bonus he's getting for a quick delivery. That's good, but it ain't enough for the coldheart bastard to risk his own skin like he's been doing. Ours, sure. He'd have no worries about doing that, but not his own. So it's got to be big."

"And he needs me? Us?"

She nodded. "Look, I've got my own reasons for being interested in tracking you people down. You can help me get to the bottom of something in my past, and—"

"You mean us? Or just me?"

"Mostly you," she said, fixing him with a level gaze. "But you're not what I thought you'd be. Still, you hold the key."

"But how—"

"There'll be time enough for that. You gotta trust me for now. If it was bad shit, I would have been happy to let you be chilled by that mutie bitch last night. No, it's complicated, but this isn't the time."

"Why not?"

"Because whatever LaGuerre has planned is imminent. We're not far from Jenningsville—another day, mebbe, and we'll reach the pesthole. That's when he'll tell me what he wants."

"You don't know?" J.B. watched her face as she shook her head. She was either one hell of a liar, or the trader really hadn't told her. "I thought he told you everything," J.B. continued. "Most of the people in this convoy think that you and him are tight."

She shook her head once more. "Sure they do. Wrong, but I can see why. He knows that I know things. Things about you people. He's wanted you for his reason, just like I have for mine. That's kinda tied us together. But once we get to Jenningsville, that's where it ends. You do what he wants, it goes off, and he rides away a rich, rich man. It don't go off, and you buy the farm, not him. You're new, hired hands. He can plead ignorance, and he's playing odds. He thinks he can charm and talk his way out of it. And he's right, mostly 'cause he will have delivered what no one else has, and that makes him someone to be took care of, not just chilled."

"LaGuerre's a smart boy," J.B. mused. "But he's reckoned without you saying this, right?"

"He doesn't know how I've changed my attitude since I've actually worked with you people. He thinks he knows me, but he doesn't. No one does. That's how I've survived so long. He thinks because I'm pussy, and not a man, he understands me. Led by his dick so much."

"So what do you suggest we do? I could get Ryan and the others, but that would look kinda suspicious, and right now…"

She sucked her teeth. "No, you do that and it could blow everything. Right now, we're in the middle of nowhere. We get to the ville, could be that what he has planned could be to our advantage. I don't want to stop it, I just want you to be aware of it. He's planning something, and it involves you. Just be ready."

J.B. nodded. He was uneasy about keeping quiet. Mildred, Ryan, Jak, Doc—this concerned them all. But what was there to tell them? At the moment, Eula knew nothing. So, by extension, neither did the Armorer. And pulling everyone together in an open situation such as this would do nothing more than cause suspicion.

She was right, as far as he could judge. Let her try to find out from the treacherous LaGuerre. Meanwhile, when they reached Jenningsville, he would find a way of alerting his friends without attracting undue attention.

"I'm trusting you, here," he said to her. "I'll wait, but if it comes to the point where it puts any of us in any danger other than we'd usually expect…"

"I wouldn't expect anything else from you," Eula said, leveling a gaze at him. "Nothing else at all."

Their conversation was cut short by the approach of Krysty and Ramona.

"J.B., what the hell are you doing sitting on your ass when there's so much to be done?" Krysty asked in perplexed tones. "That's not like you."

"Hell, hon, you ask me they ain't so much sitting on their asses as about to give them some exposure." Ramona cackled. "You should find a wag, else you'll get sunburn on your butts out here," she added with a wheezing laugh.

Eula shot the dark woman a venomous look, got up and walked off.

"Well, she sure got something up her ass, you know what I'm saying?" Ramona mused as she watched her go.

"You really don't like her, do you?" Krysty asked.

"No," Ramona replied bluntly. "There's something 'bout that girl that sure ain't right. You should stick with the sister, four-eyes," she addressed to the Armorer. "That one'll shoot you in the back soon as go down on you. Probably one for the other."

J.B. watched Eula go. Should he tell Krysty? Would he have the chance with Ramona standing there?

"C'mon, dickweed, they've just hauled Armand's pride

and joy—and I don't mean the one on his pants—out the hole. We gotta clean that fucker up and get poor Zarir in the ground."

Ramona led Krysty away, beckoning to the Armorer to follow.

The moment had passed.

How important would that prove to be?

THERE WERE THINGS that needed to be done before the convoy was finally in a position to move.

The first was the removal of Zarir's body from the driving seat of the armored wag. Rigor had set in, and it was a grimly humorous sight to behold as he was removed from the rear of the wag in a semisitting, semislumped position, carried out at an absurd angle and placed on the ground.

The men of the convoy had already begun to dig a grave for him. It was time-consuming, and LaGuerre moaned briefly about the delay, but despite the fact that their chilled were usually left to rot and provide carrion, there was something about the manner in which he had bought the farm that caused all of them to take pause and decide that a burial was right.

They dug down three feet, figuring that this would be enough to prevent his being dug up, although the position of his set limbs meant that he was not, in places, as deep as they would have wished. Short of breaking the rigor-stiffened limbs, there was little they could do. After they had lowered him in, Cody said a few brief words. Haltingly, he said all there was to say—none of them had known the silent wag jockey, but as LaGuerre's pilot he was one of them. And the way in which he had bought the farm seemed, somehow, stupe.

After he had been covered, the earth mounding up to mark the spot where he lay, they left him and returned to the armored wag.

Now, in a situation that benefited more the living, all of them felt that they could be more proactive.

The wag needed hosing down, to get rid of the stench of blood, flesh and decay that now filled it. Water was at a premium, so sand blasters were used on the rear doors to scour the outside of the vehicle. The inside was scrubbed. It took a team of six several hours in the rising heat to remove as much of the stench as was possible.

While this was taking place, repairs had to be made to the front of the wag. Ryan and J.B. rigged up a tent-cover construction that kept as much of the increasing heat as was possible off the front of vehicle, enabling the mechanics to work.

There were a few problems to overcome. First, despite the reinforced armoring at the front of the wag, the force with which it had struck the bottom of the pit, driving it into the earth, had caused the front engine cab to crumple. There was no real damage done to the engine, as the strength of the armoring had prevented any impact trauma. But the ventilation ducts that enabled the engine to cool, and maintained a flow of air around the working sections of the wag, had been dented and closed up by the impact. While members of the convoy worked to open these up, and straighten dented armoring that was resistant to the kinds of force they were able to use, those with the greatest engineering skills both checked and maintained the engine, and paid attention to the interior workings of the wag.

The steering column had maintained some damage. The actual column itself was sturdy enough to remain stable under the impact, but the force with which it had struck the floor of the pit, combined with the force with which Zarir's chest cavity had struck it before giving way, meant that some of the circuitry and wiring within had sustained minor damage. And the wheel itself had buckled, the bent metal no longer true to the pressures put on it in the course of use.

Ray took this task upon himself. Mildred assisted him, as he insisted that the repair was like a medical operation. It was a conceit that she was prepared to allow him until she saw the delicacy with which he carried out the repairs. Wires and circuits were manipulated, reconnected and replaced with pieces plundered from the old comp boards in other parts of the wag. Ray's fingers moved with a grace and deftness of touch that she would not have believed possible.

When he had finished, and his face had lit up like the control panel when he tested the steering and dash controls to find them in fully restored order, Mildred was inclined not so much to humor him as to wholeheartedly agree that he had shown a surgeon's precision in some of his work.

Finally, the armored wag was ready to move on. It looked battered, and LaGuerre complained about the smell as he shuffled in through the rear door, but it was roadworthy and showed, all things considering, little in the way of damage.

By this time, the sun was beginning to lower in the sky.

It had taken them all day to remove the wag from the pit and make it roadworthy again. But finally they were able to continue on the journey. Cody took Zarir's place at the wheel, easing himself into driver's position, adjusting the seat until it suited his smaller frame. Then the convoy moved out, heading back toward the road, with all personnel in the positions they had assumed prior to the firefight.

But other things had changed. The atmosphere between the Armorer and Eula was easier, which confused LaGuerre as he sat glowering at them. And J.B.'s attitude to the trader had changed. Before, he had been confused as to whether the man was triple stupe or cunning.

Now, he just had animal wariness. He was waiting.

And he was ready.

Chapter Sixteen

Jenningsville lay roughly eight miles from where they re-entered the blacktop. It took them some time to navigate their way back, the tracks left the previous night by the pack and by the convoy having already been almost eradicated by the ever-present, low-level swirling winds of the dustbowl. J.B. directed Cody, taking bearings and guiding them. Cody, for his part, adapted to the controls of the armored wag with ease, and by the time they hit the road once more, it was as though he had been piloting the vehicle since they had originally set out.

The ribbon, broken by time and the environment, was nonetheless consistent enough to present a black line to the horizon that the convoy settled easily into following. The wags were lined up as before, with Jak remaining in the second wag, and Ryan in the rear with Doc, Raven and Ramona. LaGuerre had been too preoccupied—both by his injuries and by the shift in atmosphere between J.B., Eula and himself—to insist that the motorbikes be taken from their secured positions on the rear of the wags and brought back into action.

Despite the fact that it was a battered and bruised convoy, with no sec at the rear, the procession made good time. Cody was less inclined to put pedal to the metal than Zarir had been, but considering where that had got them previously, no one was going to complain about that.

Except LaGuerre. He grumbled that his bonus would be cut because the convoy would be a day later than his estimated completion time. J.B. questioned him about the estimated time, and the time usually taken, and found for the first time that LaGuerre had pushed them to a schedule four days ahead of the usual run time.

"So you lose a quarter of the bonus?" he concluded. "You're sitting there giving us shit about losing part of the jack when you're still alive and collecting three-quarters? Selfish bastard. You could have bought the farm because you weren't straight with me. We could all have bought the farm."

LaGuerre was incensed. This was his convoy, and the outsider was giving him shit? He was about to say that the jack would be split among the convoy so they were all losing out, but that was only partly true, as he would keep the majority, and J.B. would know that. He was about to say that he had hired them to stop this kind of shit happening, to stop them being attacked, but he knew J.B. would only point out—rightly and possibly forcefully—that they were still alive and on the road, with a minimum of casualties and a whole lot of chilling behind them.

Frankly, LaGuerre felt that he was only tenuously in command of his convoy now, and that if he said too much then he would join those whose blood had been spilled. So he didn't make any of the answers that sprang readily to his lips, settling instead into a sulky silence as the ribbon of the road unfurled in front of them, taking them— thankfully, as far as he was concerned—to their destination. He just wanted this to be done. He wished he had never set eyes on J. B. Dix and the people who traveled with him.

If the Armorer had known that those thoughts were running through the trader's head, he would have been on triple red. As it was, he put the lapse into silence as nothing more than sulking, and returned to his task of ensuring that the remainder of the convoy's journey was smooth.

DOC AND RYAN WERE using the respite of the uneven journey to try to discover a little more about the ville to which they were headed. It was a fruitless task, as it seemed that their traveling companions were as much in ignorance as they were themselves.

"Hon, we ain't never really headed out this far before," Ramona murmured distractedly as she kept her eyes on the road ahead and the rear of the refrigerated wag that rose above them through the cloud of dust it raised. "The only thing I could tell you is what I heard from others. And we all know how reliable that kinda talk is, right?"

Doc smiled wryly. "Careless talk costs lives, and loose lips sink ships, I assume you mean by that."

"Uh, sure," Ramona replied, resisting the temptation to cast a bemused glance over her shoulder.

Raven looked at Ryan from her position on the bunk and raised an eyebrow, gesturing to her temple with a forefinger. Ryan grinned and shrugged. He knew Doc had seen her, but knew equally that the old man didn't care. For Ryan had heard Doc use the expressions before, and knew that they were phrases he had picked up on his travels through time. They had once had meaning, and from the context in which Doc always used them, Ryan had worked out what they meant. But to explain this to Raven and Ramona would only make them look at him in the same way they regarded Doc.

"So you are saying, in effect, that we know little about the place we are about to visit?" Doc continued. "Your glorious leader, having struck a deal with people he has never dealt with before, expects them to pay up without any problems? Or is that, perhaps, why he wanted ourselves along for the ride?"

"Y'know, you could be right about that last bit," Raven mused. "After all, Armand and Eula were together on wanting you with us 'cause of what they'd heard. And you ain't proved them wrong so far."

"Very gracious of you to say so," Doc demurred, "but on the other hand, you have not exactly seemed to be helpless when trouble has arisen. Which suggests to me— and I don't know what it says to you, Ryan, dear boy— that LaGuerre does not, how shall we say, trust his buyers."

"I wouldn't if I was him," Ryan mused. "When we rode with Trader, we never did a deal as big as this with a ville we hadn't dealt with in a smaller way before. Trader would always sound out anyone he could find on what the setup of a ville was, and would only deal small-time the first time around. It's the only really safe way to get a measure of who you're dealing with…at least, as much of a measure as you can."

"Makes sense to me," Raven said, yawning. She lay back on the bunk. "And I gotta say, Armand usually gives us a better briefing at the start of a run than he did this time around. Mind, we didn't exactly get this the usual way."

Ryan and Doc exchanged glances. That was something that they had suspected for a long while.

"Raven, hon, I think you're letting that mouth of yours run away with you, now that you can't fill it any other way," Ramona cautioned. "These are good folks, but we don't need to tell them all our business, right?"

"I do not think you have to, dear lady," Doc said kindly. "It does not take much imagination to put two and two together and come up with the square. Your resourceful leader hijacked another convoy, who may perhaps have dealt with this ville before. Presumably his intel told him of the fee and the bonuses, and so he now plans to collect a fee agreed with someone else. Tell me, is this a common practice for you?"

Ramona sighed. "Not exactly. He does this when times are hard, and just lately—"

"So we're carrying someone else's goods to someone else's buyer, and we're supposed to just collect like nothing's going to happen?" Ryan sighed. "Shit's gonna hit just like the sun always rises, and we're supposed to be ready for it when no one's thought to mention this?"

"Armand does things his own way, and when you travel with him, you just kinda…get used to it, I guess." Ramona shrugged.

Ryan felt an anger build within him. His people were being put into a dangerous situation. That was nothing new. But this time they were being put in a dangerous place that they couldn't possibly have known was dangerous. As with the attack from the pack, Ryan felt that his people were being forced to do their job with blasters on safety and one arm tied behind.

"Okay, so I'm not going to blame any of you for this, although I'd like to rip LaGuerre's throat out right now. Listen, and listen good—if we're going to be of any use, we need to know anything that you do. And soon. Just tell me and Doc, and we can fill the others in as and when."

Both Ramona and Raven were silent for a moment. Then Raven spoke up hesitantly. "I dunno. Armand wouldn't like it if he knew we'd told you that he stole someone else's load, and hadn't dealt directly with Jenningsville."

"He doesn't have to know. We'll talk to our people without drawing attention to it. Hell, we wouldn't want to do that, anyway, especially as we won't be able to talk privately until we're in the middle of the pesthole."

"I still dunno," Raven mumbled. "Ramona…"

"I know what you're saying, hon," the driver replied without looking around, "but you gotta figure Ryan's right on this. Listen, sweetie," she said in a slightly different tone, signaling that she was now addressing Ryan, "all we know about Jenningsville is what we've been told ourselves. The place is a pesthole, all right, but one that has jack and shit to trade. They ain't got food or clothes, or anything that can actually keep people alive. And around these parts there ain't much they can do about that. But they have got something that's as good if they can get some crazy trader to cross this desert shit they live in.

"They got weapons—blasters, plas ex, grens, you name it, honey. Armand heard all about it from one of his suppliers, who used to sell to the convoy we blasted. We took 'em, but that's how we lost so many of ours. It was a close-run thing, babes, and I'm sure as shit glad I'm still here, now.

"Anyways, they got this shit, and they seem to have been living off it since skydark. So they pay, and they pay well 'cause they have to. And that's what he wants. The pay-off. And Armand'll do anything for a big pay-off."

Doc and Ryan exchanged a look that spoke volumes. A big pay-off was one thing, but this was more than just that. Both men—along with their traveling companions— knew that a consistent supply of one kind of trade, particularly of this type, could only mean one thing. The people of Jenningsville had long ago found a redoubt or base of some kind in the vicinity, and they had been using this to buy in the goods they so badly needed to survive.

Of necessity, they had kept tight-lipped about the source of their supply, but Ryan knew from his experience with Trader that a stockpile like this, while it could not last indefinitely, could make you rich beyond your dreams. This community needed it to survive and so had been careful. LaGuerre was one greedy man, and so would use it for indulgence.

And make no mistake. Both men knew that LaGuerre had but one aim in mind. Even if his crew had not tumbled to it; even if those who had gone before had not, or had tried and failed; it made no difference.

LaGuerre was after more than a pay-off and a bonus. He was after a dream that could make him one of the richest men in these rad-ravaged lands.

And he was taking Ryan, Doc and the others along for the ride.

WHILE J.B. SUSPECTED LaGuerre for different reasons to those known to Ryan and Doc, their companions were oblivious to that. In their own wag spaces, with no need to use the comm system and no way in which they could have communicated openly if there had been such a chance, Jak, Mildred and Krysty were almost hermetically sealed from the suspicions of their compatriots.

Jak rode with Jed and Raf. Even though Cody moving on to drive the armored wag should have created more space, it felt in many ways as though there was less air within the confines of the second wag. Raf was driving, his shift in the seat meaning that the dreadlocked warrior's attention was focused wholly on the road and the wag directly in front of him. Raf was one hell of a fighter, but had never felt confident behind a wheel. Of course, he could never let this sign of weakness show through, so he sat tight-lipped, his whole being concentrated on the road in front of him, not daring to speak.

Which was a pity, as he respected Jak as a fighter after witnessing what had happened in the shanty ville. He would have been prepared to be open and friendly. This was a relative term, of course, as neither the dreadlocked warrior nor Jak Lauren could be said to be loquacious. But at least the atmosphere in the rear of the wag would have risen a couple of degrees from the ambivalent frost that settled over it.

Jed was on the bunk, Jak seated opposite. The large, shaved-headed and scarred warrior had surprisingly small eyes for such a huge man. They seemed to be further obscured in folds of fat as they bore into Jak with something that could only be called hostility. It couldn't be suspicion,

as the fat man had seen Jak fight side by side with his fellow convoy members. But why the hostility?

Jak ignored it as much as he could. Long hours spent
in wait while hunting prey both human and animal had
taught him a thing or two about being able to filter anything
around him that may be a distraction. But he was too close
to the man on the bunk, seated as he was just a few feet
away. Jak didn't care why the man seemed to dislike him.
He only knew that it was stirring an equal resentment
within him that could soon spill over into violence. The
sooner they reached this pesthole ville, the better.

Jak could not know that Jed hated muties with a ven-
geance, as one of them had taken his balls in a knife fight
some years before. This was why he never spoke. His voice
was high and squeaky, ill-befitting such a large, scarred
man. It was also the reason for his beginning to run to fat,
as no matter how much he tried to work off the weight, the
hormone imbalance always gained the upper hand.

Jed knew that both Cody and Raf had told him that Jak
was not a mutie. He trusted them…usually. But this time
the feelings that boiled within him were threatening to
overrule his respect for their opinions. He, too, was on the
edge of violence.

Jenningsville couldn't come quick enough.

MILDRED FELT PRETTY MUCH the same. The attitude of
LaGuerre sickened her in a wearying way that made her
tired. The endless dustbowl plains that spread out in all directions from the ribbon of blacktop were monotonous

and tiring, making her eyes droop, her vision spin. And she was worried about J.B. It was nagging at her all the while. His judgment was usually so sound, something she could place an absolute trust in. Yet this time she felt that it was flawed, that there was something that he was missing. It wasn't anything that she could articulate. Was it just that she was jealous of the way in which he and the young woman had suddenly gone from wary allies to the seemingly best of friends?

No, surely not. Such petty jealousies were the stuff of her youth. That kind of emotion should have been knocked out of her, both by circumstance and common sense, a long time ago.

She wished she could talk to him about it. That she could talk to Krysty, Doc, maybe even Ryan or Jak. The last was not the most articulate of men, but if ever there was someone who understood instinct...

Instead, she was stuck in the cab of the refrigerated wag with Reese. The big woman was not so hostile, or even plain unfriendly, as she had been at the beginning of the journey. But conversation was not her strength. Whatever thoughts went through her head as the landscape unrolled with an even monotony stayed firmly within her skull. In truth, Mildred couldn't remember her uttering a word since the convoy had once more taken to the road.

So she was left with her own thoughts, chasing their tails and going nowhere but circles, as unchanging as the plains beyond the blacktop. The sheer repetition was slowly strangling her, as was the silence.

KRYSTY WAS FEELING much the same as Mildred, but for a reason almost certainly the opposite. The Titian-haired woman would have welcomed the chance to be lost in her own thoughts, instead of having them drowned out by the nonstop barrage of sound that was Ray—the voice, the words, and the old music that wheezed from the speakers of the tape machine he used to play those remnants of the past that he had salvaged over the years.

There was one song that played, the sound snaking in and out of his monologue so that it seemed that his words and the sound of the music blended seamlessly into one, and its lyrics seemed to sum up what Krysty wished for.

Hush…hush…and she certainly heard him call her name as she felt herself zone out and drift away from what he was saying.

"I was listening," she said in a distracted tone.

"Hell, Krysty, I know you're not listening to me half the time, and don't think that I care too much about that. I keep on like this, even when there isn't anyone in the cab with me, but I'm betting I've said that to you before now since we've been on this road together. I do it half the time just to keep myself from falling asleep when we're out on roads like this. Hell, it'd be easy enough to do that and run this rig right off the road, and I don't think that Armand would be too happy about that if I did. But I've got something important to tell you, and I think you should listen."

"I will," Krysty said, struggling to focus her attention, realizing how the music was hypnotizing her. An insistent rhythm now, with a wailing vocalist yelling about going home before a stream of sound, a ripple of electric notes that sounded like a waterfall of molten electricity, tumbled over the rhythm at a manic pace.

"I will if you turn that down," she said loudly. "I can't hear myself think above it."

Ray chuckled as he hit the volume. "Guess I forget that I'm getting old, and my ears are even older and deafer. Is that okay?" He waited for her nod before continuing. "By my reckoning, we're not far from Jenningsville now, and I'll be honest with you, I'm not sure what to expect by way of a welcome."

Krysty was puzzled, and her expression had to have told him that.

"See, it's not as simple as you might think," he said slowly. "We're delivering this load, but they're actually expecting someone else to deliver it. We've never been there before, and a strange convoy paying off a load that they were expecting from someone else… Well, all I'm saying is that if I was them, I wouldn't be holding my arms wide in welcome unless I had a blaster at the end of each fist, you know what I'm saying?"

Krysty felt as if someone had punched her back into consciousness. Her hair tingled at the scalp; she could feel it move disturbingly.

"You hijacked this load?" she asked slowly. "You took it from another convoy, and you expect the ville to just pay up?"

"Hell, I don't," Ray said in surprise. "Why d'you think I'm telling you this, now? Armand does this from time to time, and each time I think it's gonna land us in the shit. But where am I gonna go at my age and with my crazy ways? So I just keep quiet—kinda—and hope for the best. But I'm betting that this time he ain't told your people about it. 'Cause if he had, then One-eye would have briefed the lot of you. And he hasn't, right? So he doesn't know. None of you do. And if you're supposed to be running sec for us, that's the kind of thing you should know. Am I right?"

Krysty felt more alert, more awake than she had all day. Her mouth was dry. There was no way that Ryan knew of this, or else he would have said. Chances were, none except her knew—unless, maybe, others were as loose-lipped and as concerned as Ray. But even then, how could they talk across the comm system without LaGuerre knowing that his secret was out?

They were going into a situation where they were facing a firefight with one hand tied behind their backs, and their blasters empty. It would have given her some scant consolation if she had known these thoughts had been echoed exactly. But not enough. If it blew up on them, they would have to hit the ground running and trust to the reactions of one another. Not an ideal situation on territory they'd had no chance to recce.

"Did I do the right thing in telling you?" Ray asked, a look of concern on his face. "I just thought you should know. Armand wouldn't like it, but it ain't his ass on the line. Well, not directly. And you've been good, putting up with me on this run. I wouldn't want you to face buying the farm without some kind of warning."

Krysty forced a smile, even though she didn't feel it. The old man had a secure berth here, and had put himself at a risk he usually avoided because of a sense of fairness that was a rarity. She couldn't let him see how concerned she really was.

"It's okay," she answered him. "Being warned was the

right thing. Mebbe you won't be the only one to think we should know."

Ray pondered that for a moment. "You may be right. Ramona and Raven have as much trouble keeping their mouths shut, no matter what they say about me. So One-eye and Doc might know. Mildred won't, 'cause Reese says nothing. The other two? I doubt it. But don't go by my word," he added hurriedly.

"I won't. At least one of us is ready, though. That's something," she said, noting the look of relief that spread across Ray's face. She wished she could feel the same.

Chapter Seventeen

Jenningsville came upon them just as day broke. The sun was a lazy red ball, rising on the distant horizon and making the dark brown dust of the plains look like puddles of congealed blood. An omen, perhaps...

J.B., in the armored wag at the head of the convoy was surprised by the way in which the ville broke on them, but not because it looked any different to his expectations. Indeed, the low-level shanties and cinder-block buildings that were spread in a desultory fashion across an expanse of the plains just to one side of the ruined blacktop reminded him of nothing so much as the ville of Guthrie, where Trader had found him.

No, the thing that caused the Armorer to pause and take stock was that, despite the fact that he had been looking for signs across the wastes, there was no indication of the redoubt from where the ville gained its wealth and trading power. If it was some distance, and if LaGuerre's plan was to plunder it while the trade was in the process of completion, then it was not going to be as simple as the trader would wish.

But that was a problem for later. At the moment, J.B. was torn between addressing the issue in front of him, and equally addressing the thoughts that had been bubbling under the surface of his consciousness for some time, and were now breaking for air.

There was a fearful symmetry in his ending up near the spot where Trader had found him, with a woman who claimed to be linked to his past in a way that he could not yet fathom. If he had been a doomie, he was sure he would have had one hell of a darkness descend on him. As it was, he was apprehensive about how these strands of the past would tie together. Would they form a rope to hang him?

The two issues were in balance in his head, until that balance was tipped by the rattle of blasterfire against the armor of the wag.

"Incoming," Cody said impassively, as if the matter needed emphasis.

J.B. went to the port. At the moment it was just a hail of small-caliber handblaster and rifle fire. It was ricocheting from the armor plating of the wag as harmlessly as if it had been stones flung by children. But he was under no illusion. This was just an initial volley to mark the convoy, to see what kind of armor it had, and to determine if the aggressors needed to use a larger caliber of weapon.

It wouldn't take them long to figure that out. Meantime, the convoy had to find some way of alerting the Jenningsville sec that they were friendly. Obviously, they knew the convoy they were expecting, but this wasn't it…

"Return fire?" Cody asked. It was notable that he was asking the questions, and not LaGuerre, who was watching the Armorer with no expression discernible behind his aviator shades.

"No," J.B. replied firmly. "We don't want to start a firefight with them before they've handed over their tally. We're not who they're expecting, but was there a signal that the other convoy had?"

LaGuerre laughed. "You worked that one out, eh? Didn't take you too long, sport, did it? Sure, we haven't got the same wags they had, although the refrigerated wags are theirs. So they've recognized this one is wrong. But the convoy we took this shit from had a standard."

"A what?" J.B. said, already irked by the trader's admission.

"He means they had a flag that they used on their lead wag," Eula explained.

"You got it?" J.B. snapped.

"I don't believe in trophies—no jack in 'em," LaGuerre said dismissively.

"I kept it," Eula murmured, rummaging at the back of one of the metal cabinets in which she stored armament. "I don't believe in trophies, either, but I don't believe in not covering your own back," she added with disdain, glaring at LaGuerre.

"Time to get it flying," J.B. said. "It's what they'll be expecting, what they know." He drew his mini-Uzi, switching to single shot, and leveled it at LaGuerre. If the trader was surprised, he managed to conceal it. J.B. continued. "And I'll tell you for what... If anyone's gonna put their ass in a sling for this, it ain't gonna be me, Eula or Cody. This is your problem. You sort it."

Without a word, LaGuerre rose from his seat and held out his hand to Eula. The woman placed the flag in his palm. He took off the shades, and J.B. could see that amusement twinkled in his eyes.

"Guess you're right enough," LaGuerre said. "Don't let any of you fuckers say I didn't do my bit."

The volleys of fire on the outside of the wag had ceased, but to all of them it was merely a respite before heavier fire was brought into play. If LaGuerre was quick, he might escape real danger.

There was only one way he could make the standard seen while the wag was in motion. Opening the ob port, the seal sucking and squealing as air broke the vacuum that had been so long in place, and grasping the standard firmly, the trader squeezed himself into the gap, wriggling his torso into the port with one arm held in front of him.

He grasped one end firmly, and let the wind whipped up by their momentum unfurl the standard into the breeze. It was a black flag, with a bloodred circled *A* in the center, distorted as the material was whipped by the currents of air around it.

He was risking his life. An open target, he could either have been picked off by a sniper, chilled by a stray shot, or even have overbalanced and plunged to his doom on the blacktop.

The standard had to have been recognized. As it fluttered in the backdraft, a few stray shots of a heavier caliber—perhaps even mortars—overshot the convoy on each side, falling on either side of the blacktop. These ceased, and there was no further fire as the convoy approached the edge of the ville.

Eula and J.B. helped haul the trader back into the wag.

"Which side of the road do we go?" Cody asked.

"How the fuck should I know?" LaGuerre coughed, the

dust from the road still spewing from his lungs and nose with each mucus-ridden hack.

"Take the left," J.B. told Cody, looking out of the ob port he had just heaved closed. It seemed to him that the shacks on that side were larger. If this ville was anything like Guthrie—and he was sure as hell that it was—then the larger shanties indicated the ville's leader, if baron was too grand a title for such a place.

As Cody guided their vehicle in that direction, J.B. picked up the comm mic and relayed their intent along the length of the convoy. If anyone had anything to say, their chance was lost as the leading wag hit the center of the settlement and found itself surrounded by men and women holding heavy-duty blasters.

"They're all over us like a gaudy's rash," Eula said mildly, staring out the back of the wag at those in their wake, all of which were now surrounded by men and women of the ville. They had clustered around too close to be easily fired on.

"So who's gonna explain to them why we're not who they're expecting?" Cody asked. "Mean to say, someone's got to do it."

J.B. looked at LaGuerre. "Should be you," he said, "but somehow I don't trust you to do the job properly. Ah, dark night, I guess it's shit or bust. Come with me, asshole."

The Armorer grabbed LaGuerre and opened the side door of the wag, thrusting the trader out first.

The people of the ville had not been expecting such an action, and in surprise they parted to let the trader sprawl at their feet. As the shock passed, and LaGuerre dragged himself upright, they moved forward as one. J.B. fired a burst from the mini-Uzi into the air.

"What's the problem here?" he yelled. "You don't want the trade you ordered?"

A fat, scabby-faced man with a gray-flecked auburn beard stepped up.

"Moe. Baron here. Dunno who the fuck you are, but you ain't Homer, and that's who we made agreement with."

"Homer ain't here. We are. You want we should take this shit back with us?" J.B. snapped.

"We ain't gonna let you do that," Moe said slowly. "Where's Homer?"

"I dunno." J.B. spit. "I don't care, either. This guy—" he gestured to LaGuerre "—is the trader here. I'm just one of his hired hands. Way I hear it, he did a deal with Homer, jack changed hands and he took over the run. 'S'all I know. So you pay the man, you get the goods, we're all happy."

"Mebbe," Moe said, eyeing J.B. carefully. "See, we like Homer. We deal with him a lot. You, we don't know. What's to stop us, say, chilling you ratfuck sons of bitches and just taking the goods?"

J.B. smiled, long and slow. "You could try that, Moe, but it wouldn't get you far. Soon as your people start shooting, the man in the wag there—" indicating Cody at the front "—hits the switch, and all the wags go up like it's skydark all over again. See, you don't trust us, but there's no reason why we should trust you. You try something stupe, and we blow the whole lot to fuck. Hell, we get chilled either way, but at least it'd be quick. And we'd take some of you with us for trying."

There was a moment's silence while J.B.'s eyes met with Moe's, both men trying to understand each other, size each other up and scope each other out. Except that Moe was for real, and J.B. was bluffing.

"You know Guthrie?" J.B. said softly.

Moe nodded.

"I was there years back," J.B. said. "Lived there for a while. Name is Dix. Mebbe—"

"Shit, yeah," Moe said, his attitude changing suddenly. "You were the wonder boy with blasters. That guy Trader took you with him. He was a good trader, man, never cheated you for shit so that he could come back and do more business. Yeah, I know you… The glasses… Shit, J. B. Dix. Why didn't you say who you were from the git-go?"

Moe's change of mood spread through the whole crowd, which now began to back off.

"I didn't know you'd wired the wags to explode," LaGuerre whispered in J.B.'s ear. "When the hell did you do that, man?"

"Don't be a stupe," J.B. murmured back. "When would I have had the time? Moe didn't know that, though."

LaGuerre said nothing, though the sly grin that spread across his face spoke volumes.

Moe cleared a space around the armored wag, where necessary beating back those who were too slow with the butt of his rifle.

"Okay, Dix, you get your wags right into the center. Bring trader boy with you, and we'll sort the payment before your people unload. That okay with you?"

J.B. grinned at LaGuerre. "Sure, that suits me just fine. C'mon, trader boy, time you earned our keep."

MOE TOOK THEM to the largest shanty in the ville. It was only a few moments from where the convoy had come to rest, and as they made their way through the crowd, J.B. cast a glance over his shoulder. He could see Mildred and Krysty still in the cabs of the refrigerated wags. Jak and Raf had emerged from the second wag, and at the rear of the convoy he could see Ryan and Doc. All four men were seemingly unarmed and at ease, but the Armorer could spot the signs that told him they were poised to spring should the need arise. His friends he could read from experience, and the dreadlocked warrior carried himself like a giant shadow to the small albino by his side. Whatever else he may be, LaGuerre knew how to choose his crew.

The crowd began to disperse a little, some of them drifting off to somewhere he didn't know. Others still milled around the convoy, while others followed in a loose line behind the ville leader and the convoy party.

Moe led them into the shanty, where a man and a woman were waiting for them.

"Well?" the woman demanded. "Who the fuck are they? Where's Homer?"

"Don't know." Moe shrugged. "These guys brought the stuff, they get the payment."

"I dunno…" she mused. She was squat and dark, with darting brown eyes that betrayed a sly intelligence as she eyed the trio accompanying Moe.

"Cool it," the second man said. He was as emaciated as Moe was fat, long and lean with clothes that hung off him.

"Lenny's right, Selma," Moe said. "This boy here is the famous J. B. Dix," he added, clapping the Armorer on the shoulder, "and if we can't trust in him…"

"Long time since I heard that name," Selma said, looking at J.B. in a different way. He felt like he was being sized up like a piece of merchandise.

"System works like this," Moe said, breaking a silence that was becoming uncomfortable. "You check the payment. Larry and Selma carry it out to the convoy, one of yours with them, while I check the goods with you. When I say okay, then we exchange."

"Sounds fair," J.B. agreed. "Don't take it the wrong when I say this, but any moves to fuck with that, and—"

"Same here," Moe said, looking J.B. squarely in the eye. Both men agreed without a word being exchanged.

Larry pulled back a tarp that had been covering boxes marked with what J.B. knew to be predark military insignia. They'd been opened and then resealed. But that meant nothing. Anyone would do that to check the contents. Question was, what did the boxes contain now?

"You know what the payment was supposed to be?" J.B. asked LaGuerre.

"Sure. You just tell me if it's working, and I'll tell you if it's inventory," the trader murmured.

For the next half hour, maybe longer, J.B. could feel the tension in the room from the Jenningsville trio as he and Eula checked the condition of the weapons and explosives that had comprised the payment. Frag and gas grens; semi-automatic and SMGs; ammo for these and for the crate of handblasters that also accompanied them.

LaGuerre had obviously memorized the payment inventory as he was able to recite the contents of each crate and mentally tick them off as Eula and J.B. checked them. There was the original fee, plus the rapid delivery bonus minus the lost day. When LaGuerre got to this, Moe seemed to be expecting an argument, and was a little surprised when the trader let it pass without comment. J.B. contained a grim smile. Hopefully, he wouldn't suspect the reason for the seemingly lax attitude shown by the trader.

When the check had been successful, Moe directed Larry and Selma to take out the payment. J.B. wondered how the pair of them could carry so much, a curiosity sated by the appearance of a small forklift wag, powered by an electric battery. The crates were already on a palette, and the powerful wag lifted them with ease.

That was significant. The wag was weather-beaten, and looked as though it had racked up a good few klicks in its time, over some rough terrain. They obviously used this to carry goods back and forth to the stockpile or redoubt that supplied their barter. That also had to be where they recharged the battery motor.

By the look of it, the stockpile wasn't near the ville. That was worth pondering. J.B. wondered if LaGuerre actually knew the location, or if he had a plan for obtaining it from one of the ville people.

All of this passed through his mind while he led LaGuerre and Moe back to the convoy, Eula watching their backs. There was no real need for such sec, but it did no harm to maintain the aura of vigilance.

LaGuerre began by taking Moe to the two low-level wags, indicating that the rear doors of each be opened, and the crates containing the clothing and other supplies be likewise, so that the vile leader could check his inventory.

Moe obviously still held some vestige of suspicion, as he checked carefully. And when it came time to climb into the refrigerated wags to check the food supplies, J.B. noted from the corner of his eye that some of the ville people moved surreptitiously forward. Not in a manner that would raise the hackles of the convoy, but enough to cover their leader as he made his check.

Moe took Reese's wag first, and finished his task quickly as the taciturn driver opened the rear of the wag and accompanied him inside. Ray's wag took a little longer, as the old man couldn't help but give the ville leader a running commentary on the merchandise and how hard it had been to get it to this point. When Moe emerged, he gave J.B. a quick look that spoke volumes, and almost made the Armorer lose his composure.

The fat man jumped down from the refrigerated wag, stumbling a little as he landed. He held up his hands and announced in a loud voice, "It's as it should be, guys. Larry, give these people their due. Rest of you, let's get this unloaded before it spoils." He turned to LaGuerre. "Is that okay with you?"

His tone suggested that he would brook no argument. But then again, he wouldn't get one from a satisfied LaGuerre.

"Sure, man...do it," the trader replied laconically.

THE TRADE WAS EASIER than J.B. could have hoped. The people of Jenningsville were well-versed in dealing with convoys, and they unloaded crates and boxes of chilled and preserved foodstuffs from the refrigerated wags using battered electric wags like the forklift. J.B. noted that, and figured that the battering of the vehicles had to be from constant use rather than actual distance, unless the people had moved the battery chargers from the redoubt to the ville. He wondered if he'd have a chance to find out.

While this was done, others from the ville loaded the payment into one of the refrigerated wags, ensuring first that Reese—whose wag they had picked—had turned off the refrigeration. Moe stood with LaGuerre to make sure the trader approved the change-over, and also the sealing of the wag doors.

"Cool," Moe said without a hint of irony. "That's done. Now let's tie some shit on. Every time we get a convoy through it could be the last for all we know, so it's worth getting crazy over."

HE WASN'T FAR WRONG. The exchange had taken most of the day, and the air was cooling with the dusk as the ville began to go crazy. Music issued from both sides of the blacktop as musicians started to play. Brew and jolt also started to be passed around, and that affected the musicians, whose already rough melodies became more and more random, their timing affected by the drugs or drink they had imbibed. Some slowed down and others speeded up, the music becoming a blur of sound in which it was impossible to discern a rhythm. But that was okay, as those few who danced did so to a rhythm in their own heads.

J.B. lost track of the others in the midst of the bacchanalia. He had managed to exchange a few brief words with Mildred, but nothing of any importance, either personal or to do with LaGuerre's mission. His task ensuring that the exchange went well had taken him away from them, and he had no idea if they had been able to even speak to one another. The only thing he knew was that wherever he turned, Eula was there.

The brew and jolt took effect on everyone in the ville. The dwellers also smoked a weed they grew especially, from seeds and stems they had discovered in the redoubt. A cloud of it now hung over the ville, drifting across the blacktop and into the night. It didn't exactly help anyone keep their focus.

Ryan and Doc had managed to reach Mildred and Krysty, and told them of their suspicions. But Jak had so far eluded them.

The one-eyed man, even with his razor instincts, was startled when LaGuerre seemed to appear at his side as if from nowhere.

"Hey, Ryan man, listen. This might not be the best time to ask, but I tell you, man, I got nothing but respect for your people. I know I bitched, man, but c'mon—you guys got us here, and the trade wouldn't have gone so well if not for your man J.B. I got something to put to you—"

"You want us to find their stockpile and raid it?" Ryan hissed in his ear. "Are you fucking crazy? They outnumber us, and even if you know where it is, then—"

He stopped suddenly, realizing from the startled look on the trader's face that he had misjudged LaGuerre. He didn't have the balls and imagination.

"Man, you're the crazy one," LaGuerre whispered, almost too low for Ryan to hear. "I was just gonna ask you to join us permanently."

No, he didn't have the guts. But Ryan realized who did—the one responsible for their being in Jenningsville in the first place…

"J.B., IT'S TIME," Eula whispered in his ear.

The Armorer shrugged off the emaciated gaudy who had entwined herself around him despite his best efforts, and dropped the mug of brew. He felt a little light-headed, and realized that it had been stronger than he had suspected. No matter. He could still function okay.

"I haven't been able to talk to the others yet—" he began.

Eula cut him short. "Doesn't matter. Armand will see to that. Right now, we need to get out there and scout it. They may have sec out there. But probably not. Not tonight."

J.B. nodded. "How we getting there?"

"I've got a wag. This way," she said, pulling at his arm.

J.B. followed her, allowing her to lead. He didn't see Jak.

Something had been worrying the albino youth all day. He had noticed how, since the Armorer had checked the payment, the girl had kept him apart from the others. When J.B. had the chance to speak to Mildred, it was Eula who had contrived to separate them. Jak's instincts were working overtime, and they told him nothing but bad.

Looking around, there was no way that he could find any of the others in this crowd. Jak opted to trail them himself.

Eula took J.B. to an old Jeep at the far edge of the ville. Everyone was clustered in the ville center, so it was easy for them to slip away unnoticed. Equally easy for Jak to take a motorbike from the same place—some kind of mechanic's shed—and follow.

Jak kept them in sight, but stayed back so that the sound of his bike didn't cut across their own engine noise.

About two miles out, the Jeep slowed. So did Jak. He cut the engine, let the machine drop softly to the dirt and began to move forward on foot.

J.B. and Eula got out of the Jeep. Jak could see that the Armorer was unsteady.

What the hell were they doing out here? There was nothing at all to bring them here. Not that he could see.

"THIS—THIS ISN'T RIGHT," J.B. said, trying to clear the muzzy feeling in his head. "No stockpile I've ever seen has been in territory like this. No place to—"

"Shut the fuck up," Eula snapped. "You really believed that crap? You believed that shit about LaGuerre? Like he has the intelligence or guts to do that."

Before a puzzled and senses-dulled J.B. had a chance to react, she had drawn on him. Why? And why had her tone changed so much?

"I thought for a while you were smart. A worthy opponent. That would have somehow justified the shit." Her tone was harsh, grating, as though emotion strangled the words in her chest. She sighed heavily as she caught J.B.'s bemused expression. There was no way he was going to try to draw on a markswoman with a .44 in her fist, even though the heavy blaster looked too heavy. And still he didn't get it.

"John Barrymore Dix," she said heavily. "You remember Laurel. You remember Luke. You remember Hollowstar. But you don't remember me, do you? No," she continued, not giving him the chance to answer, "and you haven't put it together yet, have you? I haven't brought you out here to recce a stockpile. There are no plans. And I don't give a fuck about the jack or the weapons. It's you I wanted."

"Why?" It was feeble, but it was all he could manage.

"Because it's time for the truth. You want to know about that? You want to know the truth about my mother?"

Even through his fogged state of mind, J.B. realized that all the strands were beginning to make sense, to be finally pulled together: Hollowstar, Guthrie, the girl… All of it formed a pattern with which his mind finally snapped into wakefulness. Too late to be of any good, as she had the blaster on him.

"Your mother… Laurel was your mother," he said slowly. "Then your father was—"

She laughed bitterly, cutting him off. "Yeah, Luke. And you chilled him as surely as you chilled her."

"Chilled…then what—"

"Happened? You'll find out. I've waited too long for this not to savor it."

J.B. watched her closely. Her trigger finger was taut. For now, there was nothing he could do except listen to her story.

Chapter Eighteen

"You didn't know I was around, did you? Didn't know that the woman you were bedding had a daughter that she left at home while she went out to meet you. Yeah, well, mebbe I shouldn't blame her so much for that. Luke was hardly the attentive father, either. Stupe, really, as if he'd taken the chance and tried to get to know me when I was little he would have known that I was like him. Always have been. I used to love going into the workshop and watch him work. Learned a lot, too, though he didn't know that as he never bothered to ask.

"See, Hollowstar was a real old predark community in some ways. Always had been. Built on the idea that women do the child-rearing and the men do the work. Even the gaudies weren't spoken of, like they were committing the ultimate wrong in earning their own living. Not that it stopped the men sneaking off to where their houses were and fucking themselves stupe. See, people are like that, aren't they, John Barrymore—liars and hypocrites.

"I don't blame my father for being like he was. Luke had no reason to figure that I'd be any good at what he did, let alone even interested. It was my mother who was supposed to be bringing me up. But she wasn't, was she? She was off dropping her drawers to anyone she liked the look of who was passing through. I suppose I was about five when you came through. And you weren't the first I knew of.

"That's got you, hasn't it? The look on your face. Though I don't know whether or not that's because you've just realized that the idiot LaGuerre has no plan, and if there is a redoubt I don't care about it. 'S'right, John Barrymore, I just wanted you to myself so I could finish off something that's been bugging the shit out of me for years.

"See, I'd like to think that you've got that look on your face because you've realized that all the shit she fed you about being in love with you was just that—shit. She didn't mean it. As far as I know, she said it to every asshole she blew. Trouble was, most of them were there and gone before anyone except me had a chance to realize what was going on. And, if I'm going to be honest with you—and why not, as you're never going to tell anyone—I didn't realize it at the time. It was only later, when it all went to crap, that I realized. Not that I could have done anything.

"See, I blame you totally, Dix. But not really, 'cause it was your dick and her pussy that chilled her and my father. But the irony is that there were things at work that were totally beyond your control. I only know about them because of what happened after. You blundered into something that was way more than a stupe like you could handle. You're like Luke. If it's not metal, carbon fiber or explosive, you can't handle it. You should keep your paws off anything else. But you can't, can you? People like you never can.

"Where was I? Shit, you're pissing me off so much I can't even think straight. And don't look at me like that.

I'm not so angry that I won't just chill you without thinking about it, if you so much as move. I want you to know
why, but not so much that I'll let you get the upper hand
again.

"See, that's the problem, isn't it? You've had the upper
hand in my life since I was five, and you didn't even
know I existed. Laurel was never really interested in
me. All my memories are of her looking the other way
when I did something. Walked, talked, drew pictures,
asked her shit. Always looking the other way, never
noticing me. At least Luke acknowledged I was there.
Not much, but that was because he was obsessed by his
work, and he was a man. It was Laurel's job, and she was
crap at it.

"Now you know that there was one thing she wasn't crap
at, and that's the thing. Luke was her type, but once she had
him, he didn't pay her the attention she wanted. So she went
out and attracted the convoy boys. They were passing through
and then they were gone. No chance of him finding out. No
chance of them hanging around to cause problems for her.

"Until you. That was when it all got a bit difficult. You
were too like Luke, and that's what fucked it up for everyone. For a start, that dickwad Emmerton had some crazy
idea of buying you off Trader and matching you with Luke.
That would have given him the best ordnance team across
the whole land. People would have traveled to Hollowstar.
There's serious jack in something like that. And Emmerton
did love his jack. Among other things.

"But Trader wouldn't have it. So Emmerton got convinced Trader wanted to steal Luke away, which was in-
credibly stupe if you knew my father. He was Hollowstar

all the way. He couldn't have lived anywhere else. Besides, it would have meant leaving my mother behind.

"She may have been a sick, scheming little slut, but he really did love her. Y'know, love is something that should have been left behind with the nukecaust. I don't know much about what went on back then, but I'll tell you what—it must have been love that caused the big war to happen. What people do for it, even when there are so many more important things to think about.

"Not that I saw much of it. Laurel didn't give a shit. If anything, I got in the way. She had to find ways of getting me looked after when she was out fucking, so that Luke wouldn't find out. I don't know how she managed that, but she did. And Luke was none the wiser. Poor bastard. I feel sorry for my father. Not for her, the slut. But him… He was an innocent in this, just as I was. So most of what happened before you arrived passed over his head without him noticing. Probably because that head was buried in some blaster.

"But you were different. Luke was your friend—at least, that's how he thought of it. I dunno what you thought, and it doesn't much matter. Except it maybe makes you more of a scumsucker if you thought you were friends and you still did that to him.

"You must have known somewhere along the line, though. And you didn't stop. Coldheart bastard. Anyways, none of that is what's really important. Point is that it went on for too long. Emmerton and Trader playing games with each other, Trader not being allowed to leave. You know all that. Mebbe you really didn't know why, but I'd bet you did. Luke noticed the way you were acting with him changed. He noticed my mother disappearing, too. And he followed, and he watched.

"Then you were gone. Laurel was like she usually was…kind of. I think that you being like my father was why she wanted you, and I really think that something inside that black, selfish heart of hers was touched. She wasn't the same after that, and Luke knew it.

"It's only looking back that it really makes sense now. I couldn't have told you this at the time, although I sensed it. But I tell you what, John Barrymore Dix, you ripped the heart out of my father. His work suffered. This was a man who only lived for his work, and that no longer mattered to him. At first, it was only a few mistakes. Next convoy through, a few months later, and there were some blasters that misfired. Some guy lost a hand. Cost Emmerton a lot of jack. The fat bastard hated that. Had those scumbags Laker and Palmer beat Luke around a little—'not the hands,' the fat fuck said as he directed it—and try to make him see sense.

"But when has sense had anything to do with it? Luke wasn't the man he used to be. He realized that Laurel didn't really give a fuck about him anymore. Mebbe he was wrong. Mebbe she would have got you out her system in time. But everything was against them.

"Luke started to drink brew. Too much. Actually, any would have been too much, as he never was a drinker. That's partly how Laurel got away with it, y'know. She went to bars, but he never did. And anyone seeing her there wasn't likely to say anything to Luke and piss him off when they relied on him to keep their ordnance in working order. So he was drinking, and the mistakes were getting more frequent, and worse. Locals, and those who came from the east and across the west to see the man they called the Ordnance Baron.

"Ha—not much of one, now... See, Emmerton didn't want word of Luke's slackness to spread. That really would have chilled trade, and you've got to remember how much Hollowstar relied on Luke by this time. He was key to Emmerton expanding the ville. Mebbe more importantly, the jack he brought in enabled the fat bastard to indulge his sick little fantasies.

"So Emmerton got sick of paying out for Luke's mistakes. He didn't know why my father's work had gone to shit, but he was sure as hell going to find out. Laker and Palmer had ways of being real persuasive, and it didn't take much digging for them to come up with what Laurel was like, and the fact that most people who knew were sure that Luke had no idea. Only about you, John Barrymore Dickhead.

"So Emmerton, being the fat, sick fuck that he is, came up with an idea to get the truth out of Laurel and prove to Luke that she wasn't worth it. He figured that if Luke could see her for what she was, then he'd realize she wasn't worth the pain, and that he could get back to being the Ordnance Baron. Which, I guess, tells you everything about how much of a triple stupe Emmerton was about people, and how much he understood about real emotion. Shit, if you'd ever met him, you'd know what I meant, Dix.

"Sick bastard had her tortured while Luke was made to watch. Started with just a beating from Laker and Palmer. Then they pulled her fingernails. Used hot irons. Hooked her up to a generator...

"I can see you're wondering why I know all this.

Simple—Emmerton thought it would help if I was there to see it, too. Actually, knowing him, it wasn't because he thought it would help, but more because he got off on me watching it.

"Anyway, none of that really matters as such. The only thing I need to tell you about that is that she didn't crack. Not once. Turns out the slut had a heart after all. Who would have thought it. She admitted to bedding you, but none of the others. And she wouldn't say that she loved you. Only that she'd made a mistake.

"Now, Emmerton thought that would help Luke, but it didn't. People are funny, Dix, and you can't tell what's going on inside them. Mebbe you know that by now. Shit, there was no way that Emmerton could know that Luke would be more hurt by this than by anything.

"By now, Emmerton was pissed beyond anything you could think of. He wanted you chilled, but you were beyond reach by then. And Trader was smart enough to never pass our way again. Just as well for you, although it always gets you in the end. Anyway, Emmerton wanted to make a point, if only to himself. Big on revenge, the fat boy...

"As an example, though fuck knows of what, he had my mother burned at the stake in the center of the ville. To the last, he was taunting her to tell the truth. Well, she did... Not that it did anyone any good.

"She said that she loved you, and that she had wanted to leave Luke, leave Hollowstar, leave me... That was really good to hear, as I'm sure you can imagine. But then you already knew that she wanted that, didn't you, Dix? She must have talked about it to you before Trader took you away. Hell, for all I know it may even have been your idea.

"Anyways, Luke didn't exactly take it too well. Shit, that's an understatement and a half. I really don't know what Emmerton thought it would achieve to do this, but if it gave him his jollies it shot him in the balls in other ways. If Luke's drinking had made his work shit before, then it really went to crap after that.

"If you didn't really know my father, you wouldn't have thought that anything except ordnance ever meant that much to him. Even I didn't realize it. I guess that's because I didn't mean that much to him. Not compared to my mother. I think she was all that he ever really cared about, y'know. Apart from blasters, of course.

"But the drink didn't blot it out anymore. He needed something else to take the edge off that pain. And there ain't nothing in the whole of these lands that can take away the pain like a hit of jolt, right? Except that it hurt so bad that a hit just wasn't enough. Not one, anyways… It wasn't long before the man was nothing more than the worst kind of jolt-head. His work—when he could be bothered to do it—was nothing more than shit. If Emmerton had thought that he was making mistakes before…

"In the end, the wise and noble bastard baron got sick of paying out for Luke's mistakes, and he'd become a pain in the ass in more ways than one. So Emmerton decided to make an example of him to other residents of Hollowstar, just in case they started slacking, as well. I kinda think that a lot of it was because he was pissed again that he couldn't get at you. You were even longer gone, and some poor bastard had to pay.

"So that was my dad, then…a public execution in the town square, chained up and flayed until he bought the farm by Laker and Palmer.

"But the thing is, it didn't end there, Dix. Not at all. That might have been okay. But I was still too young to fend for myself, and Emmerton wanted more revenge. And he likes young girls.

"I became his slave. One of them. And there were a lot. All of them girls. All of them under fifteen. Most of us weren't just doing the washing and cleaning, Dix… although we did that, too. Mostly it was what you'd call personal services. And when I got old enough, I rendered personal services, too. To that greasy bastard, and to his ratfuck sec men, too.

"I learned well about blasters at that young age from watching my father. And just mebbe I got something from his parentage, too. 'Cause I made myself some simple weapons and bided my time. One day, I knew I'd be able to catch either Laker or Palmer off guard. And when I did…

"Shit, it wasn't difficult when you knew their ways. Simple, stupe bastards. Like all men. Chilling them was good, but not satisfactory. Chilling Emmerton was better. Feeling the blade across his greasy, fat throat… Yeah, that felt good.

"But it wasn't enough. I wanted the man who was responsible for my situation, and for the events that had led me to that place. I wanted you. For Luke, who only loved his work and my mother.

"And you chilled him. As sure as you pulled the trigger, lit the fire, wielded the whip. You chilled him. You chilled my mother, and you made me a slave…."

Chapter Nineteen

J.B. listened to everything she said without uttering a word. Let her rant all she wanted. The longer she went on, the more the cold night air sobered him, the steadier he became. The longer she went on, the longer she had to hold the blaster steady on him. The blaster that looked heavy in her small hand.

The trouble was, even as the words washed over him, and he fought to gain full control of his senses, he knew that he was fighting a battle against the one thing he had no weapons against: time.

J.B. had drunk far more than was good for him, and the brew had been far stronger than he had expected. His head was still muzzy and heavy, his vision not clear. The words washed over him and made no sense beyond a series of seemingly random syllables. He had stopped listening almost from the point that the blaster had been leveled. That was all that mattered. His entire attention had been focused on that.

It was ironic that Eula had waited so long to say all this to the Armorer, and yet he heard not a word. All she was doing was buying him time.

But not, he feared, enough.

Even if he was quick enough, even if he was at his best… However focused he was, she was more so. She had waited so long for this confrontation, and she was ready to drop him at the slightest suspicion that he was ready to move. Sure, she wanted to tell him why he was in this situation, and that gave him a few extra moments of existence. But that wasn't enough, and he knew from experience of her that she was made of steel. If she had to cut short her explanation to achieve her goal, she wouldn't hesitate.

What was worse? To stand in hope, wondering at what arbitrary point her voice would stop and the roar of the blaster would be that last sound he heard? Or to try to save himself by jumping her? All that he would do was cut short the agony of expectation.

He had to try. Go out with a fight. She reached the end of her rambling speech, and he saw her finger tighten on the trigger, the extra pressure draw the blaster taut, her skin whitening in the moonlight. Could he really see her trigger finger, or was that just a trick of imagination?

No matter. It was now or never.

JAK HAD TAKEN extreme care in drawing near. After dropping the bike quietly to the blacktop at as much distance as he dared, he had proceeded on foot. It was obvious that the young woman was up to something. There was no way there was a stockpile near here. Besides, his hunting instincts were screaming at him that there was danger.

So he wasn't surprised when he saw her draw on J.B. It wasn't like the Armorer to get caught out like this. Jak could not understand how J.B. had allowed himself to be so misled, and had let his guard down. Too much brew was okay, but to then do this... It wasn't like him. But there had been something about Eula from the beginning that had led her and J.B. to cross swords.

People made mistakes. Usually, that got them chilled. But not when Jak was around. Not when a friend was in danger.

The albino youth's main problem was to approach them without calling attention to himself. Eula had her back to him. That was good. The terrain was flat, with little cover to afford him. The only good thing about that was that he would be able to make a silent approach.

If he could keep silent, she would keep her attention away from him. She was talking, and the tone of her voice as it drifted across the plain told him that she was completely focused on the Armorer.

She wouldn't be the problem. It was J.B. Normally, if he caught sight of Jak he would do nothing to betray his presence. But the albino teen knew that J.B. wasn't his normal self.

So Jak would have to be slow and use any cover he could, and just hope that J.B. didn't see him, didn't betray his position.

Jak was a hunter of infinite patience. He could wait seemingly forever. But he didn't have that luxury. He had to move as swiftly as possible.

Dropping to the earth, he moved across the ground on palms and toes, picking his way carefully between rocks and stones, moving up and down with the terrain, using the shadows of the night. As he approached, so more than just the tone of Eula's voice became known to him. He heard the whole story, and on some level understood the strange relationship between the two, and why their paths had crossed. This bubbled beneath the surface of his mind. It explained everything, but it didn't actually matter at this moment. All he could consciously focus on was remaining undetected until he could act.

It was soon obvious to him that if he could avoid alerting Eula, he had no need to worry about J.B. The Armorer wouldn't even notice he was there. Jak could see that he was trying to marshal his senses, trying to concentrate on pulling himself together to give himself a chance.

Small clouds of dust, raised from the surface by Jak's gentle forward motion, puffed up into his face, making his eyes sting, his nose smart and itch with the need to sneeze. Yet no one watching would have known this from the impassive expression on his face.

He listened to the girl as he made progress. She was coming to the end of her words, he was sure…

"You chilled him. You chilled my mother, and you made me a slave."

Fuck. He was too far away to jump her, and her words were a certain cue that she was about to pull the trigger.

Jak threw any pretence at caution. If J.B. saw him, gave the game away, that might divide her attention enough to give him some time. If J.B. didn't see him, she would never know. Not until it was too late.

Rising, Jak palmed one of his leaf-bladed knives. The sky was clear, and the moon was almost half full. The distance was more than two hundred yards, yet he could see the skin on the back of Eula's neck glistening white between the hairline where her long hair was pulled into a ponytail, and the collar of her dark shirt. It was a small target, and he would need all his skill to increase the momentum of flight. Okay, he could risk a shot with the Colt

Python, but in his current position he felt more sure with the knife.

Jak's arm was back before he was fully erect. By the time J.B. had registered the albino's sudden appearance, the knife was in the air. By the time Eula's finger tightened enough to squeeze the trigger, the knife had speared through soft tissue and muscle, avoiding jarring against the spinal column, and had pierced her neck. Artery and vein ruptured, blood welled in her throat and pumped out, flooding down into her lungs.

J.B. winced as the blaster roared in the night. But with her muscle control gone, even as the life ebbed from her, the recoil threw the blast off target, the shell spinning harmlessly into the desert night.

As the dim light of life grew less, and faded to black, Eula knew that she had failed, at the very last, in her mission.

J.B. STOOD SILENTLY as Jak approached. He didn't know what to say, and his reactions were still lagging that tenth of a second behind his normal self. That tenth that got him that close to buying the farm.

"Jak—" he said stupidly.

"Not now. Leave bitch here, cover tracks. Get back before noticed gone."

Was that possible? J.B. felt as though he had spent an eternity rooted to this spot. But Jak had a clearer grasp on things, and the Armorer knew that if the albino youth said this was possible, then it was. That simple.

While J.B. watched, Jak moved back to where he had had first made marks on the dust. Coming back toward J.B. he erased those marks, so that by the time he reached Eula's corpse, there was no sign of his movements.

Realizing what had to be done, the Armorer also began to erase all traces of his own presence, until eventually all that remained in the dust were the footsteps of the young woman, leading from the blacktop to where she lay.

Jak bent over the corpse and removed his knife, using his knee in her back for leverage, so that he wouldn't even leave a footprint on her dark shirt. He then moved backward to where J.B. stood, erasing his traces as he went.

"Bike back up road. Pick up on way," he said simply as he eased himself into the driving seat of the wag, hitting the ignition.

J.B. sat beside him without a word. The adrenaline pumping through him had cleared his head, and he knew that words were superfluous.

When they reached the bike, laid down carefully, both men climbed out of the wag, and between them heaved the machine into the back. Getting back in, Jak hit the accelerator. Tires screeched on the blacktop as they headed toward the ville at speed. Eula's corpse lay behind them, with no footprints around to tell how it got there. Chances were that it wouldn't even be discovered. Scavengers would strip it to the bones, perhaps even beyond, before more than a day or two had passed. But even if it was to be found, those who stumbled on it would scratch their heads as to how it had been left without trace. There was nothing to link it to either Jak or the Armorer.

They reached the ville without being spotted. Jak was sure of that. The important thing now was to return the bike and the wag from where they had been taken without being seen.

That was accomplished easier than either expected, as

the celebrations in the ville had caused most of the population to be supine and comatose by the time they returned. Including, thankfully, the sec force.

It was only when they had replaced the bike and the wag that J.B. said anything to Jak.

"You hear it?"

"All," Jak replied simply, shrugging.

J.B. nodded, and without a word the two men made their way back into the center of the ville. It was obvious that they should use the celebrations as cover for their departure. They only hoped they could find the others, and that they would be in a condition to travel.

Krysty was with Ryan. They had moved away from the body of the celebrations, and were deep in discussion. Jak and J.B. knew nothing of LaGuerre's offer, but it was obvious to them as they approached that something serious had occurred.

Ryan looked up as they approached.

"Good, I need to— Fireblast, what is it?"

One look at their faces, and at J.B.'s ashen pallor, told him something had happened.

"Eula's bought the farm," J.B. said. "Jak did it. He had to, or it would have been me who was chilled," he added, forestalling the obvious question.

"Need out, Ryan," Jak said hurriedly. "Only so long before shit hits. No better time," he added, looking at the drunken stupor that seemed to have fallen over the entire ville.

Ryan and Krysty understood immediately that this was not the time to wait for explanations. They could come when there was space. Right now, action was called for.

The first thing was to find Doc and Mildred. Fortunately, they were together. Doc was regaling a group of ville dwellers with a rambling story about a writer who had been snatched from the past. Mildred was trying to quiet him. Not because he was about to reveal something about his past—those even half listening were in no state to comprehend—but because he was about to tip over the edge into madness once more.

"Shit, am I glad to see you," she said as they came in sight. "The old buzzard is— What is it?" she added, her tone changing as she took in their expressions.

"We've got to get out, and quick," Ryan said in an undertone. Looking around, he could see Raf and Reese, locked together. They didn't look like they were listening to anything, but he could have been wrong, and he didn't want to take that chance.

"Why?" Mildred asked. "No, scrub that. Later will do. Plans?"

"A wag, fuel and supplies," Ryan murmured. "Enough to get us away from here and headed west. And mebbe some sabotage on the rest of the convoy, just to slow them up."

"My dear boy, I think you can trust John Barrymore and myself with the latter," Doc said, snapping as easily into coherence as he had been teetering on madness.

"Okay. Jak, you and me will deal with the wag," Ryan said.

Jak agreed. "Know where to get one without being noticed."

Ryan nodded shortly. "Mildred, Krysty—food, water and meds are down to you."

"It's done," Krysty whispered.

Their tasks allotted, the three groups of two moved off in different directions, aiming to fulfill their duties as rapidly as possible. Ryan gave everyone twenty minutes by their synchronized wrist chrons before they met up and moved out.

The ville was lit by oil and electric lamps, the latter powered by a generator that was erratic. Without a constant watch, the machine was pumping out a fluctuating current that caused the level of illumination to dip regularly. That gave the companions the kind of covering shadows that they needed to go about their tasks undetected.

The ville's wags were easy to disable. Doc's razor-sharp swordstick did sterling work, the Toledo steel piercing tires with ease. J.B. slid beneath larger vehicles, and beneath the wags of the convoy, disconnecting fuel lines and severing brake leads.

While they worked their way around, Mildred and Krysty selected supplies. Raiding the ville's stores for water, food and meds was simple under these conditions—fluctuating light, no sec and a population in a stupor. It was simple. By the time the twenty minutes had elapsed, Mildred and Krysty were loaded down. On their way back through the ville, they ran across J.B. and Doc, who took some of the burden.

It was simple for Jak and Ryan to prepare a wag that could seat six and take a stock of supplies. Fuel and spare cans came from the other wags housed in the mechanic's shed, which were then disabled.

The noise of the wag as it started, then moved out into the ville and onto the blacktop, was preternaturally loud. If not for the results of the celebrations, they would have been intercepted.

As it was, they were able to put space between themselves and Jenningsville before the sun began to rise. They traveled in silence, knowing that they were leaving behind them LaGuerre and his grand plans, a ville that accepted them as saviors, after a tremulous beginning, and the chilled ghost of a past.

No one spoke for some time. Eventually, Mildred took it upon herself to break the silence.

"So…you going to tell us about it, John?"

J.B. sighed and took a deep breath. Where to begin?

"It was all a long, long time ago…."

The Don Pendleton's
Executioner®
DANGEROUS TIDES

A wave of terror strikes the high seas....

The large cruise ship was designed for luxury and relaxation...until rogue sailors seized it. And when Mack Bolan infiltrates the vessel, he learns that it's a testing ground for a sinister chemical weapon. Up against ruthless pirates, compromised antiterrorist units and the delicate balance of international relations, the Executioner must tread lightly—and become deadlier still.

GOLD EAGLE®

Available August wherever books are sold.

GEX369

Don Pendleton's Mack Bolan®

Mission: Apocalypse

**A New Age death cult
plots its own wave of terror....**

Deep inside Mexican cartel country,
a dirty bomb is making its way north
across the U.S. border—and Mack Bolan
is closing in on the radioactive caravan,
with luck and some dubious associates as
his only allies. His orders are to find and
take out the immediate threat…but he
soon discovers the bigger, grimmer picture
in which the entire world is at risk.

*Available September
wherever books are sold.*

James Axler
Outlanders®

JANUS TRAP

Earth's last line of defense is invaded by a revitalized and reconfigured foe….

The Original Tribe, technological shamans with their own agenda of domination, challenged Cerberus once before and lost. Now their greatest assassin, Broken Ghost, has trapped the original Cerberus warriors in a matrix of unreality and altering protocols. As Broken Ghost destabilizes Earth's great defense force from within, the true warriors struggle to regain a foothold back to the only reality that offers survival….

Available August wherever books are sold.

Don Pendleton
TERROR DESCENDING

**A powerful, secret coalition unleashes hell
across the globe....**

Dedicated to a cause thirty years in the making, a powerful,
militant group has amassed a private army of weaponry,
mercenaries and a mandate of world peace—by way of mass
murder. Across the globe, military and civilian targets all
become fair game. When enough of the world is gone...they
will step into power. Unless Stony Man does what it does
best: the impossible.

STONY
MAN®

*Available August
wherever books are sold.*